CHAOS

CHAOS

BEFORE ONE

The voices used words Julie didn't always know, but the tones, the underbreath meaning, she understood well enough. They told her about death's mouths gaping open to devour her in the darkness with teeth and tongues of flame. They told her about storm clouds pressed into blade-shapes that cleave the glassy eyes of dolls. They told her about broken cats and viper pits and facial rot. And because they talked so much and so often and so dirty, dirty-ugly all the time, she knew she'd never be able to leave. The doctors, who couldn't hear anything, would never let her go. No one wanted heads full of doorways, or houses full of a head's worth of voices. Those voices said things in words so bad and dirty, she thought the owners of the voices must poison whatever invisible mouths spoke with them from the other place. Sometimes she wanted to lean her head toward the spot where she'd first heard them—the black puddle. She thought maybe if she did, though, her ear would go through the black and come out on the other side, in their world, like when she was a girl digging on the beach, trying to dig all the way through to China. She was scared her ear would fill forever with those ugly voices, compounding and multiplying until the noise was so great she'd have to dig them out with a spoon or something. Even without benefit of her rare lucid moments, she knew that would not be good.

From the window of her room on the third floor, she could see the sloping grounds of Bridgehaven Asylum's front lawn falling away into darkness. The black puddle could have spread. Beyond the small, sharp circumference of light from the eastern parking lot lamps, the world could have been eaten up for all she knew. She could be alone, floating on an isolated remnant of the human world. All around the building, alien voids could be filling with alien stars and chilling foreign emptiness, churning and swirling and crashing. She shivered. For all she knew, they had set loose the death mouths to chip away at the world she'd always known, and now they had free reign to get inside the building, inside her, and stuff her to bursting with their dark suggestions and dirty words and strange poison.

Julie wrapped her thin arms just beneath her ribs. She got pains in her stomach sometimes, and she was sure the dark from that other place had infected her when she touched it, and gnawed at her insides. The doctors said that wasn't true, that the symptoms were in her head, but when the pain yawned and then growled in her gut, she felt afraid. And sometimes the pain would be in her head, quite literally—stabbing bolts of blinding agony followed by the frenetic jumble of the whispered voices. That was worse than the pain in her gut. During those times, her mind showed her terrible pictures—a bloody altar of rock, piles of flayed skin and bleached bones stacked like firewood, the death mouths. She hated it. Even the pills couldn't cleanse the stain of those images from her mind.

***

Across the hall, Mrs. Rossi neatly unfolded her suicide note and laid it on her pillow. Then she crossed over to the door, straightening her clothes as she did. They were soft clothes: a light sweatshirt and elastic-waistband sweatpants. Nothing with zippers or snaps or drawstrings, or anything hard or sharp. Her hair hung gray-black and straight, not-quite-yet unclean but close, falling in her pale, doughy, dead-eyed face. She peered into the hallway. Julie in the room across from hers was muttering to herself. She could see the girl standing by her window, a frail wisp of a thing faded somehow, as if whatever sharpness of color or feature that solidified a person's place in the world had been bled out of her.

Mrs. Rossi hated her. It was Julie who had opened up the Pandora's door to the other place, a place beyond but somehow inside the Asylum, existing over and under and through the Asylum. It was all that little waif's fault. Skinny little straw bitch, she was, a scarecrow with a sharp pin sticking out of her heart, sharp enough to have pierced into something dark and awful.

She swallowed the anger that knotted in her throat as she crossed back to her bed. She looked down at the note, written with drawing paper and a felt-tipped marker she'd taken from the art therapy room. Her gaze traced her tight-looped, heavy-stroked script, slanted slightly to the left.

Maybe not all the waif's fault, but mostly. Mostly.

Mrs. Rossi had been committed for exhaustion, as she told it, in 1993. She'd been a very nervous sort, the kind whose anxieties took on intolerably unmanageable proportions. She didn't sleep well, nor did she eat well, which she blamed on vividly bad dreams and a nervous stomach. She'd forget things—sometimes only little things, like where she put her car keys or what she had done with her checkbook, and sometimes bigger things like working and bathing. Her skin was raw in patches on her arms and legs and the backs of her hands, where she'd scratched and then washed off and rewashed off the film of germs from the outside world. Her nephew and niece had been concerned. But all things considered, she wasn't the dangerous type. She wasn't on the suicide watch, nor was she considered any kind of threat to herself or others—certainly not on her pills, and not under supervision. She was just tired, was all—worn out—and the doctors and nurses and orderlies knew that. Maybe she sleepwalked, but she was sure that had only developed since she'd been here. It seemed a few other odd quirks had developed, too, during her residency at Bridgewood

Asylum. The anger, for one thing. And that unsettling sort of feeling she got sometimes like waking up from a dream or a nightmare, that twilight feeling of not quite being sure where unreal ends and real begins. Still, she had never been a threat. They didn't watch her like they watched most of the others. She wasn't—well, she hadn't been, until now—a problem for anyone. Lately, though, she knew what was happening. It was just a suspicion at first, but it grew and took shape in her mind. So she had prepared. The imps and phantoms that Julie had let slip across demanded blood before they'd go away. The chaotic ones. They demanded screams to drown out the moaning in the darkness.

Mrs. Rossi would make sacrifices. That girl from across the hall, that stupid little schizo bitch who'd let them all cross over—she would be the first in making things right.

True, it had been Mrs. Rossi who had found the spot where the other world bled through. She'd been taking a walk outside during recreation time, enjoying the autumn breezes, the late afternoon sun thin but warm and gold on her face, when she happened to look down and see it, pooled half under the east wing's concrete foundation, three feet away from the art therapy room window on the far shady side. It was an amorphous puddle whose boundaries shifted and changed, ebbed and flowed, breathing its blackness across a span of about three feet. Its dimensions were strange; it wasn't quite a hole, seeming to have no depth at all, and yet Mrs. Rossi was sure that if she reached into it, her hand would pass through into nothingness and keep going. It tainted the space around it, Mrs. Rossi noticed. The stucco had a washed-out quality that made it seem less a thing of substance and more a suggestion of a backdrop; the same effect leaked out onto the grass, fading it to a dull waxy yellow. Its reek made her eyes water and burned the inside of her nose like bleach, an acrid smell so strong it was almost a taste. Beneath that, warm air like a breath from a decaying throat gusted up from the black.

She'd looked around the grounds. It had been a wonder, actually, that no one had found it before her. Julie was talking to an invisible someone on one of the nearby soapstone benches. Mr. Ottermeier sat slumped to the left on another bench farther away, while Angela, a young, full-figured red-head, whispered things in his ear beneath the soft snow drift of his hair that only they two could know. Carter tossed an imaginary ball (or, knowing Carter, a radio, a bomb, an elephant) into the air and caught it, tossed it and caught it, and griped and pulled away when Janelle tried to take whatever it was from him. Orderlies milled around, keeping an eye on things.

Mrs. Rossi looked back down at the spot. She couldn't be sure, but it seemed closer, as if it had sensed her and was reaching out, flowing in her direction. She took a couple of cautious steps closer to it. She thought at first she could hear singing, very faint, coming from somewhere deep inside and well beyond the...what was it? A wound in reality? Her gut seemed to believe that. She frowned, and took a few more measured steps closer.

No...it wasn't singing, then. It was moaning. It reminded Mrs. Rossi of wind across an open bottle neck, only...sadder. Much sadder, much emptier, more hollow. The tone rose and fell, rose again, held, sank. It was heartbreaking, the sound—so much so that she began to feel dizzy, tottering at the lip of the spot, her chest tight and full of sharp things, her throat choked with the awful despair she breathed in. Her vision blurred, and she let the tears fall.

A sudden scream made her jump, uttering a little cry of her own. It cut off just as suddenly, as if that degrading throat from which it came were suddenly strangled into silence, or slit. She blinked, shook her head, and moved away until the resumed moaning seemed like a breeze that had already moved past her.

Mrs. Rossi had only wanted someone else to confirm what she was seeing. Lately, especially lately, she saw things sometimes, so she hadn't really wanted to draw a lot of attention to that, no sir. She didn't want meds changes and extra counseling. All she'd wanted was confirmation, another set of eyes agreeing to the verity of the pulsing puddle of ichor beneath the foundation. She'd called to Julie, who stopped chatting up the soapstone bench and came over. Julie had seemed fascinated, almost entranced by the wound (that seemed an apt way to think of the puddle, as a wound in the world). She had heard the moaning too, only she claimed there were words stuck in the sound like splinters in the skin. She said the words were sad and awful, worse than her other voices. When she'd looked up at Mrs. Rossi, her big blue eyes twinkled behind tears.

Maybe Mrs. Rossi had found the spot, but it was that goddamn skinny-assed bitch across the hall who'd stuck her fool hand in it to pet the sad voices. She'd reached into it, shivered, and pulled a lump of the other world out. Like sand or smoke, it dissipated in Julie's hand, first in chunky black wisps and then to nothing. But it wasn't nothing. She'd broken whatever weak membrane stretched between worlds, and in so doing, she'd let the other place in. Mrs. Rossi was sure of it; she could feel it. That wound, that soft tissue between this world and what she knew in her gut was an alien place of damaged, insane, breathing outer darkness, carried an infection. Over the weeks that followed, she could feel its abandon, its savage disregard for order and sense, permeating the bedrooms, the group therapy rooms, the hallways. It was wild, indifferent, a feral intelligence that pooled and spread and drifted like thick smoke all around them. It terrified her, and at the same time, made her feel alive and strong. Alive and dangerous. In control.

Beneath the pillow on her bed was Mrs. Rossi's knife. She reached under the cool linen and pulled it out. It was made from the handle of a paintbrush, one of those old wooden ones and not the plastic kind. She'd swiped it from the art therapy room by slipping it under the band of elastic in her bra, right under Ricardo's nose. She could have a bra. She was a lady, after all, and she had never given the staff, especially Ricardo, reason to believe she'd use it against them.

She'd spent a long time biting at the paintbrush handle, shaping one end into a point with her fingernails and teeth. Slow and tedious work, that, not to mention the nervous butterflies in her stomach every time one of the orderlies walked past the piece of loose wall plaster near her bed where she'd been hiding it. She'd whittled it down to a decently sharp point, and she thought it would serve its purpose. She'd just have to be careful not to let it break off in anyone's neck.

The time had come. She knew what those from the other place were planning: their own sepsis, their own gangrene, black-blooded chaos and orgies, cannibalistic frenzies and torn-up flesh. She heard their voices. Julie heard them, too. Julie knew. Of course Julie knew. She'd drawn the damned things out in the first place.

Mrs. Rossi touched the suicide note gently, almost fondly, like it was the cheek of a child. She wouldn't be coming back. They might never understand what she was about to do, but it seemed important to her, even in the face of everything that was going on, that she have some written record that her intentions had been good. She'd meant well. The little white square, folded neatly, an even number of times with the folds perfectly bisecting the paper into even quadrants, said all she thought needed to be said.

It read:

I tried to take it all back.

She picked up the paintbrush-handle knife, slid it up the sleeve of her soft sweatshirt, and moved out into the hall and toward the game room. She could just about smell them there, the same acrid kind of smell as that goddamned hole outside.

***

In a cold and boxy blackness beyond the east wing where the ichor had spread and congealed, beyond steel doors that required passcodes and special keys, came a sound lost in the hum of impending chaos. A figure wrapped with cloth and buckles giggled high and hysterical, its whole body shaking on its stained mattress. The manacles around its leg tittered metallically against the tiled floor. It knew; its glee was uncontainable. It waited for them to come to it.

***

For reasons beyond her conscious ability to access, Julie started to cry, moaning softly amidst the sobs as the shuffling footsteps in the hall reached their destination. The pain in her head began in earnest just as Mrs. Rossi buried the makeshift knife into dear old Mr. Ottermeier's throat, and spouts of blood pattered down onto the chessboard in front of him, and the chess pieces he never moved. Julie closed her eyes against the light of her room as Mrs. Rossi pulled back on her thrust into Carter's skull and most of his eyeball came out with her make-shift knife. Around the time Ricardo came running down the hall, Janelle and already bitten off most of Angela's bottom lip, and Julie felt the voices eating into her stomach. When in retaliation, Angela had broken Janelle's jaw, which hung slack against her neck, Julie knew the pictures in her head of all the blood were real.

Throughout the asylum, some invisible, silent timer went off. In unison, on some preternatural cue, the others understood what Mrs. Rossi believed, and started making their own lists of sacrifices. The violence swelled. The braying and howling and screaming, the merciless abandon, the tinny metallic smells of blood and fear, the organic smells of rot and urine, were all accessible to Julie, inside and outside her head. They caused her to sink to a shadowed corner of her room and rock and cry, clutching her stomach and head, until Mrs. Rossi came for her with the paintbrush.

ONE

Before tenanted apartments actually held their ground, crowding the Old Ward on the hill, there had been fire.

Fire had eaten through the original buildings comprising the apartments known as Bridgewood Estates. People in the town below, looking up at the smoking hill, whispered that it was providence, that benevolent forces in their far-sightedness had seen fit to cleanse what never should have been built on in the first place. But that land (aside from its historical significance, relegated to the last-standing main building of an asylum) was prime land, an immense span of gorgeous hilltop overlooking a clean and tidy New England town, encircled by solid oaks and maples. It didn't flood, didn't take the brunt of harsh wind, was not so elevated as to accumulate too much snow nor too steep a slope to prevent reasonable access to the jobs and stores and shops below. Despite protest, the plans to reconstruct the apartments progressed. There were petitions online and in print, the vehement arguments of the historical society, even the unspoken implication of the unexplained fires that took down millions of dollars' worth of the original construction. However, none of these could prevent the town of Bridgehaven from seeing the fiscal potential in building apartments where the crumbling remains of a historically shadowed embarrassment stood cluttering up the land.

Myrinda Giavelli knew about the fires before she and Derek Moore ever set foot on the property. She knew the asylum had something of a sordid history. Internet and library research yielded that Bridgehaven Asylum had been closed since the mid-eighties, a result of cutbacks and asbestos and the deinstitutionalizing of mental health care. There were other reasons, though, which could be found only to the persistent Internet searcher—neglect and abuse, sexual assaults and rampant drug use. There was even the hushed suggestion of cannibalistic patients running wild one night in the final year before the asylum's closing. She found it all fascinating; it contributed, in a way, to the mystique of the place.

She'd heard some of the rumors during their stay in Bridgehaven while looking for apartments; there had been the idle chat of the hotel people when she mentioned where she and her boyfriend were looking to rent, the odd looks of elderly diner patrons staking their booths out and holding court over coffee and hash browns, when the topic came up with waitresses. The people who were responsible for what happened in the decade or so before Bridgehaven Asylum turned out its inhabitants and closed its heavy wooden doors never spoke of it, but the old store keepers and bar hounds in the town below were easy enough to prod. Many of them claimed ex-staff members as friends, or ex-patients as old acquaintances. Their talk was often delivered apologetically not for the content but for the perpetuation of its telling. That those with the money and influence to make such a place go away actually did their best to do so was really no surprise. So sixteen months after the demolition crew's departure, the Bridgewood Estates were built, then rebuilt—bigger, stronger, more spacious, with slightly higher rent than anticipated, but given the amenities, worth every penny.

The Bridgewood Estates apartments stood to the right of the Old Ward. There was only one building, a long series of apartment suites encased in cream-colored brick, rising two lofty floors and stretching its arms out along the grassy acres where once the extensive eastern wing of the old asylum stood. The building's peaked roof rose slate gray against a serious sky. On lower floors, bay windows alternated with neatly New England rectangles, while those windows on the top floor curved beneath gothic arches. This was to be Myrinda's and Derek's new home.

Standing there on the sprawling grounds in the late afternoon sunshine, Myrinda shivered a little looking up at the apartment building, surprised by the sudden intimidation she felt. It loomed up over them, almost seemed to lean in toward them, inspecting them. Its sun-glared windows staring down at them gave away nothing, but she thought they didn't really need to. In every brick of the place, in the very air that it seemed to pull to it like a shroud, she could feel a sense of waiting, a sense of unemotional expectancy. She thought to mention it to Derek, to ask if he felt it, too, but decided against it. She looked up at the set of his jaw, the mouth not quite frowning, eyebrows tenting suspiciously as he studied those upper windows, too. He hadn't fallen in love with the place, but he loved her, and he knew her well. She wanted to live here; it glinted in her eyes and made her voice tremble when she talked about the place. They'd already signed the lease. Their suitcases and a few possessions they'd acquired between them waited in the trunk of his Mazda.

Mrs. Sunderman, the landlady, stood waiting for them outside the door to the main office, a small woman in an oddly jarring provincial floral top and jeans, her silver-ringed fingers patting the jumble of silver-tipped dark hair piled and clipped upon her head. On her tanned face was the polite but mildly empty airiness of one anticipating superficial pleasantries. She held a small keyring with a sibling line of similar keys—one to the outer doors of the lobby, one to their own front door, one to the fenced-in pool and tennis courts that lay off to the west of the Old Ward, one for their mail box, one for their storage bin, and one for the door to the laundry room in the basement.

"Hi, Mrs. Sunderman." Myrinda waved.

The landlady waved with the hand holding their keys. They jingled lightly, reminding Myrinda of wind chimes. Derek held out a hand to her as they approached. She looked at him a moment—just a fleeting moment, with a following glance at her—before taking his hand and smiling pleasantly. Myrinda bristled slightly. She knew sometimes she was perhaps oversensitive, and saw judgment or derision where there was none, but in that fleeting moment, she was fairly certain a sense of superiority hung around the woman's face, just as she had when she'd first met them. She could almost hear the accompanying thought: *'Well I wouldn't do it, but some folks—those modern liberal folks—do resort to some wacky things, probably for attention. Dating outside their race, throwing paint on fur coats, tossing broken baby dolls on the porches of abortion clinics. Don't want to know what sorts of trouble they like to cause, so long as they pay their rent and don't damage anything.'*

Myrinda stifled a frown.

"Well, then. Welcome to Bridgewood Estates," Mrs. Sunderman said, and held out the keys to them. Myrinda took them and thanked her. She could feel Mrs. Sunderman's eyes on them as they climbed the porch steps and entered the lobby through the neatly efficient dark green double doors.

The ground floor lobby of the building had a faint musty smell that contradicted the newness of the décor. The tiny gray and green floor tiles lay in tidy little diamond patterns. The walls were painted a soothing light gray that complemented the floor. Neat metal rows of mailboxes, lettered in silver with apartment numbers, hung against the wall to the right. To the left was a door to the staircase leading to the upper floors. Against the back wall stood the doors to the elevator, still shiny and unscuffed.

"So this is home." From his tone, Myrinda couldn't tell if Derek thought that a good thing or a bad thing. When he turned to her, though, he smiled. "Why don't you go open up, and I'll start grabbing stuff out of the car?"

The U-Haul Derek's cousin was driving up from Pennsylvania wouldn't be arriving until the following afternoon. They had packed Derek's car with the breakable stuff, the toiletries, the personal items, suitcases full of clothes and shoes. She'd wanted, at least, the cleaning supplies, so she could start washing away the invisible film of previous tenantry, if there had been any. She wanted the little odds and ends she could put out or away to stake claims on the place as being her own.

Myrinda smiled back at him and nodded. He kissed her, quick but loving, then headed back out to the car.

Alone in the lobby, she sighed, content. This was their new home, a fresh start away from the suburban repetitiveness and smallness of her home town. She would not miss generations of those people growing up on top of prior generations, everyone gathering at the local bars, the local restaurants and judging who'd gained weight or lost hair or settled for someone in a stagnant marriage formed to raise a brood of kids. Sure, they'd moved to New England, and for all intents and purposes, it was sequestered small town living at its epitome; she saw the irony in that, she really did. But here, they were strangers. Here, they were new. High up on the hill, they were removed from the town below. They were in the ivory tower, mysterious, even a little feared. She didn't think she'd want to stay forever—not if she and Derek got married and had kids someday—but for now, for what she wanted, this place was perfect, because there were no old ghosts to run into. No familiar faces. This place was their own secret delight, for her and Derek to share.

She moved toward the elevator and pressed the button. The upward-pointing triangle above the doors lit up and the shuffling hum of the car moving between floors lifted the edge of the lobby's silence. She stepped into the car and it was just as the doors slid closed behind her that she noticed the graffiti.

Graffiti seemed somehow too big a word for it, truth be told, but that's how it struck Myrinda—stark, vaguely obscene in its contrast to the sleek mirrors and metal of the elevator car. It was written in thick-tipped permanent marker, dark blue, and simply read:

I tried to take it all back.

For some reason, she found this sadly disquieting, a glimpse at someone else's private desperation. She leaned closer, her gaze tracing the neat, sharp-angled script, looped slightly to the left.

The distorted face that materialized in the mirrored surface above the words made her jump. She wheeled around, expecting against reason to see its physical counterpart: hollow eye sockets smeared out of shape down the sunken cheeks, long black hair awry and ripped away bald in some places on the misshapen head, blood smearing the pale forehead.

There was, of course, no one behind her. No one had gotten on with her in the lobby and she was only going up one floor. Her heart pounded blood into her ears. She turned back to the graffiti. The mirrored surface reflected only her wide-eyed, startled face.

With a cheerful ding, the elevator car stopped on her floor and the door opened.

The second-floor hallway stretched toward the left and right, turning occasional corners that took the doorways out of her view. The walls were painted a cool gray, slightly darker than the lobby, with a light gray carpeting on the floor. In contrast, the molding and the staggered doors were the same pine-green as the tiles in the downstairs floor, with silver letter/number plate combinations to mark off each of the apartments. She moved off to her left, toward apartment 2E, confused and shaken.

She had just put the key in the lock when a voice spoke from behind her.

"You new?"

Myrinda flinched and turned toward an old woman hovering in the doorway of 2H. The woman smiled. Her thinning white hair drifted in soft, white wisps around soft, lined cheeks. Her eyes, large and brightly blue, took in Myrinda without assessment or judgment.

"Hi," Myrinda said. "My boyfriend and I, yes—he's getting our things out of the car." She thought of mentioning what she'd seen in the elevator to the woman, but decided against it. First impressions, and all.

The woman nodded, then crossed the hall with sure but measured steps to Myrinda's door. She wore a dress, white with large daisies, and with her floated a faint scent of flowers and bleach which Myrinda felt certain wafted up from the loose folds of the linen.

The old woman extended a hand. "Agatha Roesler," she said. "Aggie. It's nice to see new faces filling up some of the rooms in this place. Happy faces. New building and all—we don't have that many tenants yet."

Myrinda shook her hand. "I'm Myrinda. Derek and I are just moving our stuff in. Nice to meet you."

"Myrinda—that's a pretty name." The old woman's eyes glazed, the comment seemingly present in the here and now, but not necessarily the speaker. Her body seemed to shiver from deep inside, rippling outward in the most infinitesimal shudder of her frame. After a moment, she returned to herself, offering Myrinda a faintly sheepish smile. "Okay, well, I won't keep you. Welcome to the building, dear."

"Thanks, Mrs. Roesler."

"Please, call me Aggie."

"Aggie." She smiled at the old woman.

Satisfied, Aggie nodded once again and made her careful way back to her apartment. Myrinda let herself into 2E.

The foyer of the apartment was a wide white space that opened into a living room on the left, behind which was an equally open dining room. To the right of that was the kitchen, behind the foyer wall. A small hallway ran parallel to the kitchen on the right, offering doors to the bedroom and, farther back, the bathroom. It was a neatly stacked and packed series of rooms that gave the impression of possessing a slightly odd shape without really having any particular characteristic to give that impression. The walls were all that same stark, clean, anonymous white, faceless canvases for Myrinda to imbue with personality. She stood among those walls, imagining what might go where, what art to buy and hang, what color to paint them for the length of the lease.

In the kitchen, she turned on the sink and let the water run for a bit before shutting it off. It was a mindless gesture, a possessive one, vaguely maternal. This was her place now, hers and Derek's. She opened and closed the cabinets, the drawers, the dishwasher door, the pantry, faintly smiling at the domesticity of the gestures.

There was a low, plaintive whine, not quite of vocal chords, and Myrinda suddenly sensed someone behind her, displacing the air and the thinness of solitude with a solid presence. She turned, expecting that Derek had come in behind her.

She was alone in the kitchen. She frowned, crossing the neat planks of hardwood flooring to the dining room entrance. "Derek?" She called through the scantly sun-lit rooms. "Honey?"

That same low, plaintive whine carried back from the hallway. She crossed the dining room and the living room to the hall. "Hon, are you up here?"

The bathroom door stood open. She thought, although she couldn't be entirely sure, that the door had been closed when she'd first let herself into the apartment. "Derek?" This time, her voice in the empty apartment sounded less tentative, a little louder in her ears.

She made her way slowly down the hall, chiding herself even as she did so that she was being silly to feel that iciness down the back of her neck and under her arms. Who else would it be but Derek? Or maybe Mrs. Sunderman?

"Hello?"

She pushed open the bathroom door and flicked on the light switch.

The bathroom was of a decent size—one of the appeals of the apartment—all beige and chocolate tiles and smooth porcelain. Toilet, tub, and shower all seemed to be in order. The apartment, she discovered as she moved back through the rooms, held to the same order and accountability, and the sweep back through proved neither Derek nor Mrs. Sunderman nor anyone else had joined her. Nonetheless, a pervasive feeling of otherness left her unsettled, a sensation that in each room she entered, someone had just left. Someone who left an imprint, not so much of ownership but of familiarity, of native locality, that she kept walking into like a light cloud.

I tried to take it all back. She felt a small, sharp jealousy well up in her, and she shivered, its unpleasant aspect like a breeze that had gone from cool to just a little too cold. *You can't have it back. It's mine,* the jealousy congealed into thought-words, and she shivered again at the absurdity of them.

The quiet in the apartment where she stood alone issued its own counter-challenge, biding time, smug.

***

"It was probably the pipes," Derek wrapped a towel around him and stepped out of the shower. "Apartment buildings like this are all full of odd noises."

Myrinda leaned in the bathroom doorway, watching him, already dressed for bed in a soft black cotton nightie. "It wasn't just that, though—that's what I mean. Those noises I heard in the kitchen weren't what bothered me. It was...I don't know, something more, something...." she struggled to find the right words.

"Baby, it's a new place, and I think what you felt was...well, not the creeps at being alone, but more the anticipation—for good or bad—of being in a place that has no history, no sense of belonging to anyone."

"So shouldn't that make it easier to feel like it's ours right away? I loved this place when we came to look at it. I still do. I just don't understand why I should all of a sudden feel like an outsider here."

Derek squeezed her shoulder as he crossed over to the sink. "Maybe it doesn't. Maybe apartments are like horses—you have to tame them, ya know? Break them in before anyone can feel at home in them."

She shrugged. It sounded plausible, she supposed, but a little anxious part of her mind felt unnerved by the thought. She didn't want resistance. She wanted...acceptance was the word that came to her mind, but she didn't quite understand why.

"It's not totally familiar. Not quite ours yet—but it will be. You'll see. We'll unpack all those boxes in the living room, get the furniture set up, put up shelves, and it will feel like yours. Mine. It'll be ours. And I bet you that feeling you had this afternoon doesn't ever come back."

"You think so?"

He glanced back at her, smiled one of those smiles that made his eyes dance, and smoothed a thin sheen of shaving cream foam onto the stubble of his jaw and chin. She watched him, his strong back rippling with muscles beneath the dark caramel of his skin. The towel was wrapped around his tapered waist. She wanted to pull it off him, to pull him close, fresh and steaming from his shower, naked, pull him to her, inside her. He had a cool, polished way about him that men envied, a deep chocolate voice and a GQ face and body that made women turn and stare. People naturally liked Derek, with his easy smile and quick wit. He could talk to anybody about anything. She was proud of him, awed by him, very much attracted to him, and glad that at least his mama didn't care that he was dating a skinny white woman. Derek often told her he loved her. He said he loved her cooking, the way her long legs felt wrapped around him when they made love, her laugh that always made him smile, too. He told her he loved the way her blue eyes swirled almost teal when she was excited or passionate about something, the way locks of her straight black hair fell over her eye or shoulder when she tilted her head, the way her lips moved when she wanted him. He made her feel smart, funny, talented, strong, and beautiful. She felt so lucky to have him. She only wished her own family saw in him what she did.

"Come to bed," she said.

He peeked at her in the mirror, an eyebrow raised, grinning through the foam. "You miss me, babygirl?"

"Terribly." She pouted prettily.

"I'll be there in a minute. Let me just wash this off."

A few minutes later, he joined her in the bed they'd put together that afternoon amidst a small scattering of cardboard boxes, and they made love in their new home, passionate and excited and slow, until they both fell asleep beneath familiar sheets and a new white ceiling.

It wasn't until hours into that sleep, some time around four in the morning, that Myrinda woke up. She remembered snippets of a dream—bloody fingers, bathtubs with chunks of rotting meat blackening the chipped and stained porcelain, burning people she couldn't save, a deep black chasm beneath the foundation of the apartments into which the whole of the building tilted crazily. She couldn't remember much else, or recall how any of it fit together, but she awoke in a sweat, her heart thudding beneath her tank top and in her ears, tears blurring her sleep-smeared vision.

She hadn't screamed, but Derek's soft snoring into his own pillow ceased, and he mumbled, "Whazdamatter, babygirl? You okay?"

She stroked his shoulder, aware of the trembling of her fingers on his skin. "I'm okay. Go back to sleep, hon."

He put a hand over hers. "Bad dream? You're shaking."

"Yeah."

He rolled over, awake now and concerned. "You want to talk about it?"

She shook her head and smiled at him. "I'm okay. Just hold me?"

"Of course. C'mere, babygirl."

She lay back down and snuggled up against him, her back to his chest, his arms around her. She lay there a long time, feeling his breathing against her, stroking his arm, until she fell asleep.

TWO

Hal Corman turned the television louder so he could block out Eda's words. They had only been living at the Bridgewood Estates apartment for two and a half months, give or take a few days, but to hear Eda go on about the new couple who had just moved into 2E, one would think she'd strode off the Mayflower and claimed the building as her own. Eda usually had something to say about their neighbors—the gay recluse in 2B, the dotty old woman from 2H, the alcoholic in 2J. It seemed the interracial relationship between the Bridgewood Estates' two newest young tenants offended Eda's highbrow sensibilities. Hal tried not to roll his eyes or sigh too loudly when she crossed in front of the Patriots game (not that he was missing much; Brady might as well have had a rubber tentacle for an arm and Pittsburgh had a 16-point lead), but he found her voice over the white noise of the television crowd grating.

"...was supposed to cater to a respectable tenantry of people, not just anyone off the street—" she was ranting, in her quiet, squared-off New England speech. She and Hal had no children, but she'd been a school teacher for years, and when she was angry, she had a way of punctuating the occasional word to make it sound like a threat just slightly gone over one's head.

"Eda, really, why does it matter?" he interrupted her. His own voice was soft from years of conceding points. "Other than their maybe getting ahead of you in line for your favorite washer and dryer, when do you even think you'll see them?"

She stopped pacing (directly in front of the television, he noticed), a thin woman graying all around the edges, her angular prettiness sharpened over the years, and sighed at him. "Hal, you really don't get it, do you?"

She seemed forever frustrated that the people that came into her life were not extraordinary, or perhaps it was that she worried that extraordinary people only kept company with their own kind and it was a company she might be locked out of. And sometimes, that drove him crazy about her. Still, he got the distinct and unnervingly more frequent impression that there were times it went further than that for her, that she hated him for every extraordinary thing he never was and would never be, and hated him for everything she thought he prevented her from ever being. And maybe, somewhere deep down where her conscious mind only brushed its fingers idly, she hated him for reminding her of everything she knew she never really was.

What she did manage to be, though, was a thoroughly efficient housekeeper, a pretty good cook, a whiz at Sudoku, and a shrewd woman who balanced the check book every month, paid the bills on time, and had saved them, between coupons, sales, and deals, thousands on everyday household items. Also, when she was inclined, which was rare, she could make him come very fast when she took him into her hands, sliding her thumbs and fingers in ways that seemed to him a mystical, orgasmic art. For those reasons—those, anyway, were the ones that immediately sprang to mind—he loved her. That was the nature of his marriage to Eda—a dichotomy of equal parts love and hate, admiration and irritation, neediness and indifference, which had kept them well if just shy of happy for a good 27 years. Hal supposed all marriages that lasted functioned with the same dichotomy.

He sighed. "I imagine you'll explain it to me."

She surprised him by storming off to the bedroom and slamming the door in that same curt, squared-off way in which she'd spoken to him.

It was a while after that, when in all likeliness, she'd changed into something soft and only vaguely feminine, climbed into bed and fallen asleep, that the man on the television advised Hal to kill his wife.

He had nearly dozed off himself in the faded green easy chair, lulled by the drone of the commentators going through plays post-game in the NFL wrap-up show. Hal was in a twilight state, the pieces of football jargon and commercials weaving their way into something that was neither purely thought nor purely dream. His mind wandered to Eda, who could be cold and sharp like a glass sliver slicing across the skin, Eda, who used to have the prettiest smile, a kind of soft and shy little sideways curl of the lips. Eda, whose parents never failed to subtly suggest in word or facial expression that he had all the intelligence and class of an ox with intestinal distress. Eda, who used to make him toast and coffee and have his paper folded open to the sport section by his plate every Sunday morning for the first fifteen years or so of their marriage.

The noises on the television rose and fell, dipped and swelled, and their cadence lulled him, rolling beneath his thoughts of his wife, the voices tapering to a monotone, almost a whisper. He shifted in the big easy chair. A McDonald's commercial ended and a man began explaining about car insurance and how Hal was in good hands. In Hal's head, he could imagine the man on the TV—a forty-something with a good head of slightly graying hair, a man of substantial presence in his build, his face carved with rugged authority. The man in Hal's mind wore a polo shirt and slacks. The voice in his ears spoke of simple conviction and inarguable instruction. Hal should have taken his V8 and gotten an oil change, the man was saying. He should have gone for a different play at the 20-yard line. He should have killed Eda yesterday while she was dreaming of men he'd never be and wishing behind his back that some lucky stroke of fate would leave her a well-off widow.

Somewhere in the back of his mind, an alarm went off. He thought he ought to open his eyes, to clear his head somehow, because the man's words were getting heavy, plodding, a methodical chant of urgent syllables boring into him. He couldn't. Other parts of his mind, more in the forefront, couldn't really see a problem with entertaining the idea. Killing Eda with a quarter back pounder hambone hand sandwich made perfect sense; he knew Tom Brady and the insurance guy would agree. He was in good hands. The sounds dropped to a low drone, and he drowsed deeper into sleep.

He was dreaming of sitting on a park bench outside the apartments, only in the dream, they weren't the apartments. There were people in pajamas milling around, some talking to low-hanging branches of nearby trees or listening to other folks speak to them in hushed and soothing voices. The man from the commercials was there, hanging upside-down from a branch of the tree across from Hal's park bench. Hal frowned, rose slowly, and took a few tentative steps toward him. He glanced around the grounds again. No one noticed the upside-down commercial man, his legs hooked over a low-hanging branch. No one was left to notice; the grounds had cleared like some end-of-lunch alarm bell had sounded that everyone heard but him. Above, the sky was bright and cloudless. There was no breeze, no sound of birds, no movement at all except for Hal, and the commercial man across from him in the tree.

Hal turned his attention back to the man. He was as Hal had imagined he might be in person—authoritative, even upside-down like that. Gravity seemed to have no effect on his hair or clothes, which underlined that air of authority. Even the absurdity of his position, hanging from that tree, somehow worked in his favor. Hal was afraid to question it, or to question him. In fact, Hal went so far as to wonder what was wrong with him that he wasn't upside down as well.

"She's waiting for it, you know. In the bedroom." The commercial man pointed over Hal's shoulder.

Hal followed the direction of his finger to a large gray stone building with wings extending bat-like behind it in either direction. The apartments were gone; the gray building swallowed up all the land in his line of view. Of the myriad windows it boasted across its front surface, all were black except one on the top floor.

He turned back to the commercial man. "Who is?"

"Your wife."

"My wife?"

The man looked at him as if it took supreme patience to be dealing with him. "Your wife," he repeated. "She seemed upset with you earlier."

"She's just huffy, is all. She...she likes a sounding board, someone to rattle off her views to. I wasn't in the mood."

"Women like to talk, don't they?"

"Women like Eda certainly do." Hal tried a smile which seemed to fall flat before the man.

"She certainly seems demanding."

Hal didn't say anything to this. He wasn't sure what the commercial man was getting at.

"Even now, she has wants."

"What does she want?" Hal finally asked.

"Nothing you can give her. Not anymore. And there lies the problem, doesn't it, Hal? Real question is, how do you fix that problem?"

The sky darkened on them then—just a shade, but enough to give Hal a chill. He didn't like the direction this conversation was taking.

"Look, pal. I don't think there's anythi—"

"But you do. You know I'm right. You knew I was right earlier. There's a problem that needs fixing and fixing things, well, that's what you do, isn't it, Hal?"

It had been, for thirty-five years in the corporate world. His little cog in the great machine had been to identify departmental problems and offer solutions. It appealed to his nature, the simple outlining of potential obstacles, and the careful planning of ways around or through them. But Eda? Did he really consider her an obstacle? Certainly not like she thought of him at times, but.... His answer came thin, quiet. "I suppose."

"So do it, Hal," the man told him. This time, the commercial man's voice seemed in his ears and very close—not coming from the hanging figure at all. "Be a man. Stop letting her dig grooves into your soul with her constant yammering. Kill her. Shut her up once and for all."

It started to rain in Hal's dreamworld, soaking him, soaking the ground around him. As the rain pelted the commercial man's skin, now somehow rubbery and unfirm, his eyes spilled out like runny egg whites, dripping down into his hair. The dyes in his clothes ran blurry across his frame and he seemed to lose substance, all the fleshy parts of him smearing and eventually running clear. What was left flattened to mere colorless pieces of cloth on a branch clothesline. This seemed to Hal both horrific and natural, that the commercial man should simply run clear like the stains evaporating in a Tide commercial or tooth plaque beneath the onslaught of Crest Whitening toothpaste. But that, like the things he had said, was inarguable. He wasn't a walking-away man. He wasn't a see-you-later kind of guy. He was a commercial man, and his message to Hal had been delivered.

When Hal woke up, he felt stiff in his neck and slightly achy in his chest. He glanced at the bedroom door and frowned.

"She's waiting for it, you know. In the bedroom."

He pulled a blanket from a nearby basket where Eda kept them, and closed his eyes. He didn't think Eda would miss him in bed tonight.

***

Their first day in the new apartment started early with cleaning. Myrinda tackled the bathroom, scrubbing down the tiles and toilet, while Derek worked on the appliances in the kitchen. Boxes stacked to different heights created a cardboard Himalayan range in the living room through which they'd carved out a pathway. Myrinda had put up curtains in the living room and laid out a few framed photos and art pictures to be hung on wall spaces which, once they were painted, seemed to call for something to fill them. She'd also cleared a space for the couch and loveseat, for when Derek's brother arrived with the U-Haul. They were waiting on other big pieces, too—the kitchen table and chairs, the TV, the small dresser. Even without these things, however, Myrinda felt that odd unease scrubbed away, as if her contact with the porcelain, the faucet, the new shower curtain, was transferring some part of her to them, some ownership by touch. Satisfied the bathroom was clean, she headed back through the apartment toward the kitchen.

A knock came just before Mrs. Roesler—Aggie from across the hall—appeared in the front doorway. "Hello! How you kids settling in? Getting by okay?"

"Hi, Aggie!" Myrinda maneuvered around a fortress of boxes and crossed to the door. "Hon, this is Aggie Roesler from across the hall."

Aggie held an apple pie, which she offered to Derek. He took it and smiled at her. "Well thank you, Aggie. This is very thoughtful of you. It's great to meet you. Please—come in. We're just unpacking."

Aggie blushed pleasantly beneath the radiance of Derek's smile. "Well, aren't you tall, dark, and handsome. Myrinda, he's a fine man." She winked.

Myrinda laughed. "This is Derek," she said, taking the pie from him to bring to the kitchen.

"Derek, a pleasure."

"Can I get you anything, Aggie?" Myrinda called from the kitchen. "We don't have much yet by way of food, but I have a few cans of soda."

"No, thank you, sweetheart. I'm just fine."

When Myrinda returned from the kitchen, Aggie was sitting on a nearby folding chair, helping Derek unpack and refold bath towels.

"So what do you think of the new place?" Aggie added a fluffy blue beach towel to a pile in a laundry basket.

"Good, really good," Myrinda answered, sitting down cross-legged in front of another unopened box. She took the box cutter from Derek and slit the tape across the top. "I think we're really going to love it here."

"Have you met any of your other neighbors yet?" Aggie didn't look at either of them, but instead concentrated on a hand-towel she was folding.

Myrinda thought she detected an odd note in Aggie's tone. "Uh, no, not yet. We haven't really seen anyone but you and Mrs. Sunderman. Why?"

"Oh, no reason," Aggie said, dropping the hand-towel in the laundry basket and picking up another from the box. "Folks here are nice enough."

"Are there a lot of other people here?" Derek moved on to a new box marked linen closet. "I mean, the building seems awfully quiet. We don't hear doors slamming, people walking, nothing."

This time it wasn't just Aggie's tone, but a strange, faraway look in her eyes that Myrinda found curious. "No, not too many folks. A good part of this floor's filled up, though I'm not so sure about the first and third floors. Probably no more than a handful of apartments, but the place hasn't been open to tenants very long either. Most of the folks are nice enough, though," she repeated.

"How about Mrs. Sunderman?" Myrinda thought her own tone sounded sufficiently amused to pass off her words as light and joking, but if Aggie were looking to issue a warning of some kind, Myrinda thought she'd opened that door.

Aggie bit her lip softly, on the verge of saying something, but then in a moment her expression, as well as her voice, had reverted to the pleasantry of the little old lady next door. "She seems pleasant enough, I'd say."

"How long have you been here, Aggie?" Derek asked her.

"Oh, almost four months now, thereabouts."

"How do you like it here?"

A flicker of that strange, faraway look. "This place is very nice. Clean, quiet, very modern. Stainless steel appliances and granite counter tops—my nephew Clarry—Clarence, but we call him Clarry—he says that stainless steel is the 'in' thing for kitchens. He thinks this place is a steal, for the price."

"What do you think, Aggie?" Myrinda persisted softly.

Aggie smiled at her, but there was something very old, very weary about the smile. "I'm an old woman—I don't need much. It's a nice place to live in, with such sweet young neighbors to humor me and give me their time. I'm just grateful to still have the wits and faculties I need to live on my own, and not in a nursing home to collect dust and bed sores while my life savings leaks through his fingers." Her smile faltered in the silence that followed.

Derek broke it with a smile of his own. "Well, let's say we take a break and cut into that pie, shall we?"

***

Wayne Tillingford of 2B stared at the laptop in front of him until the neat lines of print went a little blurry. He'd been trying to figure out what angle to take for his article. It was on the financial spending discrepancies regarding the upkeep of the historical landmark on the grounds of his apartment building, and on the rebuilding of the apartment complex itself to figuratively and literally bury over the ugly history of that particular parcel of land. He was working toward something that he hoped wouldn't make the easy slip into lurid sensationalism and yet wouldn't read like a boring budget report, either. He knew how the locals felt about the land on which his current residence stood, and how propriety and good old-fashioned sense of New England pride prohibited any kind of widespread exploration of the subject or fact-sharing. That meant getting it right would be important. And starting it right would be the key to getting it right.

So far, that wasn't happening. He'd figured out in college that sometimes writing genius would strike him if he let his mind wander, his gaze sort of daze over, and the usual half-hearted attempt in halting type to blur up. Sometimes he'd see what he'd come to think of as the words beneath the words, the truth of what he was trying to say. It would gel in his mind then and he'd know what to type.

He stared out the window above his desk at the expansive grounds below. It was hard to imagine what the drunken, lonely old folks in tucked away bars said had really happened here. He suspected most of it couldn't possibly have happened, was just dramatic over-exaggeration. Certainly, he could find no official documents to back the stories up, either in the newspapers or through connections in the records department of the police force. Stories of torture, vivisection, rape, cannibalism. And once the police got to the hospital, it supposedly had only got worse. Blood-streaked bodies of doctors and patients alike, baying and chanting in the same eerie nonsense language, biting and bruising each other in sloppy orgies or loping across the sparsely moonlit lawns. Gore splattered on the walls, the unspeakable things they found in the art building....

The art building. He closed his eyes, opened them. That little overturned tidbit of news would likely never make it to any publicly printed forum. The art building, which was demolished after the S.W.A.T. teams took down every last crawling, howling, frenzied, crazy-eyed thing on the premises, including a few of the cops, and restored order and control by utter annihilation. The art building, where nurses and patients had been strung up and slowly stripped of skin and muscle, left to dangle and drip from the heating pipes in the basement. Where lines of some kind of complex pictograph text had been scrawled in blood on every available surface of the seemingly endless hallways, floors and ceilings. Where crude finger paintings of doors and windows with stars beyond had been applied to the doors and windows. And in the art therapy rooms themselves, the atrocities continued, grotesque and obscene. What they found in the paint jars....

Wayne, who had an oddly selective weak stomach, full-figured as it was, had felt a little queasy at the drunk old man's recounting of all the horrors that had gone on at the hospital. They'd been sitting in the local bar in town beneath the shadow of the hill—an Irish place, McGinty's. The old man's intoxicated muttering had created an invisible circumference of atavistic fierceness around him that put the few other patrons at a distance. Every once in a while, his voice would rise in an unintelligible shout which would go largely unacknowledged. Wayne had sat at the stool next to him and bought him a drink. The bartender had eyed him warily and plunked a beer (Wayne's) and a shot of bourbon (the old man's) in front of the odd pair.

It had been pretty easy, considering the overall attitude of Bridgehaven's inhabitants, to get the old man to open up about the asylum's sordid history. Wayne got the impression, as the mumbling wore on, that at least part of what the old man was saying had to do with doctors and nurses and wounds. Wayne's engaging him in conversation about it caused that circumference of distance to widen, but no one stopped him from talking or even acknowledged that he was talking about it at all. It was as if the two of them had fallen into some side pocket of reality, able to see the bar around them but not really be a part of it, at least not so long they sat together. And so Wayne plied him with questions and wrote down notes as detail after gory detail poured out in a half-whisper, half moan, carried on puffs of alcohol-saturated breath. Wayne had to stop the old man when he got to the part about the paint jars, fearing that if the story continued, his three or four Sam Adamses might lurch up from their tentative place in his gut and onto his relatively expensive shoes.

But now as he went through the story in his mind, recalling the pictures that the slurred cadence of violence had conjured, he felt an odd tingling beneath his skin, a kind of nervous anticipation.

It hadn't just been the night at the hospital. There had been the series of freak accidents during building, the high incidence of brawling among the workers. And the fire, of course. There had been the fire.

The fire burned so hot and fast that it took down the newly-sheetrocked shell of the building in less than seven hours. Investigations into the cause of the fire proved inconclusive, although the general consensus was that it had been some faultily installed wiring. That was the general consensus, but it was the belief of the old man (and others, he'd been told) that the bad of the place had never left, and those crazy enough to build up and through that kind of bad had to expect it to cause problems.

Warner, a sleek black and white cat who had been confidante and sidekick to him for about seven years, hopped up on his desk. Wayne stroked its back absently while it investigated Wayne's work in progress. Behind the cat, he noticed a spider crawling across a yellow legal pad. He got up, carefully curling the pad to keep the spider contained, and walked it to the window. He didn't like to kill bugs if he didn't have to, or leave them to Warner's predatory devices. He was just borrowing the planet, after all, like the rest of the creatures on it, and they had as much right to be there as he did. Balancing the legal pad on the window sill, he hefted the storm pane and screen up quickly, keeping an eye on the confused little spider skittering hesitantly in one direction, then skewing slightly off in another. He picked up the pad and brushed the spider out the window and out of sight.

"Saved another one, Warner," he told the cat, who responded with an indifferent stroll across his keyboard before jumping off the desk.

Wayne turned to the window again to close the panes, and that was when he saw a girl standing out on the expansive lawn. She was shadowed, almost smoky, even though she stood in the bright gold of late morning sunshine.

He frowned. She hadn't been there a moment before. He rose to get a better view.

She looked maybe fifteen or sixteen, tall and bony, her features all sharpness barely contained, hardly softened by the flesh stretched over them. She stared up at him, a smoldering hostility obvious, but for no consciously discernible aspect or expression. It was instinct, a gut reaction Wayne had to her—that she was toxic, and quite possibly dangerous. She wore a grayish hospital t-shirt and sweat pants with large, irregular dark stains. From that height, Wayne couldn't see her face clearly enough to discern details, other than high, pale cheeks streaked with blood and dark hair that dangled in thick, wet strings. The part of him that remembered what his mother taught him considered calling out to her and asking if she was okay, but everything about her discouraged the thought. How was it the sun didn't light any part of her? He felt the very wrongness of her in his chest and the first real weight of fear in his gut before the his brain registered that she had no shadow, that—

—Oh God, she has no, she—oh God, she's missing—

Her hands. She was missing her hands. Her long, slender arms ended in heavily bruised wrists, and beyond those, nothing. Wayne felt his stomach tighten. That wasn't all. She stood perfectly still—but only on the ankled stumps of her legs. Her feet were gone, too.

"Warner," he whispered to the cat. He needed the reality of his own voice, the sense of another familiar body in the room with him. He felt very shaky. "Warner, check this out."

Warner complied, hopping up on the window sill, and Wayne absently stroked its fur. He didn't realize how tightly he had been gripping the cat's back until it yowled, twisting away from him and jumping to his desk. Wayne barely registered it. His attention was fixed on the girl.

Her face seemed to have come unhinged from her head. It slid to an odd angle, her crooked gaze watching him, then started to rock slowly back and forth, a layer somehow separate from her head. Suddenly it stopped, and the jaw stretched. The mouth gaped open, a dark chasm impossibly large, and black tendrils of smoke drifted upward out of it. The sound that swelled up from that narrow throat and out that gaping maw wasn't human. In fact, it didn't sound like any creature of this earth at all. Her skin, which had taken on a dirty grayish cast, suddenly spiderwebbed with skin-splits from which rivulets of red dribbled away.

Wayne gripped the edge of the desk, unable to move, his breath a small, hard ball in his chest. His hand groped the desk for his cell. He wasn't sure who he planned to call—Mrs. Sunderman, the police—but he had to call someone, had to get help before...before what?

He imagined that thing down there, that horrible mockery of a person, jerking itself closer to the lobby door on its stumps, its face swinging, that air-raid howl shattering the glass of the doors. He could see in his head the stumps of her legs crunching over the broken glass, leaving untidy splatters of blood and clots on the tiled floor as it made its way closer....

He thought he might throw up. With the one hand not blindly groping for the cell, Wayne gripped the window sill, waiting for the feeling to pass. Where was the damn phone? He glanced down and saw it knocked askew by the cat. He grabbed it and tapped the phone to bring up the keypad. He looked up, his finger hovering over the "9."

The girl was gone.

THREE

Detective Jack Larson of 2J had spent the better part of his leave of absence watching his new neighbors move in. There had been the old lady first, who had moved her two suitcases, some folding chairs and end tables, a couch, and a few old boxes into 2H with help from a tall thinking reed of a young man who came and went like the wind. There was the terse woman and her tired-looking husband from 2A who followed next, the hum of tension between them nearly palpable, followed by the recluse writer in 2B ("I think he was one of those club kids in the 80s NYC scene," Mrs. Sunderman had informed him one day in a conspiratorial hush, followed by a meaningful look and a gesture like she was sniffing something off the cupped underside of her long ruby-painted pinkie fingernail). There were also the newest editions, the couple in 2E. They were beautiful people, both of them, and seemed, from the subtle and intimate gestures between them, to be very much in love.

He was most fascinated, however, with the new woman in 2C. In Larson's experience, there were two equal but very different kinds of beautiful women. There were some whose beauty warmed you, invited and comforted you, women you fell in love with for their smile, the flow of their hair, the gentle slopes of their curves. And there were women whose beauty chilled and intimidated others—a rarer kind of beauty, the kind that almost made you look away for fear of somehow being mocked by a thing you knew could never belong to you. Those were not women who were truly and healthily loved, but obsessed over. Fretted over. Women whose intimacy and most secret lives were forever out of reach.

One could know the destructive force these kinds of women could be, Larson discovered, and still find oneself succumbing to the inexorable pull of them.

He'd known a woman like that once and lost her. Julia had been that rare latter kind of beauty—just like the woman from 2C. The striking resemblance between them hurt his heart. It made his hands ache, his head ache. The little details were different—this woman's hair was blond and short and her style of dress less aggressively sexy, for example—but it was her, down to the subtle self-aware way in which she moved and stood.

It had been that first woman, Julia, who had sent him from Boston to Bridgehaven in whiskey-laced grief and abandon, lacking sleep and food, indifferent to names and dates. He'd used up his vacation at the behest of his chief, a C.O. in every sense, and then dipped into his short-term disability. There had been psych evaluations and a half-hearted attempt at AA, but no more than three weeks had passed before he was blowing both off and dodging the increasingly impatient follow-up calls. He needed time, dammit, time to himself, to grieve and to think. When he looked in the mirror, he saw dark whiskers just going gray, the strength gone out of his football-player bulk, the fight gone out of his blue eyes. The former two things he didn't care much to do anything about, but the latter—the latter had to be rectified for his own sake. His own sanity.

Larson thought the fix lay with the woman from 2C. He wanted to (possess her) meet her, get to know her. It was something he'd realized one morning in the kitchen of the new place. She had been put there for him, a second chance. The idea made every cell in his body sing with emotions—elation, relief, excitement, love. He could win her over—he thought could make it happen in a way he never could with...the other woman.

The evening that Larson stood out on the front lawn looking up at the window to the apartment of 2C, the curtains confirmed he was right. A series of small but obviously connected events, a breadcrumb trail of clues, had led him to the curtains. The need for complexity was obvious; this woman, like the last one, surely had a man. Women like that always did. Larson wasn't jealous; women like her deserved someone to protect them, to take care of their needs. Those men served a purpose. And once Larson could be with her, he would serve that purpose and she wouldn't need other men anymore. He would do it all for her, give her everything she could ever need or want.

In the meantime, the breadcrumb trail served the purpose of discretion, and also gave him an opportunity to prove his devotion, his patience, and his intellect. He'd follow her little subtle clues and in the end, he'd go to her with open arms.

First, there were the sticky notes. He'd shuffled into the kitchen one morning to get coffee and milk—a mugful of each usually settled the rot in his gut and the dry pounding in his head. The first of the sticky notes was on the fridge; he saw it when he went to get the milk. He frowned, squinting through the pain in his head to read it.

Today's the day, the note told him. Just three words, unprecedented and unsigned.

He had no recollection of writing himself a note about anything, nor of there even being such sticky notes in the apartment. And he didn't think that day was momentous or anniversarial in any way. It was Tuesday, the 11th. What had he wanted to single out today for? The day for what? He couldn't remember. His head throbbed as he leaned in, peering closer at the tight-looped, heavy-stroked handwriting, slanted slightly to the left.

Handwriting, it dawned on him, that most definitely wasn't his.

Today's the day.

For a moment, a flare of alertness set his head turning sharply, scanning the kitchen for signs of intrusion. He made a swift check of the door (locked and bolted, as it should be) and of the windows (unopened, second floor) and found no evidence of attempted entry, or of any other presence than his in the apartment. He went back to the kitchen. The sticky note still hung there with its simple proclamation. He grabbed it, crumpled it, and threw it away, wiping his hand on his robe, knowing it was silly but still feeling like his hand had touched something unnatural, something poisonous. It was just a stupid sticky note, he told himself, and probably one he'd written himself in a drunken stupor, the booze rendering his handwriting strange and unrecognizable.

Seventeen years of police work, much of which had been in district A-1 and the last seven of which had been as Sergeant Detective with the BIS, had taught him to hone the natural instinct he had to understand possible subtext beneath the elements, sometimes unusually disparate, of a case. Usually, the train of logic made neat little mental stepping stones in his mind. Once in a while, though, some of those stepping stones would lie submerged beneath the surface of missing facts, or more lately, beneath swamps of alcohol. He'd learned to bridge those gaps pretty well, gathering seemingly unrelated snippets of conversation, paper trails, crime scene photos, and the like. His mind tried connecting the pieces together quietly in the background, keeping what fit and reworking what didn't, while the forefront of his thoughts worked on other things. It had been that process which led him, hours later as he napped on the couch, to realize what the note meant. He sat upright suddenly.

Today's the day. It sure was, goddamn it, and he'd almost slept it away!

He hopped up and made his way into the kitchen, crossing to the counter by the cordless phone. A stack of papers—folded take-out menus, mostly, along with unopened bills, bank statements and credit card offers—lay in a messy heap next to the phone. He rifled through it until he found what he was looking for: a small daily calendar. Each day presented an uplifting saying and above that, a colorful image—spirals, mostly. He'd had it on his desk at work—some generic stocking stuffer he'd gotten at the precinct Christmas party the December before. One afternoon, Feehan had walked by carrying coffee in a foam cup and a Twinkie (Larson didn't even know they made Twinkies anymore; he suspected, in fact, that the remaining Twinkies of the world, the "fruitcakes" of the snack set, were simply regifted until someone like Feehan came along and ate them) and Feehan had stopped.

"Julia sets," he'd said through a mouthful of spongy cake.

"Huh?"

He'd nodded down at the calendar. "Julia set fractals."

Larson had stared at him, unsure if Feehan was pulling his leg. Julia (that other woman) was a name he'd repeated so many times in his mind that he'd felt, explored, understood every aspect of it, could taste it. A flood of thoughts made it difficult to respond. He wondered if the other guys in the precinct could sense those thoughts, and the emotions behind them. It was crucial to staying on the case that they did not.

He was about to ask, "What the fuck you talking about?" when Feehan waved his Twinkie dismissively and walked away.

As it turned out, Julia sets, named for French mathematician Gaston Julia and not for his own Julia, were functions used in the making of fractal art. Julia sets were such that slight permutations caused drastic changes in the pattern, he'd discovered. He didn't know much about math—cared even less—but the art had kind of a soothing effect, a pattern repeating to infinity, God in mathematical art form. That they were created from something bearing the name of the most important woman he'd ever encountered seemed pleasantly fortuitous.

Gazing at the calendar, he saw the transport from office desk to box to car trunk to new apartment to counter had weakened the binding, and many pages had fallen out or were hanging like loose teeth by thin strands of glue. He gave the calendar a little shake and the loose pages, too, fell away, fluttering to the floor. The new top page revealed today's date.

The message of encouragement: *Go after something you've always wanted. Today's the day!*

The image above it: a Julia set fractal. Blue, like her eyes had been. Blue had been her favorite color. Fractals. Glorious patterns from the slightest of evolutions. Vivid and emotional and breathtaking art made from the colorless fact of repetition. There was something here, some step to be taken, some message to be read and understood.

Messages. Sticky notes. But who...how...? He looked up from the calendar and turned to the fridge, his breath a tight fist in his chest.

The slightest of evolutions. Lighter hair, darker eyes.

He thought he knew what to do next.

***

Mrs. Aggie Roesler knew they were from the other dimension, the word for them something she suspected her vocal chords couldn't quite pronounce, though she dared not try out loud. In her head, it was a hissing word for them: *hinshing*. She knew what they were the same way one knew things in dreams, a certainty no less trustworthy for its sourcelessness. Since she'd moved into 2H, she'd seen them often. During the day, they were a mottled sickness-yellow, but as night came on, they darkened to a tumor-black. They were humanoid, but completely hairless and sexless. They were essentially faceless, too, except for an angry red schism of a mouth running the vertical length of the facial plane. Lipless, the mouth opened to several rows of small, sharp teeth that made Aggie think of serrated bear traps stood on end. The backs of the creatures, as well as the backs of their trailing, pointed heads, smeared outward, producing a strange optical effect that suggested motion caught on film. Their movements were jagged and to Aggie, jarring. It was as if they skipped frames of reality, slipping along from one conscious moment to the next. Their long fingers had no nails or claws, but rather, ended in sharp little points. Their knees bent backward, their wiry legs able to pivot in multiple directions from high-set hips.

What bothered her more than their unfathomable alienness was that they could, at times, look quite familiar. Sometimes, they looked like memories, and that was worse than any foreign aspect of their true forms. When it suited them, they could look very much like everyone else. But she could see. Oh yes. She could see.

Sometimes they surrounded her in the dark. They'd come up behind her in that shadowed corridor that led to the laundry room, or surround her bed in the surreal early-morning hours when night first begins to fade to a pale silvery-blue. They smelled kind of like death flowers, that stomach-churning sweet smell that reminded her of funeral parlors, nursing homes—all the end-of-the-road places that the people who had grown bored with her oldness wanted to put her in. Those creatures smelled of the end of things—which, for all intents and purposes, she supposed they were.

She knew these were beings that suggested awful ideas and made them sound okay. These were things from a wound between worlds, that puddle of darkness, drawn into this dimension. However, these also were things that well-meaning neighbors might call her senility, or the onset of dementia. She couldn't tell anyone. She didn't want to wither away in one of those end-of-the-road places, where death hovered close and loneliness came and went like a tide.

She never spoke to the hinshing nor they to her, but she felt their insanity rolling off them in waves like heat. They had never touched her, not yet, but they, or maybe just the contagion of their mere presence, had lately begun to change things around the building. She'd only noticed little things at first—their moving the hands on the clock to confuse her, moving her slippers, her keys, her reading glasses. Once they'd mixed up all her pills in different orange bottles. Luckily she'd memorized pill colors and dosages together, or God only knows what kind of terrible damage she could have done to herself. That had really shaken her—it seemed clear to her that they had gone from unnerving to threatening—and had made her more aware of those creatures closing in on her periphery in the darkness.

Lately, bigger things had been changing, things she couldn't tell herself might be just an old lady's forgetfulness. Moving the doors and windows was particularly upsetting. So were the faces in the elevator, reflected in the metal. The hinshing rippled pavement, moved trees and then moved them back again. They called on the phone with the stolen voices of dead people. They had even warped the windshield of her car, the very car she'd fought to prove she needed and could take care of. And once, she could have sworn they had made it rain up instead of down.

She could see them now as she sat in the old rocker by her window, looking down over the grounds. She hadn't stayed long at Myrinda and Derek's, finding she couldn't bring herself to do what she'd come to do. She glanced at her pill bottles and bit her bottom lip. She was *not* senile. She knew that, but instead she'd gone home, curled up on the rocker with a blanket and a mug of tea, and watched the afternoon sun wrestle the shadows on the Bridgewood grounds. That was when they came, skittering in and out of the moments of the afternoon, gathering beneath her window. Their distorted stances seemed threatening to her, but she didn't dare move. She pretended she was lost in thought and wasn't seeing them, but they were already working their suggestions inside her, working stomach-wrenching images and ideas into her thoughts. It was all she could do not to scream.

Aggie tried to yank her own thoughts out from the tangle of alien ones. She wondered if the others living in Bridgewood Estates could see the creatures too, or feel their oppressive madness. She worried about the new couple that had just moved in. She had liked them both right away—enough to want to warn them, but....

"*Mother, I really don't think your living on your own is a good idea. There are plenty of lovely facilities for people your age—*"

No. The thought of living anywhere that anyone could call a facility made the loose and wrinkled flesh of her face pull tight in a grimace of disgust. She was not something to be stored in a facility.

On the grounds below, one of them caught a rabbit and tore it in half, tilted its head as if studying the dripping insides, then dropped the ravaged pieces on the ground.

The new couple would be all right, she told herself. Smart, strong. They would be just fine. Maybe the hinshing would leave them alone.

She pulled the quilt on her lap over her chest and squeezed her eyes shut, but the tears dampened the thin white skin of her cheeks anyway.

FOUR

Myrinda first heard fingernails scraping inside the walls a few days after they had settled in.

Derek had gone to the gym and to run some errands, and she was making what he liked to call her "Friday Fish Dish," which usually consisted of tilapia in some kind of butter sauce. The fish baked placidly, tucked beneath a layer of sauce and spice in the oven. The apartment carried its own pregnant silence: the barely audible tick of the oven heat, the low grumble of the pipes, the soft settling of the new walls and flooring. In the kitchen, Myrinda hummed to herself as she chopped up green peppers for the salad. Above the quiet buzz of life and occupancy, a tiny thud and a sliding sound from the living room caught Myrinda's attention.

She put down the knife, her thin, arched eyebrows knitting momentarily in surprise. A second, louder thump and scrape made her jump. She took a few cautious steps toward the living room.

"Derek?" No answer, no keys on the table, no jacket over the back of the couch.

Scrape. Scraaaaape. It sounded like it was coming through the vents, somehow. From behind the walls, maybe. She took a step into the living room and looked around.

At first, everything looked as it should. The couch and loveseat, the end tables, the lamp—

Scraaaaape.

There under the window, down by the baseboard heating vent.... She looked back at the kitchen, considered getting the knife, and realized that was silly. What could possibly be in the vent that she'd need a knife for? The worst it could be was a mouse or rat, some kind of critter trapped behind the wall somehow, and if that was the case, it wasn't like she was going to stab it. Hell, no. She'd wait for Derek to get home, and have him get rid of it.

In the fading afternoon sunlight, it was hard to tell for sure, but it looked to her like something was growing out of the vent, some kind of plant or vine with long black tendrils. She crossed the room to the window and crouched down, then grimaced in distaste.

A glistening patina made the long, thin tendrils look amphibian and somehow sticky. An odor arose from the whole area that reminded her of unclean cages and animal neglect, of lake grasses left to rot in the sun. It was an unwholesome smell in the new apartment air, out of place just as those dirty tendrils were, plastered against the bright and newly painted wall. She wished she had gone back for the knife. She wanted to scrape the tendrils off, but didn't want to touch them.

"What the hell...?" she muttered to herself, and the tendrils shivered. She made a surprised little gasp, and would have sworn that the tendrils responded to that as well, their tips reaching out in her direction. She had to work to suppress the shudder of revulsion they inspired.

"Oh, God." She gave a cleanish space on the wall above them an ineffectual thump with the heel of her hand. Immediately, the tendrils retracted, leaving wettish trails as they recoiled into the vent. She reached a hesitant hand out toward the oily smears on the wall, then pulled back.

Maybe they responded to sound. She thought she'd read somewhere that some plants did that. Hopeful, Myrinda tapped the baseboard vent in a series of dull metallic thunks.

Something from inside echoed back the same.

She frowned, peering as close as she would dare into the dark vents. She supposed it was possible that someone was messing with her, someone from downstairs who could hear her through the vents, but.... She drummed on the vent again, three quick taps followed by two slow ones.

Taptaptap...tap...tap echoed back from inside the vent.

She tried a different pattern, one tap, followed by three quick ones. They were returned in the same sequence. Myrinda pulled back a little.

"Uh, hello?" She didn't really expect an answer, but found herself glad all the same that none came. She let go of the breath in her chest and stood up, debating in her head if she ought to get the weed killer or bleach (*the knife*) or maybe just Windex, and tackle those stains and whatever had retracted into the vent.

Something gray but fleshy pressed against the crack in the vent through which the plants had recoiled. It twisted a little and then withdrew. A moment later, the grayish tip poked out again, and Myrinda saw a long, ragged fingernail emerging from a black nail bed. She swallowed the bile rising in her throat. In horror, she kicked at the vent. It was pure reflex, her foot lashing out to loosen that horrible little fingertip from the vent opening. The vent sucked the fingertip back into it like the tip of a tongue disappearing between lips. She shuddered, a sickening lump forming in her stomach. She had to call Derek now. She—

Three fingertips, all gray, with ragged, overgrown nails and blackened beds, popped out of the vent opening. She let out a choked cry and watched, horrified, as the fingers wriggled like blind, jointed worms toward the sound of her voice. The fingernails scrabbled against the baseboard, using it to leverage themselves farther through the opening. The gray flesh glistened wetly where it pressed tight against the vent. They escaped two, then three inches and Myrinda's breath caught. They had to be fully extended now, and the knuckles would keep them from getting farther, wouldn't they? They wouldn't be able to drop onto the carpet and flop like little dead fish in her living room.

Of course, her mind told her, the idea of knuckles supposes those fingers are connected to a gray-fleshed hand in there somewhere—a hand maybe connected to an arm, which would be connected to some terrible dead-skinned torso deep inside the wall— She cut the thought off right there. *STOP it.*

It was something of a moot point, she saw, when the fingers inched themselves farther out of the opening, far enough so that the ragged edges of the nails grazed the carpet. Too stunned for a moment to move, she watched as the rough ends of the nails caught carpet fibers, strained and twisted through the vent, and plunged into the plushness beneath them. Seeing them touch her carpet, a part of her home, her sanctuary, spurred her to movement. The revulsion ignited a simmering rage and an instinct to destroy every part of their foul little presences. Unable to bear the thought of feeling their bones crush beneath her thin-socked feet, she darted back into the kitchen and grabbed the knife. She thought it over a moment, then reached under the sink for the wasp killer. It was in a large gray and red bottle with a sprayer connected by a hose, and the remnant miasmal smell of fast-acting chemical death clung to it. Armed, she jogged back out into the living room.

The fingers were gone. She felt the bottom drop out of her stomach. Her head swiveled in every possible direction as she crossed the room. They had escaped. *Oh God, oh God,* they had escaped and were loose somewhere in the room, hiding beneath a cushion of the couch or a magazine on the coffee table, wrapped up in the hem of the curtain, maybe, or inching their way along the baseboard somewhere to access the rest of the apartment. She'd never sleep if she didn't find them. The thought of them writhing in the sink or tub or hoisting themselves up the bedsheets under her blankets to her legs, making their way toward her pillow—it was too much. A wave of nausea enveloped her and for a moment the room went fuzzy. She took several slow, steadying breaths, closed her eyes, and opened them. She would find them. *Kill them*, was the thought that immediately followed. But could she do that? Was it possible to kill disembodied fingers?

That the stain those plant-like tendrils had left was also gone only managed to cross the periphery of her awareness, and even then, only fleetingly. That the fingers might have retracted into the wall, back down into the fiber of the apartment building, never crossed her mind at all. Panic wouldn't allow for such thoughts. Her mind did reason, however, that those fingers couldn't have gotten too far. Chances were, they were still in the living room somewhere. She stopped, listening for the scratching of the fingernails, the small, subtle sounds of movement. She didn't think she'd be able to hear them on the carpet, but if they brushed a chair leg or one of the baseboards, she might be able to catch them. The silent hum of living once again washed over the apartment, and she strained her ears through the faintest of natural noises for unnatural finger-sounds.

Nothing came to her as out of the ordinary. So then they probably were moving across the carpet, dammit, with slow and silent inchworm drags beyond her lines of sight.

She made a careful, circular inspection of the floor, starting with the baseboards and spiraling in toward the center of the room. She lifted the couch cushions. She nudged at the papers and magazines on the coffee table with the knife, then lifted them to check underneath. She shook out the window curtains, eyeing them from top valance to bottom hem. She checked the potted plant in the corner of the room, giving the branches a little shake. When it came time to check beneath the furniture, an involuntary shudder coursed through her. Setting the jug of wasp killer down on the coffee table, she got down on her hands and knees in front of the couch and lifted the flap of fabric to (*wait for the fingers to spring out and claw her face with their ragged nails*) look beneath. playing them as a means to a piece of packing tape there, but otherwise, nothing. She turned her head, her hand tightening around the knife, and peered under the coffee table. It, too, was clear. She crawled over to the love seat and then the big chair, and came up with nothing both times. She stood, brushed her hands off on her pants, and looked around. Where could they be?

The sound of scratching made her jump, a flash of revulsion making her flesh hot all over, and she turned in the direction of the noise. A moment later, the scratching came again—from inside the walls. She had a strong but transient desire to bury the knife in the wall up to the hilt, to spear those little fuckers to a support beam. She walked over to the wall and gave it a good thump instead with the palm of her hand.

"Go away," she growled at the spot. "Whatever you are, just go away."

In answer, the scraping of fingernails from the other side dragged down the length of the wall.

She slammed the wall with the palm of her hand again, and then again and again until it hurt.

When a knock at the door followed a few minutes later, she jumped, convinced for a moment that it had come from the wall, something big and angry, the fist those little bastard fingers belonged to.... The knock came again—from the front door, thank God—and she exhaled in relief, setting the knife down next to the wasp killer on the coffee table.

As she crossed to the door, it occurred to her that she must have made quite a noise, and supposed one of the neighbors had come over to complain. She opened the door and was relieved a second time to see that it was Aggie, and that rather than looking annoyed, she looked concerned.

"You okay, dear? I—I heard the banging, and—"

Myrinda's hand fluttered up to her heart, still pounding so loud she thought the old woman had to hear it. "I'm so sorry, Aggie. Really, I'm fine. I'm sorry to disturb you."

Aggie waved the notion away. "No, no dear. No trouble there. I just wanted to make sure you were all right. You're not hurt, are you?"

Myrinda shook her head. "I'm fine, really. Just—" she looked back toward the living room, "—hanging up some pictures."

"Well, okay, then. So long as you're okay...." The old woman lingered uncertainly, eyes crinkled in worry despite the grandmotherly smile.

After a moment, Myrinda shook her head and said, "Forgive my rudeness. Would you like to come in? Maybe have a cup of tea?"

"That sounds lovely, dear, but if all's well, I must be getting on back." Aggie smiled apologetically. "Wheel of Fortune in—" she checked her delicate little lady's silver watch "—nine minutes. I never miss Pat Sajak. He's quite a looker, in my opinion." Her accompanying laugh was light, almost girlish.

Myrinda laughed with her. "Well, far be it from me to hold a woman back from viewing a good-looking man. Good night."

"Good night, dear. Ring if you need anything." With a wave, she turned and headed for her door.

"Will do. Thanks, Aggie." Myrinda watched to make sure Aggie got in okay, and then closed her own door behind her. She turned to the stillness of her apartment and listened for several seconds, but could not make out even the faintest scratching along the carpet or knocking inside the walls. She crossed to the vent under the window, vaguely aware of how the carpet shushed the sound of her footsteps, and peered down. Nothing out of the ordinary. She shook her head slowly. Lack of sleep was catching up to her. Tonight, she'd make sure to take it easy and get some rest. The rest of the unpacking and decorating could wait until the morning.

She turned to the coffee table to clean up the evidence of (*the hunt for little dead child-sized fingers*) what had to be stress or an overtired imagination and started a little when she realized the kitchen knife, which she'd placed—well, had *thought* she'd placed—next to the wasp killer was gone.

Myrinda frowned, checking under the table, on the window ledge, around the baseboards, retracing her steps. A back part of her mind registered a panic not yet fully-realized. She forced herself to inhale and exhale slow, even breaths. She was simply hunting for a misplaced kitchen knife. And she had to have misplaced it; there was no other acceptable explanation. There had been no near-silent scratching across the carpet, no thud of the knife falling, no clanging of metal against the vent. There was no oily residue like there had been on the wall. Further, there was no smell of unclean cages and animal neglect, or of lake grasses left to rot in the sun. Nothing in the apartment suggested the faintest traces of those things. She nodded grimly while she inspected everything and then reinspected it, so as to set her conclusion in stone in her mind. The possibility that those grotesque, dead-flesh fingers from inside the vent had crept out to take the knife or sent some tendril of slimy vine out to grab it could only be rejected.

She swept up the wasp killer in her hands and nevertheless sprayed the hell out of the vent and the wall, then plastered what was left of the roll of packing tape over the whole spot.

***

Over the grounds outside the apartment, the night came on quickly. Under the night, the grounds began to change. The changes were subtle and gradual: shifting boundaries between grass and gravel, trees creaking and sinking their roots into new patterns in the ground, moonlight manipulated into distorted finger-shapes by the surrounding shadows. Beneath the apartment building, the black puddle spread outward again, pulsating, breathing, bleeding, pumping its reckless abandon into the world. In the spaces between things where night gathered thickest, the chaotic ones that Aggie knew as hinshing moved and chattered their own half-nonsense language.

The residents of Bridgewood might have seen movement if any of them had been looking out a window toward the Old Ward. They might have caught blurred glimpses, or heard the irregular cadence of the chaotic ones' speech. As it turned out, the few residents of the Bridgewood apartments were busy with their own thoughts and their own nighttime rituals. But the night wore on, and the chaotic ones were felt as chills, as ideas gone too far for comfort, as memories, both real and faulty. Also, of course, the chaotic ones were seen in dreams, beneath a handful of masks, a number of costumes. It was a common early symptom of the black puddle leaking through.

The hinshing themselves did not sleep, and so did not dream.

It was only a matter of time before they got inside.

FIVE

For the week following his discovery of the sticky note on his fridge, Larson set the foreground (and at times, simply the background) of his mind to figuring out two very important things. The first was the question of who was leaving him the notes. The second was how to decipher the hints the notes offered, and so have the woman in 2C for himself.

Regarding the former, all the most likely suspects in his mind raised questions that left him largely unsatisfied. Mrs. Sunderman, the landlady, ostensibly had a key to every apartment. It was possible that she could have let herself in during one of his whiskey naps and left the sticky notes on his fridge. He was no longer the light sleeper he used to be. But why would she be leaving him notes? It was possible that maybe she saw a grieving man in him, a loss-stricken man, and wanted to offer him encouragement in a way she felt was unobtrusive. It was unconventional, even off-putting, but it had been his experience that New Englanders often had a quirky way of conducting affairs that they felt no need to clarify or explain to those outside. Still, how did she know what to say? How did she know about the fractals?

The man in 2B was a writer, and the connection between writer and written notes seemed a possibility, though to what end, Larson couldn't say. Maybe while Larson had been focused on watching others, others had been watching him. Maybe the writer from 2B had written the notes.

Then there was the woman in 2C herself. She could have left the notes to encourage him. To entice him, maybe. Of all the possible leads, she was the one he hoped was writing the notes, even though it meant she was playing games with him. He didn't mind games; he liked them, in fact, especially when beautiful women were playing them as a means to a most desirable end. Aside from games of chance, which were, in his opinion, foolish wastes of time, Larson thought of most games as puzzles. And solving puzzles, after all, was what he did best. It was what the city of Boston had paid him to do for so long.

One of the things Larson had picked up in his years as a detective was that the solution to a puzzle was most often written between the lines. And the little details, abundant once one knew what to look for, pointed right to it. It wasn't just the devil, but all his answers to everything, that were in the details.

While his mind worked on that piece of the puzzle, he reread the next three notes where he had stuck them in a row across the fridge. They, too, had appeared overnight, but this time in different locations throughout the apartment. The first note he found stuck to the bathroom mirror. Its little yellow square with matter-of-fact print was inarguable.

Follow the pink and gray lines. He smiled to himself. "Follow the lines," he asked the empty room, "or what's between them?" He didn't know what the note meant. Was he supposed to follow specific train lines, like Boston's Ell? Did it mean lines in a book? A line drawing of pink and gray? And what was significant about those two colors? He thought brains were gray, at least. Organs were pink. The body was constantly creating and recreating its own patterns. Pink and gray patterns. It was a stretch, but he supposed the instruction given in the note made more sense in conjunction with the others.

The second note he found stuck to one of the kitchen cabinets, where he kept the coffee mugs. Larson thought it had something of a fortune cookie vibe to it. *Catch the clouds while you can.* In the context of the second note, maybe the lines had to do with something in or about the sky at sunset or sunrise. Perhaps where the first note indicated a direction or a place, the second indicated a time. When was the best time to catch a cloud?

The third was, to him, the most puzzling of all. Although it was written in the same handwriting as all the others, the tone of it was different. The sentiment did not strike him as in keeping with the previous notes. It had a forlorn, almost desperate quality to it, not in the words so much as in between the lines.

Take it all back.

Yet somehow, this seemed the most important bit of advice of all, and the clearest. He'd lost so much over the last few years...so much. If he were to be brutally honest with himself, he supposed there was a big part of him that thought he'd deserved to lose it all. He'd had no family for some time; he believed one of the things that had made him a good cop was the time and freedom to be dedicated exclusively to the job. He could hone in on an idea and ponder it from every angle, study it in every light and thoroughly involve himself in it. In the end, though, that focused dedication had worked against him, particularly when such a precision tool was turned on another person. He'd been forced to take leave of absence from his job. He'd lost friends. Respect. Credibility. Sleep. He'd lost whole nights and days to alcohol. He'd lost the crucial ability of homicide detectives to detach from things when necessary. He'd lost Julia, if he'd ever really had her in the first place.

And in spite of that big part of him that thought he deserved to lose everything, there was just as big a part of him, maybe bigger, that still wanted it all back. But wanting it and going after it were, and had always been, two different things, and therein lay the problem.

That last note, though, somehow felt like a go-ahead, like he was being given both permission and encouragement at the same time. To have it all back again.

To take it back.

There was something very freeing in knowing providence, albeit in the form of anonymous sticky notes, was absolving him for whatever he needed to do to take it back.

He found himself walking the sidewalk path around the apartments without any real conscious thought of having gotten outside. It was a cool night, its edges sharper only when the wind blew. He walked with hands thrust into his jacket pockets, head bowed. The sun was low but the sky still clung to the deep blue of the day.

It was something internal, part gut instinct and part psychic connection, maybe, that suddenly drew his eyes upward to a window on the second floor. He was standing just below apartment 2C. The curtains were drawn. No light shone through from inside, but it didn't matter. He stood there, transfixed and buoyed by his own internal illuminations, the discovery just above his head bringing all the notes into one focused message of crystal clarity.

The gray and pink threads made fractal patterns amidst the cloudy white of her curtains.

More importantly, there were suggestions between the lines. Come-hither suggestions. Soft commands. Ideas. Promises. He could read them as clearly as he could read the sticky notes.

The sunlight was just so, at the beginning of its descent behind the hill on which the Bridgewood Estates stood—not too dim to miss the threads of charcoal gray and baby-pink and the subtler patterns between and beneath them, but not so bright as to blind the eye to them, either. He would have missed them, he knew, at any other time of day or night.

The message in the curtains was clear. Pursuing the woman in 2C and winning her over would be the first of many achievements that would put his life back on track. The events of the next few weeks would all be unfolding permutations in a larger plan of life and love and elements greater than any one person. Whoever his anonymous benefactor was, whether the woman in 2C herself or someone else, he had been issued the greatest of all challenges, the most significant of all puzzles to solve, and at the heart of the solution would be what he needed. The idea of redemption seemed both smarmily melodramatic and out of reach, but a helping hand extended from the darkness to give him a leg up into a life of visible spectrums of happiness seemed possible for the first time in months.

He realized that the sky had gone a kind of blue-gray, finished with streaking pink sunset clouds across its breadth. It was quickly settling into the deep of twilight, its moving darkness nestling and shrouding the landscape. He had been standing there under her window far longer than he'd realized. But he'd caught the clouds just in time.

With a final glance up at her curtains, he smiled to himself and made his way back around to the front entrance. There was a bottle of whiskey waiting for him on the table by the couch, and he wanted to celebrate.

***

Mrs. Sunderman, who had been living in the Bridgewood Estates longer than any of her tenants, had reached her fill of breathing poisoned air, drinking tainted water that ran through pipes suffocated by tainted ground, and eating food rotted internally by exposure to the insanity that clung to everything like an invisible second skin. She didn't know—not consciously, at any rate—that she was being poisoned in these ways, nor did she realize that she had reached the saturation point, but there she was, poised on the brink of fireworking her own particular issues in imminent, unavoidable, unpredictable ways.

Livie Sunderman, whose salutary title was an insisted remnant of respect for twenty-five years of mostly blissful marriage suddenly ended by a heart attack, lived alone in an apartment on the first floor. Her Marty, passed on some six years ago last May, had been a shareholder of the corporation which owned and maintained the new apartment building on the old hill, and had been appointed manager of the building with a bonus and his choice of apartment to live in. As another remnant of respect for dedicated and loyal service, Mrs. Sunderman was asked to step in as manager after her husband's passing.

She did not care for the sordid gossip which had nearly destroyed her chances of living her approaching golden years in comfort and modern style. She refused to listen to the rumors about what had happened on that land, nor lend any credence to the whispered notions that any part of the cause could linger to permeate her apartments. And they were her apartments in her mind—she was responsible for them, and while she felt no maternal or even professional responsibility for the tenants beyond what her job dictated, she was more than a little concerned for the well-being of the rooms those tenants occupied.

What she did know of the Bridgewood Asylum's history, the token of which those uppity nerds at the historical society had managed to preserve in the form of the Old Ward, she had simply shoved down and away from her conscious thoughts. She was not a particularly imaginative woman nor a superstitious one, and any silly suggestion that even the worst of tragedies could have an effect on the impenetrable cleanliness and respectability of new wood and glass and fiberglass was preposterous and unacceptable.

The only element of that horrific past that she entertained in any way was a public statement attributed to one of the doctors of the old asylum: if the best trick the devil ever pulled was convincing people he wasn't real, then the second best was endowing the dangerously insane with the uninhibited confidence to carry out their own internal logic—logic of a sort that self-validates their sense of sanity in an otherwise mad world. This was somewhat in keeping with her view of other people, many of whom she believed were blatant in their impropriety and illogical, at least to her, in their thought processes. That they were driven by a logic of their own only they and the devil could understand brought some sense to the senseless for her. That it was a subjective application of the doctor's sentiments had never occurred to her.

The first match to the fuse of her mental fireworks was the maintenance man. She had first seen him when she padded out to the lobby in her sweats and slippers to get the morning paper. She may not have understood the internal logic of the forces driving the world toward headline-making tragedy, but it didn't stop her from reading about it every morning over coffee. Some complicated system at the local newspaper office prevented the delivery man from leaving each tenant's paper with his or her mail; instead, he stocked a newspaper dispensary near the tenant mailboxes from which those so inclined could take a morning paper. Mrs. Sunderman was so inclined.

She didn't notice the maintenance man until she had begun the return slipper shuffle back to her apartment. In fact, his sudden presence half-inside and half-outside the inert, darkened elevator made her jump.

"Um...excuse me...excuse me there...can I help you?"

A balding, middle-aged man sat up with a mild expression of surprise at being interrupted. His hands, she noticed, were unusually big and brown and lightly hairy, the fingers of one wrapped around a screwdriver while the other held a flashlight. He kept a tidy paunch tucked beneath work pants and a company shirt whose breast-pocket logo read Kintner & Sons Elevators.

"Can I help you?" she repeated dumbly when he didn't answer. Already, the encounter felt awkward and uncomfortable.

"I'm here to fix the elevator," he said, blinking at her. His voice had a kind of friction that reminded her of rough and gritty things—sandpaper and garbage disposals and five o'clock shadow.

"The elevator?" She looked from him to the steel box surrounding him and back to his impatient face again. "I didn't call anyone about fixing the elevator."

"You didn't need to. The corporation sent me. Scheduled maintenance for six months after installation was part of the agreement."

Flustered, she opened her mouth to reply but then closed it. Scheduled maintenance? Why hadn't anyone from the corporation or the elevator company told her? Strange men working on her building seemed important enough to mention. And how had he gotten in. Was the Godfrey Corporation now handing out keys to any old joe that claimed some job on the premises? It was outrageous. Still, she found an uncharacteristic reticence holding her tongue. She wasn't sure if it was the sparkless look in his eye or the way he clutched both the screwdriver and flashlight, but the thought of arguing, of making a scene with this man, of even questioning how he'd gotten in let alone attempting to propel him out, seemed utterly out of the question.

"I found a system bug, ma'am. I'm fixing it now." He blinked his right eye rapidly as if trying to free an irritating eyelash.

"Oh," she said, and clutched her newspaper tighter. It was all she could manage. Most of her mind was already focused on composing the angry tirade the corporation's president was going to get on the phone later that morning. This kind of ridiculousness would never have been allowed to happen when Marty was alive.

"It's a wiring issue. It's nothing catastrophic. I can have it fixed in twenty, maybe thirty minutes." Each of his statements was delivered as simple and inarguable fact. For just a moment, she thought she saw something small and thin swim beneath his eyelid, raising it slightly like a sea serpent cresting just beneath the surface of the water. Before she could be sure, though, the eye began to twitch again and he blinked it hard, trying to bring it under control.

She gave him an uncertain nod. "I'm in 1B, when you're done."

He nodded once, his right eye still twitching, and then resumed his fetal curl around the side of the elevator, ostensibly working on something beneath an inner panel. She peered over him again and for just a moment, she thought she saw the distorted image of an eyeless man reflected in the shiny interior. She squinted, frowning, and took a step closer. There was no man—only the twisted shapes of light and shadow that constituted the reflections of shapes in the lobby. She hurried back to her apartment with her paper, her slippers making quick shushing noises against the tile.

Before she closed the door, she heard the man say, "It's only a matter of time, cupcake." The door swung shut, though, before she could ask him to repeat or explain himself.

She padded to the kitchen, muttering her indignation at the corporation's thoughtlessness. As she poured herself a cup of coffee, she did her best to ignore her shaking hand, or the cool, sick feeling in her stomach.

Cupcake. Only Marty had ever called her that, and not even him for the past six years.

Cupcake. It was unprofessional and inappropriate—*if* it had been meant for her at all, that was. It was possible the man had been talking to...what, the elevator? Did maintenance people talk to their buildings the way sailors talked to their boats? Regardless of whether he had been talking to her or the elevator or an imaginary friend (*an eyeless man, maybe*), she might have been able to chalk up the nickname to coincidence. It was more than just the nickname, though. It was all of what he'd said.

"*It's only a matter of time, cupcake.*"

She had a flash of recollection she had done her best the last six years to avoid. In it, her Marty had been sitting in his favorite recliner, feet up, as he peered at the newspaper through relatively new bifocals. One of his habits, both irritating and somehow endearing to her, was to read the most depressing or shocking headlines, shake his head, and comment about how the world was falling apart. He was not a survivalist type who stockpiled guns and canned goods, nor was he given to belief in the supposed portents signaling the end of the world—the end of the Mayan calendar, the conspiracies claiming that the government was supporting terrorist bio-weapon attacks, the statistics predicting a meteor hit, a solar flare, the timely eruption of Yellowstone. Marty didn't think the end of the world would be a bang or a flash of bright nuclear light or celestial fire. He didn't think the earth would be knocked out of orbit and go spinning off into space to be swallowed by a roving black hole. But Marty did believe the world as its people knew it would come to an end with a whisper or possibly, in simple stubborn silence. He thought the pestilence that would wipe out humanity would be indifference. The explosions that would take out major cities would be those internal kinds of individual and inexplicable violence. The genocide of millions would start with the rotting of their brains, the degeneration of their education, their desensitization to the ugly, violent acts that fenced them into their own private pens of pseudo-safety and blissful ignorance.

Six years ago that past May, they had gone another round of debating his theories. She had joked with him about it, but he'd returned both an expression and an answer of almost sad gravity.

"It's only a matter of time, cupcake," he'd told her, and she had shaken her head, neither dismissive nor conceding.

He'd had the heart attack minutes later, while reading, of all things, the obituaries.

Her recollection and subsequent consideration of the maintenance man's words took less than five minutes, and within that time she'd already crossed the kitchen on her way back to the front door, intending, she supposed, to ask the man...something. She hadn't fully formed what she wanted to ask him; she only knew that she couldn't let his words go.

She opened the front door and stepped back out into the hall.

The elevator doors were closed. The halo of greenish light around the Up arrow button to the right of the doors was lit. There was no sign that the man was or had ever been there at all. She frowned, turning to survey the lobby, then went to the main doors and scanned the front lot for a van or truck with the elevator maintenance man's logo on the side. There was nothing but the usual collection of tenant cars.

She frowned, turning back to the lobby. There had been no follow-up of paperwork, no mention of the bill. There hadn't even been enough time, by the maintenance man's own estimation, for him to have finished the job. So why had he packed up and left?

It occurred to her then—she didn't know why she hadn't thought of it right away—that the man very likely hadn't left. He was probably up on another floor. The second floor, maybe, where the majority of her inhabited apartments were.

She crossed the lobby to the elevator and pushed the button. The upright triangle above the doors lit up. The muted hum of the cables lowering the elevator to her floor was punctuated by a cheery *ding!* as the doors slid open. The elevator was empty. With only a moment's hesitation, she stepped in and the doors closed behind her. She had never been a fan of elevators, and for a second or two following, she felt an overwhelming rush of panic, as if she were being swallowed by some large, gleaming silver fish that would swim with her down into the black depths of the ocean to drown and digest her. The panic passed as quickly as it had come, as quickly as it took her stomach to bottom out and then right itself while the elevator lurched upward.

The interior of the elevator was brightly lit, the mirrors polished and the steel panels beneath them reflecting the overhead light in strips and slashes. *No eyeless men here*, she thought, and a grim smile twisted her mouth a little. She found herself glancing at the mirrors anyway, just to be sure no one was reflected behind or beside her. To her relief, she was alone, and she chided herself for having been silly enough to think otherwise even for a moment. The possibility of some ghostly figure with gaping red eye sockets hovering just over her shoulder or close enough to her reflected self to reach out bone-sharp fingers to touch her—

The elevator doors opened, and she hurried out. She did not look behind her.

The hallway on the second floor was empty. Aside from a few muffled voices and the occasional bump or creak of unidentifiable movement from within the apartments, the hallway was quiet, too. She moved a little way down the hall, trying to be quiet for reasons her conscious mind could not quite access. It seemed important, though, not to get caught...well, prowling, she supposed. Spying on the tenants. It was important she use stealth so that this elevator man, intent on eluding her, could be snuck up upon, and his true purpose discovered.

She paused. That thought sounded absurd even in her own head. It was a crazy thought, an alien, un-Livie thought. *Keep it together, cupcake,* she told herself, pinching off the headache starting in the bridge of her nose.

Nothing indicated the maintenance man had come up here. She shook her head, little twitches of a tight neck, and made a frustrated clicking sound with her tongue. It was ridiculous, chasing a mystery maintenance man from floor to floor to ask him why he had called her cupcake. She'd already wasted more time than she should have. Something inside her had driven her to pursue the issue this far, but it was gone now. The man had left, the elevator obviously worked, and the bill would probably come in the mail.

She turned back to the elevator.

The doors now stood open, patient, inviting her back in.

She frowned, looking around the empty hallway. She was sure no one had come up on the elevator behind her. She peered inside. It was empty. The doors remained open and silent, waiting.

With a final glance around the empty hallway, she stepped inside the elevator and turned to push the first floor button. Just before the doors slid closed, she thought she saw something man-height flash by, a pale sickness-yellow blur of mottled skin rippling over inhuman musculature in jerking, rapid movements. She gasped, her heart thudding, and stabbed a ruby-red nail at the Open Doors button. The elevator whirred internally but the doors did not open, despite her repeated jabs.

"Dammit," she muttered. The elevator car began its descent with a pleasant little *ding*. The tight thumping in her chest spread to her stomach.

When the elevator approached the first floor, she felt an overwhelming sense of dread anticipating what might be waiting for her in the lobby. She took several deep, measured breaths while she listened for the cables to brake. When the doors slid open, the relief at finding the elevator car secure on the first floor and the lobby empty drew a little cry from her lungs. She couldn't get out of the elevator fast enough. As her shaking hand closed around the doorknob to her own apartment, she felt the sweaty heat that sheathed her, heard the silent thrumming of her heart in her ears and the raggedness of her breath.

She opened the door to step through to safety, and fell into a hole in the earth.

SIX

Wayne cursed as the Internet connection went down for the sixth time that morning. Each time he lost access, the irrational semi-hypochondriac part of his mind offered it as proof from the universe that his self-diagnosis of early onset dementia was true. No other explanation could be obtained.

He was sure he'd seen something—a mutilated girl, dead or almost dead—out on the lawns below his window. But just because his eyes had seen it and his brain was backing the image, that didn't mean what he saw was real, or that what he saw was what he thought it was. That kind of uncertainty was never a good sign. He'd been working long hours picking mundane facts from a mire of particularly unpalatable horrors, and the contents of which were suggestive to even the strongest-willed mind, but still...hallucinations? He'd left a life of varied party substances behind twenty years ago. Hallucinations were no longer supposed to be part of the deal. Looking back over the last couple of years, he couldn't imagine any event that might have catalyzed the deterioration of his mental state. However, the World Wide Web was not forthcoming in offering any counterargument to his insanity theory, either—even when it was accessible.

The little hourglass turned over and over on his screen, his PC's version of on-hold music. It connected to the Internet for a moment and promptly froze. He swore at it. Warner glanced at him from his lion stance on the windowsill and then went back to lazily watching birds.

Wayne sighed. For a place so brand new it practically goddamn *shined*, nothing ever seemed to work. Cell reception was non-existent everywhere except for a six-inch square patch of carpet just to the left of Warner's window. The power went out for random ten- to fifteen-minute intervals even on perfectly clear, sunny days. There were thumps and groans in the plumbing pipes. Occasionally he caught crossed cable signals on his television in the form of muttering voices and high-pitched singing over whatever was being broadcast, something he found to be even more prevalent on the higher-range empty channels, where static took a back seat to actual clear phrases and snippets of eerie pipe music.

Once, he'd found a website where reviews of apartment buildings could be posted for those looking for a place to live; he'd been tempted to post anonymously about the amenities never working right. He'd ultimately decided against it, though. It seemed premature, early enough in the building's history to seem mean and self-serving rather than justified and helpful. He assumed many of the problems were due to the building being so recently built. He'd spent enough time in Corporate Cubicle

America to know that anything new, from technology to business to people, had to be troubleshot sometimes, and ultimately had to work out a few kinks and flaws before functioning at full capacity.

That didn't make it less frustrating, however, when deadlines loomed—or when possible mental breakdown and the deterioration of his faculties of perception hung like low clouds around his brain, stratus anxieties whose details even now were blowing off, losing shape and substance.

Wayne clicked on the red X between his network and the Internet and tried to repair whatever was wrong. The system spun its wheels a moment and then informed him that the connection could not be repaired. He sighed, glancing over at Warner curled up on his window sill.

"Looks like we're off the 'net again, buddy," he said to the cat. Warner, who had given up bird watching in favor of curling up in a ray of morning sunlight on the windowsill, lifted his head, blinked sleepily, and twitched an ear indifferently.

"Damn." Wayne pushed away from the desk and rose. The chain bookstore down in town had free wireless; he'd have to email his article (and browse for mentions of something like the hobbled creature he'd seen the night before) from there.

He glanced out the window over the cat's back, but found he couldn't look too long. He hadn't been able to all day. He half-expected to find someone dragging stumps of legs across the grounds below, its jerking body inching closer to the front door, its stench of rotting skin still on the bone clinging to it like its shabby, darkly-stained clothes.

There was a part of him that hoped if he did see it in the light of day, it would reveal itself to be harmless, an easily explained thing—a zombie-walk reenactor, maybe, or an early Halloween decoration. Or possibly, it had been a girl, hurt but not nearly in so severe a state as the shadows around her limbs suggested. Maybe Mrs. Sunderman had taken care of her, had taken her to the hospital or patched her up and sent her on her way. A second glance could prove what he had seen to be no more than a host of mundane, safe realities the night had perverted into horrors.

A much bigger part of him didn't want to see it at all, ever again. That part was sure the figure was exactly what he had perceived it to be, and seeing it again would prove he was crazy, especially if glimpsed during the day, when perception did not have the kid gloves of low visibility to handle the sharper facts.

He glanced at the window again, nervous, only skimming the view for something out of place.

There was, however, a third part of him that entertained another possibility. If the woman had been gravely injured out there on the lawn, and if she had been looking for help and was now missing, it was a story. The local papers wouldn't print it if he made the Bridgewood Heads into bad guys or suggested their newly renovated patch of paradise was rife with violence once again. But there could be a story there. A ticket, perhaps, back onto a bigger paper, and in more than just a freelance capacity.

He needed the security of a newspaper office job. Working without insurance benefits was like tightrope walking without a net, in his opinion, plus a regular journalism job would mean a regular paycheck. He'd steered away from the gory history and more hot-button sensationalist angles with the article on Bridgewood's financial bang-ups because he needed to. Pissing off the Powers That Be who worked hard to bury the negativity surrounding his hilltop home would mean no publication, and worse, no paycheck. So he had slogged through a lot of false starts and frustrating slumps, but he was finished now, with a check and a publishing credit on the way (if he could get his connection to the Internet up and running long enough to email it to the editor). He was free to pursue other stories. More lucrative journalism, maybe.

He crossed to the window to scratch Warner behind the ears (that was what he told himself, anyway), and casually looked out the window. Nothing on the grounds except one of the men from the landscaping company Mrs. Sunderman hired to mow the lawns. And the man wasn't doing anything more horrific than sitting on the tailgate of the landscaping truck and unwrapping some kind of sandwich for his lunch.

Wayne found himself well into wondering what that dirt-dusted little man would look like without benefit of hands and feet before he realized what he was doing and shook himself free from the thought.

He turned back to his desk and packed up his laptop, the afterimage of the mutilated landscaper superimposed over his vision. Wayne had never had a stomach for blood and guts—he had, in fact, turned down a field reporting job once in the early nineties because of its proximity to gangland territory—but the picture in his head had no ill effect on his stomach that he noticed. Rather, it seemed grimly satisfying for underlying reasons that would not quite surface in the conscious part of his mind.

Grabbing his keys from a hook by the front door, he and his laptop swung out into the hallway. Warner yawned and stretched, indifferent but not oblivious to the change in Wayne's mood and routine, and went back to sleep.

***

The expanding of the wound between worlds, pooling with its own viscous black liquid chaos from somewhere on the first floor, awoke Aggie from a mid-morning nap. It had been part dream, part voice, an idea as certain in her mind as her own name.

She found herself in the rocking chair by the window, where she so often nowadays lost hours to frequent and sudden naps. Something felt wrong. It came to her as a dull ache in her legs and hands. Her chest felt like a fist closing tightly in on itself and her head felt light. More alarming than the physical aspects was the distinct sensation that she was drifting in a dark ocean and all around her, shadows as sharp as knives were slicing through the water, closing in. These apartments were supposed to be safe, but she was old and slow and she lived alone. If those shadows swam closer to her, grazing her with their sharpness....

A sense of presence turned her head to the dark corner by the end table. A strange man stood across from her, staring not just with his mismatched eyes, but with the intensity of his whole mixed up face. She jumped, her hand fluttering to her chest. A flare of panic seared through her.

It was hard to describe exactly what was wrong with him; the asymmetry of a blue eye and a brown one was surprising but not unpleasant. It was a character of wrongness in the combined other features of the face that made Aggie feel ill at ease. The crookedness of the mouth, the way one corner sagged just a little—that was part of it. It gave the impression of a half-cocked sneer. The nose was a shade disjointed, the protrusions of the cheek and brow bone just slightly out of proportion for the face. The chin was long, pointed, and hairless. The vaguely lopsided head was shaved, the ears small and sharp. None of the distortions of the man's features individually were so pronounced as to suggest congenital deformity, but together, the effect chilled her blood and stole her breath.

"Agatha," the man said. The gravelly voice seemed awkward in his throat, the cadence suggesting words in general were out of place there.

She opened her mouth to say something, but could find nothing to say. She swallowed what felt like a dry lump of paper.

The man's head gave a spastic twitch and then tilted as if in curiosity. He reached a hand toward her and she flinched. The hand hovered there a moment, the long fingers undulating in a kind of wave.

"Agatha," he said again. He took a lurching step toward her, widening that crooked grin to show teeth tinged with red. She pulled in on herself. She was pretty sure she wouldn't be able to move fast enough to outrun him but her gaze trailed to the front door nonetheless.

When she glanced back at him, he had closed half the distance between them. His legs were long but seemed attached to his hips with an uneven, almost painful rigidity. That he could move so fast even with such jerking motions only confirmed her certainty that she'd never make it to the door before he was upon her, that off-kilter face taking her in, those unnaturally long fingers digging into her clothing, pressing into her flesh.

"What do you want?" she whispered.

"I want to taste the candy pictures behind your eyes. Your skin smells like light and dark and it intrigues me."

She frowned. There was an underlying sinister suggestion to what he said, but the words themselves made no sense. "I don't understand."

"I want to experience your mind," the man said. She wasn't sure if he was explaining, or continuing in rattling off a wish list. "I want to be the voices in your head and the shadow from the corner of your eye. I want to spike your folly and read the sheets."

She shook her head, her arms rising protectively to her chest. "Stop it. Leave me alone. I'm an old woman. I have nothing you—"

"You have everything I want," he replied, and with bone-grinding strides, he advanced on her.

***

Myrinda's mother had told her once that animals were not safe to touch when they were feeding. When she had asked her mother why, the reply had been that they didn't like being caught off guard, for one. More importantly, they didn't like anyone potentially threatening their food source. Myrinda found this to be true in an ornery cat named Socks she'd once rescued from a shelter. The cat wouldn't come to her, would swat at her if she tried to pet it, and chewed holes through just about everything not made of metal. They were quirks Myrinda found tolerable if not vaguely endearing. But when it came to feedings, Socks would hunker over his food dish with the desperate, protective air of a starved prisoner. If startled while eating, he'd look up with his lip raised in a fanged snarl, his eyes narrowed to concentrated points of hate. If touched—Myrinda had learned this the hard way—he'd emit this crazed yowl, his fur spiked to make him look meaner. He'd bite and claw in a fury that genuinely seemed reactionary rather than driven by spite. That cat had died suddenly, the vet attributing it to expansion and subsequent rupturing in his stomach. Whether that was brought on by a tumor in his gut or poisoned food from the crazy asshole who'd lived next door, Myrinda couldn't say. But she couldn't help remembering all those meals Socks had so possessively defended, as if his stomach ruled him. In the end, it hadn't been enough.

Myrinda had seen that look in people in the years that followed—not often, but she had seen it from time to time. The type of hunger itself varied, but she had come to find that behind it was invariably the fear of some kind of loss. If she were to be honest, she supposed a part of her could understand that fear, and the backlash of violent desperation that drove people to protect and hold onto that which they were most afraid of losing.

She never would have expected to see that look on the face of Aggie Roesler, but that's how Myrinda found the old woman late that next morning, crouched against the cement walls in a corner formed by two perpendicular dryers in the basement laundry facilities. The floral housecoat she wore was torn at one shoulder, with dark smears like haphazardly dragged fingerprints streaking toward her breast. She wore only one slipper, its fuzziness matted and specked with flecks of dark brown. Her fingernails were torn and dirty, the cuticle beds crusted with more of the dark substance. It wasn't quite the right color for blood, but it was close. Myrinda couldn't see any injuries to account for blood, either, which wasn't much of a relief; she had obviously been badly hurt; no visible external injuries could mean Aggie was injured worse than she looked.

Aside from a lock drenched in a thick, congealed glop of the dark-colored substance and plastered to Aggie's forehead, soft wisps of her hair floated away from her scalp, forming a soft halo in the slant of sun that came in through a high window above the dryer. Wide eyed and clutching her trembling roundness with tensed arms, she mumbled and hummed to herself, occasionally trailing off and shaking her head violently as if expelling thoughts or images uncomfortably lodged there.

The deliberateness of her low-spoken syllables, though, suggested a mantra, their repetition either to help her remember or to convince herself of something. She looked very much like a woman trying to hold on to the last of something.

Myrinda approached her with light, cautious steps "Oh my God, Aggie, are you okay? What happened?" Crouching beside her, Myrinda gently touched her arm. Aggie flinched as if she had been pinched, the murmured syllables snapping off. She closed her eyes and shook her head.

"It's okay," Myrinda told her. "Shhh, it's okay. Aggie, I'm here. Everything's okay. Can you tell me what happened?"

"It's a wound," Aggie said, her voice trembling on the edge between fear and hysterical giggling. She repeated herself, pronouncing "wound" as a two-syllable word—"wooo-nnnd." Her eyes seemed to wink out, gazing beyond the space over Myrinda's shoulder.

"Where? A wound? Are you hurt? I don't—"

Aggie gave an impatient shake of the head, waving off the younger woman. "A wound that bleeds over—bleeds up from the ground. If you were to find the place, the exact spot, and put your hand through, it would come out on the other side, in another world, an alternate herespace which is really nothing like here at all. In the other world, idiot gods rule, and insanity is the norm. There's no sense or symmetry or logic or physics— to them, over there, our unarguable rules are the stuff of wild dreams. To them, life is chaos, indifference to responsibility, to rhyme or reason."

"To who? Who are you talking about?"

Aggie leaned in closer, a darting glance sweeping the otherwise empty laundry room. "You're a good girl. Good girl. You need to know. I—I can see them. I can. I didn't want to say, but I see them because they really exist. They, who come from there, who reach through with their slippery, slender bodies, oozing up from the wound. Their lunacy pollutes. It gets in the air we breathe, the water we drink and bathe in and wash our hair in and wash our clothes with and brew tea with...everywhere, everywhere. It gets inside, that other alien place, and the alien things that breathe and writhe and slither through. It poisons us. It sickens us. And the sickness is contagious."

Her voice had dropped to a low and lilting spillover of words that conveyed an urgency to Myrinda. She rubbed her arms, chilled all over, and leaned away from Aggie. She needed distance, both physically and mentally, from the old woman and her overlarge eyes and thinning wisps of hair and her vague smell of bleach and flowers. Crouching so close to her was making Myrinda feel suffocated. The old woman was in shock or sick, maybe. Whatever had happened, Aggie needed a hospital.

"Don't you see?" Those overlarge eyes filled with tears. "Don't you see what they've done? Building an asylum on top of such a place...and all those poor crazy souls leaking their own human kind of crazy on top of it, their dementias and psychoses and neuroses and disorders. This place, the very land on which they poured the cement foundations of this, this—" she gestured around them helplessly, seemingly at a loss for what else to say. The tears flowed down her soft, overblushed cheeks, drawing faint lines in her face powder. Myrinda put a hand on her shoulder, and she flinched under the touch.

"Aggie—I think maybe we ought to get you upstairs. You don't look well, you're clearly agitated, and I think—"

"Of course I'm agitated," Aggie said, pushing the words out through a matter-of-fact impatience. She dabbed at her eyes with the side of her finger. "Of course. We've made it worse. Not you and me, maybe, but somebody. Somebody pulled open the wound, set the blood flowing fresh again."

Myrinda nodded at her, murmuring soothing agreements as she led Aggie to the elevator.

Suddenly Aggie's whole body went rigid and she cried out, jerking from Myrinda's arms.

"Aggie?" Myrinda cried out, catching the old woman awkwardly in her arms and lowering her to the floor. "Aggie, what's wrong?"

The old woman shook violently, her legs spasming and her hands clenching into fists. Her eyes rolled back until only the whites showed beneath half-closed lids. A hum came from deep inside Aggie's throat, a low, ugly, animal sound. And it was *spreading*—that's what it sounded like to Myrinda at least, that the sound was not so much growing in volume but picking up reception inside Aggie's chest, her skull, her stomach, even her hands and feet.

A gut instinct compelled Myrinda to back away from the old woman, who was now not just shaking and humming but somehow *vibrating*; everything in her bones, everything in her flesh screamed to her to escape that terrible alien internal buzz, that flesh-jarring shiver that held Aggie in its grip.

As Myrinda watched, thin, dark pink lines began to form around Aggie's neck, wrists, and ankles. It looked as if invisible fishing line were wrapping tighter and tighter around her, biting into her flesh, but Myrinda could see nothing to cause the seams. They strained a moment, waxy and tight, before indenting into tiny furrows, and then with small popping sounds, began to fill with blood. Similar lines began to form across her face, and from the looks of the blood lines taking shape on her housecoat, they also crisscrossed her body.

"Aggie! Oh my God, Aggie!" Myrinda fluttered helplessly nearby, still afraid to touch her, to stand too close to that awful hum. "Aggie, we need to get you some help—"

Aggie's eyes grew wide and for a moment, the hum grew louder. Then she broke apart at the seams, the pieces sliding away from each other wetly. Myrinda screamed. The bisected pieces of her chest rose once and fell like two halves of a gourd, then lay still. The wide eyes grew glassy. The hum faded. The pieces of her didn't bleed, and somehow, that made the sight of her carved up like that more horrible.

Myrinda backed away. A helpless sound lodged in her throat. It tried to be a word, a call for help, but it failed. She glanced at her basket of untouched laundry, then back at the stairway behind her. She couldn't quite bring herself to look fully on the pieces of flesh that used to be the nice old lady from across the hall.

She bolted from the laundry room and took the stairs two at a time, her head a tornado of confused thoughts. What could have possibly cut her up like that? She'd been—well, not exactly fine, but physically *whole*, at the very least, less than ten minutes before. Or had she been? Was it possible that whatever cut her had been so thin, like fishing wire maybe, that she'd managed to hold herself together inside and out, at least for a while? She frowned, shaking her head. That was absurd. She wouldn't have been able to talk, to breathe. No, whatever happened to the old lady had begun after the convulsions. Myrinda had never heard of convulsions strong enough to create

flesh-rending vibrations, but then, she was no doctor. Maybe....
It didn't seem right, either, though.

It had looked like something had diced her up right in front of Myrinda. Something invisible, precise, deadly. Something that hummed. Something that had been so very close to Myrinda that it was a wonder it hadn't sheared off layers of her own skin.

She reached the first floor, her heart pounding and her mouth dry with the heaviness of her breath.

"It's a wound...."

She crossed the lobby to Mrs. Sunderman's apartment and banged on the door. Seconds ticked by with no sound from the apartment. Impatient, she pounded on the door again. "Mrs. Sunderman? There's been an accident," she called. She pounded again, her voice cracking with tears. "Please, Mrs. Sunderman. I need help. Mrs. Roesler's...she's dead. Please, call 911!" With each phrase, she paused, listening for some sign of the landlady. No sounds of movement or life beyond the door.

She huffed, turning to the elevator. Her cell phone was upstairs. She'd just call 911 herself.

The elevator doors opened almost immediately, and she was thankful for that. As she rode up to her floor, she burst into tears. Every muscle in her body was tensed, thrumming with fear and urgency.

Almost humming. She shuddered at the thought, crying harder.

The elevator doors opened and she ran to her apartment and into the kitchen, grabbing her cell phone off the charger on the counter. She dialed 911.

In the basement laundry room, the pieces of Agatha Roesler cooled, their perfectly severed edges unshrivelled and painted with unspilled blood, and in the silence where the hum had been, frenzied whispering of a half-nonsense language echoed between the cement walls.

SEVEN

Derek held a protective arm around Myrinda as she gave Officer Rusker, a husky, middle-aged man with a thin shock of brown hair, her statement. Around them on the grounds, police moved with quiet, purposeful efficiency. Two uniformed officers relegated their curious neighbors, some of whom Myrinda recognized by sight, to the parking lot. Others moved in and out of the lobby, conferred quietly with the uniformed CSIs and EMTs. Flashing lights from the three police cars and the ambulance in the parking lot behind the onlookers twirled red and blue against the wall of the apartments.

She told Rusker about finding Aggie in the basement and how she had seemed terrified, even hurt, how she had rambled incoherently about nameless threats and poison, and how when she tried to get her to her feet and back to the elevator, she had begun to convulse.

Myrinda stopped short of telling Rusker what she had seen next. There was no conceivable way she could explain how a woman had literally come apart in bloodless chunks. The thought of it, let alone any verbalization of it, made her sick to her stomach. So instead, she told Rusker it was when Aggie had begun to shake uncontrollably that she had gone for help, first to

Mrs. Sunderman's apartment, and then back to her own for the cell phone.

"Was there anyone else in the laundry room with you and Mrs. Roesler?" Rusker asked.

Myrinda shook her head. "I didn't see anyone."

"No one on the stairs? Lurking in the lobby, maybe?"

"No, no one."

Rusker took notes, nodding. "You said she was scared of someone?"

"Someone...something," Myrinda shrugged beneath Derek's arm. "I don't know. She wasn't very clear."

"Woman her age, could have been dementia. She might very well have gotten herself worked up into an aneurism."

Myrinda frowned, confused. "An aneurism could do all that?"

"That's the preliminary guess, although we can't be sure until the autopsy, of course. Yeah, right now we're assuming dementia. Hallucinations, maybe that drove her to cut herself like that. Drove her to near hysteria, gave herself a brain aneurism—"

"Cut herself?" Myrinda couldn't imagine an 80 year old woman cutting herself clean through to pieces like that. The woman had been diced alive, for God's sake. Couldn't they see that? No brain aneurism she'd ever heard of could cause *that*.

"There were superficial flesh wounds when we found her. Nothing serious, just scratches on her face, her arms and legs. Like she'd been clawing at herself. You mentioned she seemed hurt, that there was blood on her clothing?"

"Yes...." Myrinda was barely aware she'd spoken out loud. Scratches? *Scratches?!* Just what had she seen down in that basement...or thought she'd seen?

"Maybe from a prior convulsion, like the one you said you witnessed." An uncomfortable pause followed that Rusker finally broke with a clearing of the throat. "Well thanks again, ma'am. Here's my card if you remember anything else or just need to reach me. I appreciate your time."

Myrinda took it in fingers that had grown numb and nodded. Two men wheeled out a gurney on which a long black bag had been laid. Its contours indicated something the size of an intact Aggie Roesler lay inside.

"You okay, baby?" Derek asked once the officer had moved on to a hush-toned conversation with three men in suits. He watched them watch him with a well-practiced unperturbed cool.

"I'd like to go inside now," she said. "Lay down a bit. I'm not feeling well."

"Of course, baby-girl. I got you. Everything's going to be okay." He pulled her into a quick, tight hug, kissed the top of her head, and guided her toward the lobby door.

***

Wayne pulled into a mess of flashing red-blue lights, anxious onlookers, and a body bag being loaded from a gurney into the back of an ambulance.

"What the—?" He put the car into park and got out, trotting over to the nearest uniformed policeman, a young kid maybe a year on the force if that, who ushered him back to the crowd.

"What's going on?"

"Please sir," the young officer told him. "We need you to stand over there with the others."

"What happened? Is that...is that someone from the apartments?"

"Please sir, we would appreciate your cooperation in standing over there with the other tenants of the apartment building."

An older man with an unshaved jaw going gray, a football-player build, and the stance and presence of a cop himself, stood off to one side with a husky, dark-haired officer holding a small notepad. The former he recognized from the building; Wayne thought his name was Carson or Larson. The latter was an on-scene police officer. He watched them a while, gesturing casually with their hands and leaning in toward each other to talk in hushed tones. Then he scanned the crowd for the landlady. He couldn't imagine that busybody Mrs. Sunderman letting such a hub-bub go down on the grounds of her precious building without being all up in cops' faces, demanding answers. Strangely, though, she was nowhere to be seen.

Wayne watched as a uniformed officer emerged from the lobby and crossed over to the husky cop and Carson/Larson. The officer said something, shook his head, and gestured back toward the lobby. The other two men looked off in that direction. Finally, Larson/Carson returned to a small group of onlookers near Wayne.

"What's going on?" a thin woman with severe features asked him. Her bony arms were crossed over her chest as if to self-comfort, but Wayne noticed she curtly yanked one from the grasp of a paunchy, dark-haired man next to her, ostensibly her husband, when he reached out to her.

The tenant who struck Wayne as a police officer (Wayne felt sure he'd seen the name somewhere as Larson) shook his head. "Sunderman. They can't find her. She's not in the apartment, and when they tried her cell, one of the uniforms—the patrol cops over there—heard ringing coming from inside the apartment."

"What about the old woman?" the paunchy man asked.

"They're not sure what happened, exactly. Stroke, aneurism. Maybe something with fits, given her injuries."

"What do you mean?" The woman's bony hand fluttered to her thin chest.

"Cuts," Larson told her, gesturing across his face and chest. "Scratches. In fact, they think—" he stopped, his attention suddenly fixed on something off-center from the front entrance of the building. Wayne followed his gaze to a small cluster of tenants he didn't recognize. They were ostensibly from the first floor, none of the faces familiar in the slightest. Nothing about any of them struck Wayne as particularly attention-worthy. Wayne glanced at Larson, then back at the cluster of tenants. He put them in their early seventies, their slight stoops from latent muscle-ache and dry grayness of face and hair reminding him of his parents. Their clothes, faded from overwashing and drying, hung loose around their chicken skin arms and legs, tight over their softening midsections. They were, so far as he could tell, unremarkable. Well...except that maybe they seemed less shaken than impatient. He frowned. That was the way of people up in New England, Wayne had discovered. Patient impatience. Polite exasperation. It got under his skin in general, and more so now in the face of a poor old lady's death. What was so important, waiting for them back in the building? Their L.L. Bean catalogs and Jeopardy? A sudden heat rush of anger flared in their direction, and he found himself imagining them trying to flip through their magazines with the shredded flesh of bloody wrist stumps slapping wetly against the pages, or watching TV with blackened, hollow sockets where their eyes had been....

Larson's voice broke through Wayne's thoughts, which vanished with the anger as suddenly as they had come. He finished with, "The girl who found her said she had been incredibly distraught moments before. She was trying to tell the girl what was happening to her, I guess, but from the sounds of it, she wasn't making much sense."

The girl, Wayne supposed, was probably the one he'd seen talking to the police, the one with the hot boyfriend who seemed so attentive. And he had known the old woman by sight, had seen her around the building. She always smiled and said hello when she passed him in the hallway or shared an elevator. He hadn't known her, but he'd liked the vibe he got from her, the grandmotherly warmth she exuded, light and airy, like her floral perfume. Poor old lady. She'd come apart.

"Pardon?"

Larson was watching him expectantly, as was the couple beside him. The woman, in particular, seemed to be sizing him up.

Wayne hadn't realized he'd muttered anything out loud until Larson had spoken. It took him a moment to recover from what felt like a sudden invasion into his personal musings. "I—I said she came apart, sounds like. Onset of dementia. Sad."

Larson nodded. "Sad indeed. By all accounts, Mrs. Roesler was a nice lady. It's a shame."

A nice lady, yes. Wayne shifted his weight and glanced at the door. Cops seemed to be conferring on how best to manage the people waiting to get back into the building. Sure, the good people of Bridgewood thought Mrs. Roesler was a nice lady...and an unfortunate and unpleasant incident quickly and neatly cleaned up, while people not much younger hurried on to their lives. The group of faded gray people that had arrested Larson's attention were already gone. *There but for the grace of better meds,* Wayne thought unkindly, and the image of them coming apart, too—quite literally—respawned in his head.

A lot of waiting followed, while by degrees, the CSI, then the nonessential police personnel, finished their tasks, packed up, and left the scene. Finally, one of the detectives who had spoken to Larson announced to the milling tenants that they could return to their apartments. From their spot in the parking lot, Wayne, Larson, and the old couple (Larson introduced them as Hal and Eda Corman) watched the others pass through the front doors. There weren't many yet in residence at Bridgewood Estates, but there were enough to deter Wayne from joining the jostled, largely confused line as it filed into the lobby. Wayne's profession (like Larson's, he supposed) suited his natural sense of security and his inclination to people-watch.

He didn't register the limping figure in dirty, loose-fitting gray clothes right away. She was a good deal shorter than the people ahead of and behind her, and seemed less substantial somehow than the others in the line—more like an afterimage of someone than a real person. Ultimately, though, it was the limp—it was pronounced and arrhythmic—that tripped some inner alarm, wading through his non-thoughts to trigger a sense of familiarity. A heavy lump dropped from his chest and into his gut.

—Oh God, she has no—

The wet, stringy dark hair of her bowed head hung forward, obscuring her face. She was shorter...shorter than the others, because—

She—oh God, she's missing—

He moved closer, not quite at a jog, craning his neck and impatiently dodging police and other tenants who obscured his view of their feet, but he knew. He *knew*. It was the way she limped, dragging what he remembered as rabid stumps ending around the ankles. He vaguely heard Larson calling to him, but he ignored it. He had to see—and to make sure others saw.

Just before she passed through the front doors and into the lobby she looked up and right at him, stopping him short. The lump in his gut rolled heavily, painfully.

Filmy cataracts clouded the eyes but he could feel their precision focus, their malevolent glare. A long lash from the corner of her bluish lips opened up her right cheek to reveal graying teeth clotted with something he didn't want to identify. Her head jerked slightly as if its supports were wrenching away from her neck. In the next moment, she had passed out of sight and into the lobby.

Revulsion sat like dead weights in his shoes, solidifying his legs and arms so that he felt welded to the spot. It took several seconds for feeling to return to his limbs and allow movement again, and even then, it took a supreme effort on his part to half-walk, half-jog to the lobby doors where the last of the tenants were filing in. His gaze swept frantically around the lobby, taking in a glimpse of torn cheek and black hair by Sunderman's door before a man passed between them. Then the girl was gone. There was no sign of her at all, and no indication, given their bored and placid expressions, that anyone else had seen her.

He moved inside, the lump in his gut dropping to a painful place just above his groin. What the hell was going on?

With a trembling hand, he stopped a middle-aged woman heading toward the elevator. She turned and offered a small, polite smile.

"Excuse me, ma'am," he said, aware that his voice sounded small and scared. "Did you see a young girl, uh, dressed in gray sweats? Black hair, pale face, a limp...." His voice trailed off. What else could he say? A slash that opened her mouth almost all the way to her right ear? Cataracts over dry, dead eyes? A girl missing her hands and feet, and yet dragging her corpse toward the landlady's door?

The woman seemed to sense there might be more forthcoming from him, but when he didn't speak, she shook her head. "Sorry. I don't recall seeing anyone like that." She walked away from him.

He tried again with an elderly man shuffling across the lobby floor, describing the black-haired girl in gray sweats as "sickly-looking, and with a bad limp." That seemed sufficient.

The old man hadn't seen her, either. Wayne knew he wouldn't have. No one here had. He waited until the lobby had mostly cleared before getting on the elevator. The others in the car got out on the first floor, and he rode up one more floor alone. For just a moment before the doors opened, it occurred to him that the footless, handless girl might be limping toward the elevator, smearing her bloody stump of an arm across the wall between apartments, leaving a gory double-trail behind her as she dragged her legs forward. That and the lurch of the rising elevator threatened to double him over and force up his lunch from the depths of his stomach. He swallowed several times, a technique he'd learned in childhood to calm his insides and return order to his mind. Usually, it worked.

The doors opened, and with one final suck of air, he stepped out.

The second floor was empty. He felt tears of relief well up in his eyes, and he let go of the breath in his chest. He made his way to his apartment, glancing around to ensure the hallway was still empty as he unlocked his door and stepped inside. Immediately, he locked the door behind him, sighed, forced a smile at the cat, who purred against his legs, and then stumbled quickly to the bathroom to throw up.

***

Derek had accepted early on that the women in his life were complicated, and that their complications made them both strong and fascinating. This extended from his mother and two sisters to the love of his life sleeping in the other room. And they had all taught him that it took a strong, multifaceted man to handle women like that without going crazy. Derek had known a lot of women in his life. He knew his way around them. He knew how to make them smile, to turn them on, to pique their interest. He knew how to read them. But the women in his life now knew and understood him—they knew how to wow him, how to move him, how to infuriate him and how to soothe him. Weighing the passion, the excitement, and the great memories against their soapboxes, their fits of passionate discourse, their unpredictable moods and whims, these women intrigued him, captured his interest as well as his heart and mind.

He often thought it was a shame that his mother and sisters had such a problem with Myrinda being white. They were all so much alike, and it ought to have bonded them. But then, maybe the very qualities he found so interesting, those they shared in common, could only naturally push them apart, like similar magnetic poles. He accepted that, too. So long as they were civil, even if it was cool politeness and guarded respectfulness, he was okay with it. He was a grown man, in control of and happy with his life. The army had put him through college, where he'd earned a Master's degree in National Security, and had gone on to build up an impressive reputation in private security for a small handful of powerful clients. He attributed these successes to the strong women who had raised him, and to the beautiful, remarkable, strong woman he now had to share them with. He felt pretty strong and pretty remarkable himself for achieving—and balancing—a good life.

His mom and sisters hadn't been thrilled that he was moving so far from Philly. To them, New England was too far and too white, and he supposed they thought he would have to fight for acceptance so far away from his old, familiar stomping grounds. They were fairly insulated, though, in their community, and didn't realize that in more than one aspect of his successful, happy life, he'd had to fight for acceptance anyway, in passive and sometimes even in direct ways. It was, by now, naturally assimilated into his social interaction. That he was black meant something to him, but he knew it made many people uncomfortable if they thought (or believed he thought) it was his sole defining feature. That was one of the reasons he loved Myrinda; all the things that made him who he was, she loved and respected. She wanted to know all about what mattered to him because *he* mattered to her.

He glanced in the direction of the bedroom as he got a beer and a Tupperware container of leftovers—one of Myrinda's "chicken surprises"—from the fridge. He was worried about her. It wasn't just that she'd been quiet. He'd expected that, after what had happened down in the laundry room with Aggie Roesler from across the hall. He'd expected her to be troubled—distracted, moody, even. But she was different in a way that unsettled him. Different in a way he couldn't read, couldn't understand. He'd always prided himself in knowing what she needed almost before she did, but this brooding, jumpy woman with shadowed, far-away eyes exuded a kind of alienness to him. She wasn't distant and distracted; she was there with him, all right, but she was...not herself. It was almost like whatever she had seen had loosened some pipe inside her, and she was dripping, dripping, filling up slowly with someone else. Someone darker. Someone he couldn't quite reach.

At the kitchen table, he ate the leftover chicken cold, right out of the Tupperware container, thinking about her earlier request. When he'd denied her gently, she'd gone off to the bathroom. She wasn't angry, he'd seen, but anxious, like her thoughts were already ahead of him and on to other things. As an afterthought, she'd called back that she was going to go soak in the tub, and Derek had let her go. He'd figured it was a possibility she was just hormonal, and maybe feeling the natural stress of moving away from family, friends, and familiarity. She took baths to ease menstrual cramps sometimes, or when she wanted to relax alone. Also, she got anxious nearly to the point of obsessive-compulsive for a day or two when she had PMS, and sometimes presented odd distresses to him that seemed constructed of a logic only she could follow. He didn't always understand the origin of her worries, but he was and had always been a fixer, so he did his best to reassure her, and it passed quickly enough.

It was really her request more than anything that had thrown him off. She'd wanted him to leave the packing tape she'd plastered all over the heating vents. She wouldn't tell him why she'd done it, other than that she thought there was some sort of infestation. However, she'd denied seeing any insects in the apartment, and jumped up when he moved to call the landlady about sending someone up to check the vents out. No, she emphatically insisted he not involve the landlady. She just wanted him to leave the tape on the vents for a few days. Like fly paper, she said. Just in case, just to see. When he'd explained to her that it was probably a potential fire hazard, she nodded, and reluctantly let him peel it off. She'd still insisted no one needed to be called, that she'd let him know if any other problems with the vents presented themselves.

Usually her stress revolved around the cleanliness, order, and structural integrity of the things in her charge. The sloppy, excessively applied wads of tape over her beautiful living room vents made no sense to him. Derek knew this apartment meant a lot to her. It was more than just a place to live. It was meant to be a soothing sanctuary, an inviting and comfortable hang-out, and a neat and orderly command post. To her, it was a collection of treasured possessions and furnishings, which in turn, displayed a lifetime of cherished memories. Myrinda didn't ask for much, really; she had only ever wanted a home of her own. To her, an apartment meant home in all its warmest connotations, and home meant family, security, and a future.

Maybe he was overthinking it, but this move seemed to be more stressful than anything to Myrinda. He wondered if they should have just stayed in PA.

Soft mewling sounds coming from the bathroom threaded through his thoughts. At least, he thought he heard something, though he couldn't be sure. The way this building was, the sounds could be coming from another apartment, up through the floor, or through the ceiling maybe. He put down his fork and listened. A distinctive thump from their bathroom confirmed it, followed by little cries of pain, and a wet dripping sound.

He rose and moved out into the hall. At the far end, the bathroom door was closed, the sliver of space beneath it dark. He listened again, and thought he heard water running in the sink. It stopped, and there was another thump, a kind of crystal sound like a fist (or face) hitting glass, and a small cry so heartbroken, so forlorn, that it made Derek's own chest ache a little. What was Myrinda doing in there in the dark? He moved quickly down the hall to the door and knocked, his hand already on the knob. "Babygirl? You okay in there?"

There was no verbal answer, but he could hear the sucking of the drain in the sink being released, and the wet splash of liquid hitting the floor.

"Myrinda, baby, what's going on? Talk to me."

"She isn't here," a faint female voice said from the other side of the door. It had a quality to it he didn't recognize at all.

Derek frowned, trying the knob. It was locked. "Myrinda?"

"I said," the voice from the other side replied, dropping octaves with each syllable, "she isn't here."

Derek jiggled the handle, then threw his weight against the door. A cold fear spread quickly from his chest, enveloping his arms, rising up his neck and fanning down into his gut. Myrinda didn't—couldn't—sound like that. He slammed a shoulder against the door again, and then a third time, but it wouldn't budge. Beyond it, he thought he heard a low kind of chuckling, devoid of humor. He shouldered the door again. "Open this door, or I'm gonna break—"

He tried the knob again, and the door swung easily open, breaking off his words. He tumbled through, his hand flicking the light switch and bathing the bathroom in bright white light. His gaze darted between sink and toilet, then across the tiled wall to the tub and shower.

The room was empty. Well, nearly empty.

In the mirror, Derek's forehead bled. Still confused, he frowned, his fingers rising to feel the spot. They came away clean. He blinked, and the blood somehow refocused, appearing smeared on the glass. He glanced down and saw that there was also a dark smear of blood, like dragged fingers, across the tan counter, spilling into the sink. Grabbing a large wad of toilet paper, he turned on the faucet, wiping the blood from the counter and mirror and rinsing it out of the sink. He chucked the pink wad of paper into the small trash bin between the counter and toilet, then turned off the light.

He quickly crossed to the bedroom, opening the door. The bedroom was dark. A shape lay beneath the covers.

"Babygirl?"

EIGHT

Myrinda lay in the darkness, willing sleep to take her. It didn't. She could hear Derek moving around out in the kitchen—soft sounds, lithely confident. She imagined him heating up the leftovers or brewing up some coffee, and it was soothing. His solid, sure presence, his thereness made her feel better. There, but not on top of her with questions she couldn't answer just then. Whether or not he knew she was awake didn't matter; he knew she needed to rest, alone in the dark. He was good like that; it was one of those endearing qualities about him that she found herself appreciating a lot just then. He knew when to be there, but not *too* there.

Her thoughts turned to Aggie. She'd heard people murmuring about her as she'd turned to go, and it had hit a nerve. It had been idle talk, clueless and unfounded, about how the way she was dressed suggested she might be going senile, about her being too old to live on her own, about strokes and heart attacks and even terrible accidents that could befall little old ladies when wandering basements alone.

At first, Myrinda couldn't quite put a finger on why such talk got under her skin the way it did. No one had looked at her like she should have or could have done more, or that she had somehow done something wrong. And it wasn't that Myrinda felt a comparison to her own current life. She was young, strong, and certainly not alone. She had Derek. She had been growing quite fond of Aggie in a grand-daughterly sort of way, and she supposed gossip about the sweet old woman was part of what bothered her. Despite her current situation, she could imagine what it might have felt like to be an old woman living alone, learning to balance what her mind could still do with what her body could, learning to accept increasing limitations and relinquish certain freedoms. On top of that, to feel like the world was watching her, waiting for a sign of unmistakable frailty, waiting for any shred of evidence to prove it was time to give it all up and accept infirmity....

She turned over, frowning as she felt for a cooler side of the pillow. That was it, maybe. She could relate to the feeling of being watched, of being scrutinized by people waiting for the pretty little prom princess to fail at something, anything to make them feel better. She'd never told anyone she felt like that—she worried it made her look conceited, another thing to criticize her for—but there had been dirty looks in high school hallways, and whispers trailing after her from bowed heads of gathered girls. More often than not there were the dull looks of girls dating her boyfriends' friends, assumptions made about her motives and her sexual history, the slights and snubs of friendships already formed and unwilling to expand to accept "John's new bimbo" or "Greg's flavor of the month."

A misdirected flare of anger made her cheeks hot. She felt a sudden hatred for those clueless, gossiping idiots outside, making narrow-minded judgments and pronouncements about Aggie based on their bored and limited world view. Fuck them. Who were they to label her senile? Who were they to say she couldn't handle anything on her own that she set her mind to?

A throb of pain above the bridge of her nose made her grimace and then close her eyes. From what Aggie had been saying, Myrinda supposed the old woman had been having delusions. Wounds in the earth that opened up from another dimension, for God's sake, with chaotic creatures crawling through it to spread their insanity sickness in this world. It sounded crazy.

But crazier than severed fingers crawling out of a heating vent into her living room? Crazier than hallucinating that Aggie Roesler's body had split itself into bloodless chunks of flesh as she lay dying on the floor?

She heard the door open softly, just a little, and a wedge of light from the hall made the room a shade brighter.

"Babygirl?"

Myrinda didn't answer him. There was still something nagging at her, something tangled beneath her conscious thoughts that she felt somehow needed processing, and she wanted her thoughts clear before she tried to voice anything to Derek.

She heard him enter the room, felt the movement of the bed as he sat on his side and leaned over to her.

"You awake, babygirl?"

She turned over to face him. In the semi-darkness, she could see a worried glint in his eyes. "Mm-hm," she said.

"You okay?"

She offered him a sleepy smile. "I'm okay. Just...tired."

"You hungry? Can I get you anything?"

"No, baby," she said. She felt a surge of unexplainable annoyance, much like a monthly hormonal tide. Derek was only trying to take care of her, and yet his presence was starting to feel vaguely like an intrusion. "I just want to get some sleep."

"Were you in the bathroom just now?"

"No," she replied. "Why?"

He stroked her hair, looking into her eyes for some time before answering. "No reason. Get some sleep. I'll be in later to check on you." He kissed her forehead and got up, and she fought the annoyance at the thought of a future intrusion from washing over the warm, comforting feeling of his kiss.

"Okay," she murmured. "I'll probably be out before you come to bed."

He nodded, paused in the doorway as if he had something else to ask her. He didn't. "Good night, Myrinda."

"Good night," she replied, turning over.

He shut the door behind him, cutting off the light.

***

The upside-down commercial man appeared on the television again after Eda had gone to bed and Hal had settled in his chair to doze in front of a late-night western. The man's voice, a presence in itself, cut through the first layer of sleep, and Hal's eyes opened.

"Good evening, Hal."

Hal blinked, the taste of sleep still in his mouth, and squinted at the television.

"Now that she's gone to bed," the man said, glancing at the bedroom door from the TV screen, "we can talk."

"Talk?" Hal, still groggy, took in some of the background features on the screen—a stretch of green lawn like the apartment grounds behind the commercial man's head, and a large, Victorian-style building with massive staggered wings seeming to envelope the man's broad build. This time, instead of the polo shirt and slacks, the upside-down commercial man wore a sharp, expensive-looking business suit. "What do you want to talk about?"

The bright, buy-this-from-me smile shrank to a smirk. "I believe you already know. Wake up, Hal. You've been asleep for too long. I need you to focus." Behind him, on the grounds, orderlies in scrubs with sets of metal jaws stretching their faces wide open were assisting slow-moving, dazed-looking people in pajamas. Many of the latter had blood streaking down from their hair or in long smears across their pajamas. One woman passed directly behind the upside-down commercial man; from the frame of the television, Hal could only see her from the hips up, but by the way she dragged herself, he could tell she was hurt badly. Her head was tilted forward and dark hair hung in her face, but as she shuffled by, Hal thought he caught a glimpse of her neck, the skin gray and dirty.

Hal leaned forward in his chair, glancing around the room. It was one thing to dream of the upside-down commercial man, but quite another thing entirely to be wide awake and watching him converse in real time from the TV screen. "What's going on here? Are you some kind of hacker broadcast or something?"

"No, Hal, I'm not."

"Well, look—I don't know who you are, then, but if you don't leave me alone, I'm going to call—"

"Mrs. Sunderman? I'm afraid she won't be able to come to the phone. She's occupied elsewhere. The police?" The man shook his head, his hair dangling. "I don't advise putting yourself on the police's radar. It will only make things messy later. I suppose you could call one of those...those places you have here in this world, the ones for containing those like us, but I suspect they greatly limit your personal freedoms."

Hal considered just getting up and unplugging the television, or just walking right out of the room, but he found he couldn't. He didn't want to get close enough to the television that one of those solid arms could reach out and touch him, and he was afraid to turn his back, even for a second, on the commercial man. He couldn't quite discount with reason the notion that if the upside-down commercial man wanted to pull himself bodily right out of the television screen, he could do just that. And then Hal would be without the gossamer safety of the screen glass between him and the whims of figure before him. "Are you...somewhere in this building? A tenant?" He fought to restore reason to his thoughts, to identify this man for what he was—a hacker, maybe, broadcasting from boosted Radio Shack equipment stashed in one of the first-floor apartments. A colleague messing with him. A nut-job stalker with a very real presence and a very real address.

He found it difficult to make any of those explanations work to his satisfaction.

"A tenant, no," the man answered. "But in this building...yes. In a manner of speaking. We're all in and out of this building, aren't we?"

"Where are you broadcasting from?"

"I come from chaos. From chaos, erebus, and from erebus, the roads to death."

"Death?" Hal wasn't sure he understood any of what the man was getting at, but he did get the distinct feeling that the conversation was taking a bad turn. He surreptitiously felt along the seat cushion for the remote, and when he discovered the hard oblong of plastic, his fingers closed around it slowly.

The man's smile disappeared. "I wouldn't do that if I were you." The twinkle in the man's eyes was swallowed by a blackness that made Hal think of sharks. Hal let go of the remote.

Just as quickly as it had darkened, the man's expression lightened again. "Now then. Let's get down to the business at hand."

"I don't—"

"Your killing of your wife, I mean."

Hal glanced at the bedroom door, his hand flying to the remote again, to turn down the volume. A moment after, he drew his hand away, recognizing the move as both silly and useless. This man wasn't really being broadcast on the television; on some level, Hal understood this without being able to explain what that really meant. Moreover, he understood that if this man wanted to talk to him, he would find a way, regardless of Hal's powers with the remote. In fact, Hal got the distinct impression from those eyes and that terrible shark smile that the man had more ways than just the television to invade his life, and that he wasn't going anywhere until Hal heard him out.

He thought again of the man peeling himself off the television screen and dropping into his living room, and the thought made the dinner sitting in his stomach a heavy, gurgling thing.

"I can see from your expression," the man said, his image dissolving for just a second into static pixels before reforming into perfect, slightly graying hair and rugged face, "that you need me to walk you through your reasoning. Maybe help you come up with a plan of execution. Which, of course, can be arranged. After all, that's what I'm here for."

"Why do you want me to kill my wife?"

The inverted brow crinkled innocently. "I don't want anything for you, Hal, that you don't want for yourself. I'm here to help you. I recognize in you what I know in me."

"Who are you?"

The man smiled broadly. Upside-down, it looked like an obscene frown. "Why, I told you. I'm part of chaos. And you, my friend, are part of erebus. So you see, our roads lead inevitably to death. Eda's death."

Hal thought about this for a moment, unsure how to respond. He didn't feel as frightened as he thought he should, or as horrified at the thought of killing Eda, either. He knew that was wrong, that it signified something wrong with him. The longer he talked to this man, the less he was really sure of, though. Again, he considered the possibility that maybe the upside-down commercial man wasn't really coming through the television at all. Maybe he was being broadcast from inside Hal's head, a visual hallucination. Maybe he was part of a tumor, or an early sign of the onset of dementia. Maybe...but he sounded pretty real to Hal. Hal pinched the bridge of his nose. It was harder, he noticed, to read body language and facial expressions of a man who was hanging upside-down.

"In other words, I'm what you need."

"What I need," Hal said, "is a head-shrinker. Or a better cable provider."

"I think you need to understand something, Hal. I'm not asking you to commit murder. I'm asking you to act in your own self-defense."

"What are you talking about?" Hal scoffed. "She's not trying to kill me."

The man looked knowingly at him, head slightly tilted. "Isn't she, though?"

"No, of course not. She...."

"Loves you?" the man asked when Hal's voice trailed off. "Is that what you were going to say?"

Hal wasn't sure he was going to say it, wasn't even sure if it was really true at this point in their marriage. He didn't know what she felt, and it had sparked the faintest idea that maybe his fervent protests of her intentions (or lack thereof) were buoyed by...well, nothing substantial.

"We have history," he said instead, sighing. He leaned back into his chair.

The man nodded—up-down-up-down. "And you don't think history, by its very nature, is woven through with unbreakable habits, inescapable patterns? That it's soaked, even saturated with years of disappointments and subsequent resentment? Of slights maybe forgiven but not forgotten? Or are you so confident your good times have outweighed the bad, at least so far as she's concerned?"

"Okay, so what? She doesn't love me anymore? She's not happy in this marriage? We're both too old to change. It's not like either of us savors the idea of starting over alone at our age."

"I think," the man said, the words already chosen carefully from somewhere dark behind that perfect mask of salesmanship, "that you'd do well not to assume she thinks just like you do."

"I've known her a long time," Hal argued. "I know how she thinks."

"Do you know she cheated on you?"

Hal was, for a minute, stunned to silence. Eda? Eda, for whom sex was handed out like a gold medal for the few and far-between things he did to appease her?

"You're lying." It was out of his mouth before he could stop it, and immediately after, he felt a cold unease.

The words hung ugly and heavy between him and the man on the screen for several seconds, before the man replied, unperturbed, "In fact, I'm not. She never made it a habit, but there was a man she met three times while you were on business trips. Three times she slept with this man. He's dead now. He died in a fire. You didn't know him. No one in her personal life did."

"Wh—when?" Hal, still too stupefied to process this new piece of information, found that surprise took the lead ahead of hurt or anger. He hadn't thought the old girl, even when she wasn't old, had had it in her.

"Seven years ago. She meant to leave you for him. Not because she loved him, mind you, but because of his money. He had a lot of it at one time. He was a local politician, a man of small favors always owed to him. Some influence. But there was the fire. You may recall his death on the news. Gerald Wycoff."

Neither the name nor the newsworthy item of his death in a fire rang any bells whatsoever. Hal had never cared much for politics, and even less for the men entrenched in them, but he did know it was always an interest of Eda's. She was always trying to get him to watch the news, always snorting at his confusion over political issues on the voting ballot, his oblivious indifference to most current events. For years, it had been a chisel to the wall of their marriage, chipping off little pieces.

She thought it made him dumb, or at the very least, uneducated and uncultured, that he couldn't and didn't care to follow politics. He thought her volunteering for local political campaigns and fundraisers was a vain and shallow attempt to ingratiate herself with better company. It was an interest of hers that had never cultivated more than resentment.

Well, he thought with a spike of bitterness, *resentment and a damn dirty affair with a local political snake.*

"It's a matter of perspective," the commercial man said placidly, making Hal jump. He'd almost forgotten the commercial man was there. "There are more ways to look at things than what resignation to your life has brought you to. And, of course, other solutions than simple resignation."

Again, his hand closed around the remote, if only to try and regain some sense of control over this increasingly unpleasant conversation. A dull ache was beginning to form behind his right eye. "What do you want from me? God, what the hell are you?" He leaned forward, the remote in his hands. He wanted to hurl it at the television, to brain the man and make him fall from his inverted perch off-screen. Instead, the man pixelated again, static scrambling the rugged features, and for a few seconds, Hal thought he saw the thing beneath the salesman's mask, a blurred kind of creature with a gaping mouth like an open zipper, except the teeth were sharp and the gullet beyond them an endless black abyss. The now-familiar form of the upside-down commercial man returned suddenly, like a figure emerging from the swirling depths of a snowstorm, but for another second or so, the afterimage of his true shape remained, a ghost imprint that gave an unpleasant cast to his features. Then it was gone, too.

"I told you, Hal," the commercial man said, "I'm what you need. Think about the life you want and how to get it. I'll be in touch."

The television screen went dark.

***

In the night, the Old Ward stood silent. It had been silent for a long time. Faded memories of dusty voices and blurred faces echoed down the hall. Rust crusted the hinges on the heavy wooden front doors. Layers of gaudy spray paint marred the testaments to order that the administration building's walls used to be. Cracks interwoven through the graffiti found water stains and those of something darker. Paint chipped and peeled like dry skin, flaking off from time to time to drift to the gouged floor tiles. File folders, long emptied of classified contents, lay strewn and rotting on cracked and chipped desks, the muck of blown-in dirt and seeped-in rain beneath them making them pulpy, leaving them stuck in pools of their own kind of blood. Doors that had regularly stood locked now hung open, uneven, splintered by fingernails, chipped by rabid mouths of broken teeth. The Old Ward had indeed been silent, left untouched, for a long time. But it was not empty.

There were plans for restoration made by the Bridgehaven Historical Society, but they had yet to be started. The corporation who owned the surrounding land had insisted that the tenants of their new apartment building have time to settle in first, before that monument to depravity drew noisy work crews and dust and heavy equipment to trample the lawns. So The Old Ward stood as it had for nearly thirty years, with the Narrative in the tunnels beneath and the chaotic ones moving silently in their jerky, blurred way, around the debris. They went there when there was nowhere else to be; they found the idea of containment for creatures possessed of unbound insanity fascinating, and the ruins of such a place felt fitting to them.

What the chaotic ones had come to think of as the Narrative had opened the way. Through the Narrative, all questions were answered, all sights were seen, all words were given extra dimensions, and so, extra meanings and truths. The chaotic ones didn't much care for these powers, had no interest in possessing the Narrative, but had always responded to the opening of the way. It called to them across the abyss and brought them into new worlds, and those new worlds gave them what they needed.

Because of the Narrative, they had found they could traverse at least one way through the abyss even though someone had dropped a structure on it on this world's side; mass and solidity were concepts of logic, a reasoning that didn't matter to them, nor to the powers contained in the pages of the Narrative. The abyss could be filled with all the structures of this world and just keep going on and on, limitless, bending around corners and taking up space where it pleased.

Tonight, the chaotic ones moved forth again from the Old Ward, trying on new faces. There were minds in the nearby structure that were like the inside of the Old Ward. Minds steeped in the essences of the abyss that had been spilling through. Minds to play with, let fester, then to taste.

Beneath the apartments, the black pool pulsed excitedly.

NINE

What Wayne eventually found at the library regarding the early days of the Bridgehaven Asylum was unusual, to say the least.

At first, he couldn't find anything to add to his base of knowledge about the apartments or the asylum. There wasn't very much on the Internet; he'd found an obscure reference on a website about abandoned asylums that linked to a 1992 article on the 100th anniversary of Bridgehaven. It mentioned a Dr. Eagan Fullbright, brilliant psychiatrist and firm supporter of the theories of mental healthcare purported by Dr. Thomas Story Kirkbride and his design-as-therapy buildings. Dr. Fullbright had been appointed Director of the new Bridgehaven Asylum, to oversee a staff of 70 and a patient body of about 450. By the mid 1900s when Fullbright retired, budget cuts had reduced the staff to 50, although the number of patients crammed into the asylum was closer to 520. Development of psychoactive drugs rendered some of Kirkbride's (and thus, Fullbright's) methods obsolete. But the staff didn't quite bridge the gap between the method of treating patients as human beings by building them up body and soul and medicating them for their psychiatric disorders. In the chasm in between, a lot of patients fell prey to victimization, abuse, and neglect.

This wasn't what really interested Wayne, though. He'd done extensive research for his article on both the apartment building and the asylum, so he knew all that already.

The only item of importance to him was the fact that despite the deteriorating conditions, the lack of funding and such, there was no record of significant tragedy or scandal to mar the reputation Fullbright had worked so hard to build until the massacre in the 1980s. That, Wayne knew, had been bad enough to encompass years' worth of tragedy and scandal. However, little was reported on that particular event, either. Article after article on the asylum told the same story: the promising humanitarian start and subsequent fall of a mighty historical landmark, a briefly touched-upon tragic end, and the highways of progress that reclaimed valuable land to build apartments.

What Wayne was looking for, he supposed, was a connection to something possibly more...supernatural. Maybe some mention of the mangled girl he kept seeing—who she was in life, maybe how she died. He thought it easily possible, given the tragedies that happened on the grounds, how much blood and horror and violence had soaked into the place, that the apartments could be haunted. He felt pretty sure of it, actually, especially after what he'd seen the day before in the parking lot, when all the tenants had been gathered after the death of Mrs. Roesler. Wayne was pretty sure he was the only one who had seen the girl. In a way, the idea of a ghost was easier to accept than the idea of a brain tumor. So he went that route next.

After some digging and cross-clicking, he found an entry on HauntedAsylumsofAmerica.com. He scanned through it, looking for mention of the girl. There were no specific individuals mentioned, but in his mind, the whole entry supported the idea the apartments might be haunted. He printed an excerpt of the entry which read as follows:

Bridgewood Asylum

Official records indicate Bridgewood Asylum was closed due to funding cutbacks, asbestos, and the deinstitutionalizing of mental health care. However, evidence exists of higher rates of neglect and abuse, sexual assaults, and drug use among both patients and staff, and impending investigations into the alleged misconduct may have played a part.

Those official records, according to sources, claim that the real reasons for the facility closing are downplayed if not flat out denied or ignored. The rumors of the locals in the town below indicate a massacre involving both patients and staff in the early part of the decade caused such a scandal that town officials were compelled to bury the truth—literally—under brand new concrete and stone. The details of the massacre are wild and sometimes conflicting, but invariably report orgies, cannibalism, human sacrifice, and torture. The few survivors of the massacre, when interviewed, claimed that monsters "from the black puddle of space and nothing" drove them to kill. It is worth noting that this answer was given consistently by both patients and staff involved in the incident. Medical tests indicated no presence of chemical substances in their blood streams, and subsequent inspections of the building found nothing in the building material to cause auditory and visual hallucinations (high levels of asbestos were discovered, though asbestos is not known to cause hallucinations).

Nothing of the asylum's residency wards, treatment areas, or isolation areas remain; the entire structure of the asylum has been torn down with the exception of the Old Ward (the central building of the asylum), where offices, registration, and patient files were kept. A majority of these files, particularly the patient medical files and the staff employee files, were removed by police after the massacre. Sightings of illuminated offices (although the Old Ward has stood without electricity since the '80s) have been reported, as well as the occasional pretty nurses wandering the hallways. The most frequent sighting is of a balding man with a mustache and a briefcase entering and leaving the Old Ward. He is said to vanish through the chained front doors of the building on overcast mornings, and around sunset, has been seen to hurry down the stairs and disappear on the lawns between the Old Ward and what used to be its staff parking lot.

It is also interesting to note that the apartments were built on the site where the art therapy wing used to stand—the site where the worst of the massacre incidents took place, and where survivor reports claimed the "black puddle" was.

Bridgewood Estates Apartments

Evidently, the hotly debated construction of apartments on so notorious a landmark site was not without strangely coincidental portends. Unseasonably rough weather conditions, worker accidents on site (some fatal and some without determinable cause), manufacturing blunders, and permit snafus all delayed the original building plans. Further, upon completion of the building, a massive fire broke out less than a week after. Although no one was hurt, the building was completely leveled.

Reconstruction commenced late the following spring, and met with less of the original obstacles, although it is said the turnover in work staff was unprecedented, many workers citing "unacceptable conditions" and refusing to elaborate.

He read the printout again, paying closer attention to the noted details regarding patient and staff motives, and his gut lurched.

In all his previous research on the massacre at the asylum, he had never found any mention of motive for the killing. But here was an account of both patients and doctors claiming a "black puddle of space and nothing" drove them to kill. Wayne was used to trusting journalistic instincts, but there was something more than even that here, something he felt spoke to his own feelings of aggression and imbalance lately. A black puddle, or pool, a surge of darkness, adequately explained the feelings he'd been having, the sense of being drowned, washed over by a liquid hate whose surface he couldn't quite break through.

Wayne didn't feel like he was being haunted, exactly. He felt like he was being poisoned.

He poured through the excerpted entry again, highlighting every mention of the black puddle. He wasn't quite sure yet how this new information might be able to help him, but it certainly seemed worth more research. Maybe there were toxic chemicals in the ground that caused hallucinations. Maybe there was a cover-up here between the corporation that had built on the land and one that had dumped dangerous chemicals onto it. Maybe—

"Ahhh, Bridgehaven. One of La Claviére's gates."

Wayne jumped, turning in his chair. "Excuse me?"

Behind him, looking over his shoulder, was a short gray-haired man in a flannel shirt and slacks. Wayne recognized him as the head librarian, a jovial septuagenarian with a nearly eidetic memory for book titles and covers and a propensity to tell rambling stories related to books with often quite interesting diverging branches. They were nodding acquaintances, but the man's warmth, the glow in his eyes when he talked about books, endeared him to Wayne.

The old man nodded a hello. His professor's mustache billowed over an unlit pipe clenched (as an affectation, Wayne supposed) between the old man's teeth. Deep laugh lines bracketed the man's eyes behind thin-rimmed glasses.

"Sorry to have startled you," the man said. "Couldn't help but notice you're highlighting the 'black puddle' references in that article." He gestured at the computer screen. "That old asylum where all the massacres were. Those patients there and even the doctors and police all claimed a crazy sickness poisoned them and made them do those horrible things. Something that came out of a black puddle. Just reminded me of something."

"About a gate?" Wayne asked.

"Ayup." The man took the pipe from between his teeth and held it, his expression thoughtful. "That last Director before the place closed down, a man named Symmes, was a big bibliophile. Particularly interested in very old, very rare books. We've got a section here in this branch; you need a special library card and you can't check them out or anything, but he had a card. Came in here asking for all kinds of things. Primers, old Bibles, travelogues. Oh, and of course, books on spirituality and the occult. 'Specially liked them."

"I'm not sure I follow," Wayne said.

"Well," the old man said, gesturing again at the computer screen in front of Wayne, "we don't have it here, but a few times he'd asked for this one book called *Livre des Portes*, or the *Book of Gates*, by an occultist and alchemist named La Claviére. It was written in the late 1500s in France. Probably worth a small fortune. From what I've heard, much of it was a translation of parchments brought out of Egypt by traders during the Renaissance. The parchments themselves weren't Egyptian, though. They supposedly predated Egyptian hieroglyphics, were in some language the traders claimed was older than Sumerian, even. Lord knows how they were even translated; I've heard tell the characters of the language had...extra dimensions, aspects that made it unlike any language known to expert linguists. Anyway, supposedly, this Frenchman, La Claviére, got a hold of these parchments by murdering the trader carrying them. The translations then began to come to him in dreams and nightmares. In a fever, he wrote the *Book of Gates*. There were five—gates, that is—that La Claviére knew of, five he saw in dreams, though he thought there might be more. Gates to other universes, other dimensions, worlds beyond imagination, he said."

Wayne nodded, confusion crinkling his brow, and waited for the old man to continue.

The old man put the pipe in his mouth as if smoking, removed it, then continued. "I guess it comes to mind now because Symmes died not too long ago. Around the time of the grand opening of those Bridgewood Estates apartments, where the Asylum used to be, actually. Suicide—sad affair. Left behind a family. Anyway, everyone here knew it was sort of a quest of his to find this book—this went all the way back to when he first took the job in '79—and then one day, he just stopped. Stopped coming here altogether. Mid-eighties, I believe that was. Right before they closed the asylum down." The old man shrugged. "I saw him once at the market and asked after his health and all. He told me he was great. Found that book he was looking for."

"So, forgive me if I'm being dense," Wayne said, fully turning in his chair to face the old man, "but what does this *Book of Gates* have to do with the massacre?"

"Nothing, if you believe sane folk," the old man said, offering him a smile and a conspiratorial wink. "Coincidence, maybe. But this one nice fella on the police force—used to come in here to borrow children's books for his kids—told me Dr. Symmes claimed in interrogation that he had used the book to open up one of La Claviére's gates to another dimension. That was right after the massacre up there, he said that."

"And this gate—?"

The old man leaned in with a conspiratorial smile. "He said it looked like a 'black puddle of space and nothing.'" He clamped the pipe in his mouth, and with a clap on Wayne's shoulder, he moved on.

"Hey, uh—?" Wayne called after him.

The librarian turned around.

"Where is Symmes's copy of the book now?"

The old man shrugged. "Don't know. I don't think anyone knows. Heck, maybe it's still in the Old Ward." He winked again and walked on.

Wayne sank in his chair and turned back to his papers. A gate to another dimension, one where something alien, something infectious and crazy had poisoned the minds of patients and staff alike. Where this black puddle had driven them to such frenzied heights of violence that even the shocker sites wouldn't post pics or give out details. It was absolutely absurd. Insane, really. Wild and *Weird-Tales*-esque.

But then, it was no crazier than seeing the ghost of a handless, footless dead girl. It wasn't so far a leap, if he kept with this chemical-dumping theory, that Symmes read from this book or performed some kind of gate-opening ritual and coincidentally, his patients took crazy to a whole new level shortly after because of exposure to toxins. If Symmes believed in all that occult mumbo-jumbo, it was possible he thought he'd caused the massacre. And that kind of guilt, combined with the belief that they were building apartments on a dangerous gate he had never managed to be able to close, might have driven him to suicide. It was certainly all possible.

Or...Symmes had opened a gaping maw in reality as he knew it, and what leaked through was a kind of toxin of its own.

Either way, Wayne felt pretty sure that his mind was not right when he was home. Away from the apartments, it was like a smog cleared from around his head, and he could put things in perspective again. But when he was home...there were the thoughts. The ones he didn't really want to admit to his conscious mind he was having, the ones that followed sudden and uncharacteristic flashes of anger—violent anger.

The kind of thoughts that stuck in his head like a sinus infection, caught from some nasty exposure to craziness on the apartment grounds.

Either way...though even in the library, where knowledge abounded, only one of those two possibilities gripped him as being the truth.

"Don't know," the old man had said. *"Maybe it's still in the Old Ward."*

Wayne gathered up his print-outs and rushed out of the library.

***

In the crowd gathered outside after the death of Agatha Roesler, Larson saw the woman from 2C. It was only briefly, as she passed by a group of old-timers on the way to the lobby, but it was enough to move him. She had found his gaze, but her eyes, her whole facial expression, had been so hard to read. And there was something else off about her, something he couldn't quite put a finger on.

Seeing her did confirm two things to his satisfaction, though. First, she had left him the notes to find. It had to be her. That distracted coolness he'd seen in her eyes had to be disappointment that he hadn't yet acted on the suggestions so subtly interwoven in her curtains, certain steps to prove his feelings for her. Second, if he did, in fact, follow her love notes, whether on paper or in curtains, that he would finally know real, true, lasting love.

He'd all but convinced himself for decades that true love didn't really exist. Experience had shown him that any number of things, big and small, could eat away at any kind of love, even the kinds that happened at first sight, that surpassed the loves that had come before—hell, even the kind that compelled people to label each other with the overwrought term of soul mate. Money and boredom were, in his view, the usual top two reasons. Both had destroyed his first marriage, back when he was just out of the academy and long hours for low pay had prevented him from bringing in enough of the former or providing a respite for the latter, in his wife Cici's eyes. She'd had an affair, more emotional than physical, but evidently strong enough to send her packing and into Brett Whateverhisnamewas's arms. The juxtaposition of "amicable" and "divorce" was a pitifully obvious oxymoron, even when there was no disagreement on terms, and the ugliness of theirs wore enough of love's shine right off that it was possible to fall out of love with a woman he'd once promised before God, family, and friends to love forever. His second marriage had ended with an aneurism in his new wife Callie's brain a mere three years into their wedded bliss. He'd loved her so, so much. Callie, with her beautiful white smile and green eyes and that lock of red hair that was always in her face. He thought he'd never love again, but time had blown enough dust over his memories of her to bury whatever romantic love he'd had. Nothing sustained love, whatever is was really, to make him believe it was forever.

But then he'd met Julia, and he finally understood. The only kind of real love—the only backbone that anything like true love could ever be supported by—was what others called obsession. It was intoxicating and all-consuming, but in Larson's experience, it had a tenacity and immortality other kinds of love only grasped at.

He'd never really let the idea of Julia go. But this woman in 2C had brought it all around full circle. With her, he wouldn't have to. It was fate, inexorable. It was one of the things the curtains had told him, that whatever was left of Julia, her spirit, the energy and essence of her, was in this woman. It sounded impossible, but he felt it and knew it to be true, knew it the way he knew air he couldn't see was there, and there to sustain him.

As he lay on the bed, his own shades drawn, he thought about the other messages in the curtains. He'd gone back just before dark that night once the parking lot had cleared of milling tenants to check the curtains. He had to be sure he wasn't just imagining things.

He wasn't. The colors of the threads, their placement, the fractal order in the chaos of their 3-dimensional patterns, formed ideas in his mind. He could read them, the literal and the layered meanings. Some of the suggestions were...intense. Some were criminal. Some were horrific. And yet, as he stood there gazing up, studying the patterns, reading the truths tucked inside ideas, none of them seemed impossible to carry out. Not for her.

Larson had never been a stickler for rules, exactly, but he had always been a basically clean cop. His methods were, in his mind, outside the box, but they got results. He was good at what he did. The only time he had ever crossed any lines legally, and then, not so much in his opinion as in the opinions of his superiors, was with Julia. But out here in these apartments, he wasn't a cop. He was only lovesick Jack Larson of 2J, trying to rebuild his life and find that little glimmer of happiness with a woman that so many times was given and then taken away.

And if mutilating a hand was step one in that direction, so be it. Even some of a hand could still deliver the thrill of touching her body.

He got up slowly, his body creaking. There was no time like the present, but he'd have to prepare first. He was not as young as he used to be, and it would do no good for him to bleed out. He moved down the hall to the kitchen and stood over the knife block, considering which knife would be best for the work. After a few moments, he chose a non-serrated butcher knife whose blade, thanks to his adventures in take-out, was still very sharp. He let it clatter to the counter and went to the liquor cabinet for a new bottle of whiskey. His hand closed around the neck of a Jim Beam Devil's Cut 90 proof bottle he'd been saving for a special occasion and he pulled it out.

Forgoing the glass, he twisted off the cap and took a swig right from the bottle, then settled down in one of the kitchen chairs set up next to a folding card table where he ate. Just about half the bottle should do it—not too drunk to see what he had to cut, and not too sober to feel the bulk of the pain. Realizing he'd forgotten something, he got up again, took another swig, then rifled through his kitchen drawers until he found Ziploc bags. He considered using one, thought better of it, and kept looking. In one of the cabinets, he found a large box of long matches, the kind where the box slides out like a drawer. He dumped the remaining matches onto the shelf and measured the length of the box against the side of his hand. It would fit, with a little squishing. He also found duct tape, which he thought might come in handy. He brought the empty box and the tape back to the table, sat, and took another swig of whiskey.

When the bottle was a little more than half empty (*or a little less than half full*, he thought with a dull grin), he got up again to get the knife. By then, he felt light and kind of tingly all over, and though he expected it to hurt, he didn't think it would be unbearable. Reaching into a cabinet below and to the right of the sink, he got out a cutting board. Then he laid everything out on the table.

A towel. He ought to have a towel for the floor, and maybe another for...after. He went and got a bath towel and a hand towel, spreading the former out on the floor beneath the table and the latter alongside the cutting board.

As methodically as the whiskey would allow, he taped the cutting board firmly to the little card table. Then, he taped his left hand by the wrist just as carefully to the cutting board. He took one more swig of whiskey (*for luck*, he told himself), and picked up the knife. He angled the point between his middle and ring finger, then brought the blade down on an angle toward his wrist.

Blood immediately spritzed up into his face and sprayed across the cutting board. The pain was immense, even through the haze of alcohol, and his wrist jerked against the tape as if he could pull himself away from the feeling. His vision swam before him and he had a terrible notion that he might just pass out, collapsing to a heap on the floor with his arm still taped above his head to the table. He took several long breaths, trying to right the world again, and when he could see, albeit somewhat more soberly than before, he picked up the knife again. He glanced at the bottle near the towel, considering another swig or just forgetting the whole thing, wrapping up his hand and passing out in front of the TV, but dismissed it.

He studied his hand a moment, tracing the welling blood line and the angry pink skin around the cut. He'd broken the skin and cut through part of the tendon in his ring finger, but hadn't cut through all the way. It might take two or even three more tries to take off those two fingers and that end chunk of hand.

Larson positioned the knife blade to match the blood line, looking to cut the same place. He didn't want it to be a hack-and-saw job if it didn't have to be.

He closed his eyes, opened them, and sucked in a breath to hold through the pain. Then he brought the knife down again.

His vision burst into sparks of light but cleared itself quicker than he expected. The pain became a throb, and blood that had been collecting under his palm now spilled off the edge of the table and pelted the towel below.

Without giving it too much more thought, he brought the knife down and sawed a little. The sensation was a hot silver pain that ran across the back of his hand, his wrist, and up his arm all the way to his armpit. Surprisingly, the tape held against his body's natural reaction to flinch, and he enjoyed a modicum of pride in his forethought. He didn't think he would have gotten this far with a free-flinching hand.

The knife blade, now sticky with blood and bits of white despite its smooth, non-serrated edge, rose and fell again. He was almost there, could feel when he hit the inner layers of his palm's skin. It was a weird sensation that overlapped the pain. One more....

The fifth and final time, both his ring and pinkie fingers, as well as a slant of flesh, came away from the rest of his hand. It leaned wet and glistening on its side on the cutting board. Immediately, Larson cut away the tape and brought his mutilated hand and the bottle of whiskey over to the sink. He poured some of the alcohol over the wound and the burn set off every pain sensor in the area with blazing sparks of agony. He took another swig as a reward for accomplishing his goal, then moved quickly to the table to wrap up his hand. He laced it tightly, binding it with more duct tape until he looked like he was wearing a puffy silver mitt. Then, with his good hand, he brought the piece of himself he'd cut off over to the sink, rinsed it off with water, and dried it with a paper towel. He then wrapped it in more paper towels and tucked it into the match box. It fit better than he'd expected.

He used the bath towel to wipe most of the blood off the table, the chair, the cutting board, and his face. After freeing the cutting board from its tape bonds, he dropped it and the knife into the sink, and the wadded-up tape into the garbage.

Finally, he sat to finish off the bottle of whiskey. As he took the last few swigs, he stared at the box, willing his hand to stop pounding out blood and pain.

She'd see the sacrifice he'd made. She'd know his heart. She'd have to know.

When the bottle was empty, he pulled the match box to himself, holding it in his good hand. Seeing the stains forming on the sides and bottom of the cardboard, he reconsidered the Ziploc bags after all. Before he left the apartment, he slid the box into a quart-sized plastic bag and did his best to seal it with his one good hand.

Then he brought it out into the hall. A woman's seductive laughter, echoing from behind a door, caused an instant flare of jealous rage to heat his chest, neck, and face. If she had another man over, after what he'd done for her....

He realized, though, as he listened, that it was from a television in a different apartment. Not 2C. No, 2C was perfectly silent, perfectly dark.

He crossed the hallway to her door, as nervous as a young boy bringing flowers to his first crush.

She'd see. She'd have to see.

He knocked once, fully expecting her not to be home, but half-hoping she was. There were no sounds of movement from the far side of the door, and after several seconds of staring at the unmoving 2C plaque affixed slightly above eye level, he put the first token of his love, boxed and bagged and leaking just a little pinkness against the plastic, on the floor by the door. He turned, willing himself not to look, not to keep checking every five minutes to see if she was home and had picked up his present. By the time he made it to his couch, he was convinced he'd be helpless *not* to check. He surprised himself, though, by passing out soundly into a depth of pain-addled, alcohol-blurred darkness.

TEN

The thing in the tub that suggested terrible things to Myrinda yanked her out of sleep, leaving her heart thudding in her chest, an icy-hot off-kilter sensation tingling in her extremities. Derek, sleeping beside her, awoke at her sudden bolting out of bed. The room was still dark. The digital alarm clock on the night table looked, at first glance, to read 3:78, then reformed itself properly to 3:13 a.m.

"Babygirl?" His eyelids were half closed. "What happened? Are you okay?"

She took several deep breaths before she could manage words. "I—I'm okay. Just a bad dream. A nightmare. It was awful." She crawled back into bed and snuggled back against Derek's chest. He put his arm around her, and immediately she felt safer.

"Want to talk about it?"

She thought about that; she could tell from the looks he'd been giving her ever since Aggie's death that he knew something was off with her.

"No...not now. Maybe in the morning. Go back to sleep, baby. I'm okay, really."

He mumbled something, already half-asleep again anyway, and in a few minutes, the sound of his breathing slowed.

Myrinda, on the other hand, lay wide awake in the darkness. She trusted him completely; she'd wanted to tell him what was wrong with her. She didn't really know what it was herself yet, though. She could feel herself changing from the inside, could feel tumorous thoughts growing like pearls around specks of dust in her mind. It was like Aggie had said in the basement: *"Their lunacy pollutes. It gets in the air we breathe, the water we drink and bathe in and wash our hair in and wash our clothes with and brew tea with...everywhere, everywhere. It gets inside, that other alien place, and the alien things that breathe and writhe and slither through. It poisons us. It sickens us. And the sickness is contagious."*

Aggie had said there was a wound in the ground, and if she were to put her hand in it, she'd be able to touch an alien world. She implied some kind of creatures had come through from that wound, bringing a kind of poison with them that would infect everyone exposed to it. Of course the whole idea sounded crazy...but so many things, *real* things, had been happening that she'd have otherwise discounted as crazy, too, if she hadn't experienced them herself. If Myrinda was going crazy (and she was not completely oblivious to that notion, either), it had been before Aggie's dementia could set her own wheels spinning. There had been those fingers in the vent. The whispers of her name she kept hearing when Derek was out. She wanted to believe things would right themselves again when she and

Derek both started their new jobs in a week or so, but the incident in the basement with Aggie seemed to suggest otherwise. The old woman had sounded so sure about what she was saying. That she might have been in the throes of some dementia couldn't explain what Myrinda had watched happen to the old woman's body. And if her falling apart like that was real, then maybe what Aggie had been saying was real, too.

And how was she supposed to explain all that to Derek?

The more she thought about it, the more the dream upset her. In a way, it consolidated all the weird things that had been happening into a single, horrible experience. In it, she'd gotten up to go to the bathroom. She needed air, needed cool water to calm her and help her think. She remembered checking the clock, and it had read some impossible time (like 3:78) that digital clocks, unless they were broken, would never form. The time had made sense to her, though, the way dream-logic offers its skewed rationality to the strangest dream experiences to keep cohesion. The time was an association with the Old Ward, a frightening indication of something imminent, and although she wasn't sure even in the dream exactly what that something was, she knew it had to do with the chasm beneath the apartments, gaping open like an untended wound, and the near-hysteric excitement of the other ones, those in the Old Ward.

She'd gone to the bathroom and flipped on the light, bathing everything in dazzling brightness it took her eyes a few seconds to adjust to. Then she'd glanced up at the vanity mirror hanging above the gleaming sink.

In the dream, she'd seen a face behind hers. She'd whirled around to find a figure standing in the tub. It appeared sexless, motionless, even lifeless. It held long black tangles of hair clenched in its hands and bald patches, marred by cuts and scrapes, showed through the sparse stringy locks on its head. Very pale skin stretched tightly to the point of splitting across the sharp bones of the emaciated frame. It wore a torn gray sweatshirt and sweatpants, smeared with long brown stains. Myrinda took all this in and though her stomach twisted, she felt pressed against the sink by some heavy weight.

It had looked up at her. Where its eyes should have been were tiny inkstorms waxing and waning, shifting with their own internal tide. It was not a person, nor had it ever been.

It opened its mouth and like a fault line, its face split vertically, halving the chin, bisecting the nose and forehead. The gaping lipless maw revealed hundreds of tiny, sharp teeth. From the original mouth, new tears ripped the flesh of its cheeks nearly to the ears. The two halves of jaw unhinged and fell with a wet plop to the chest of the sweatshirt. Blood and something thinner and blacker poured over the lolling tongue, carrying the bottom teeth, its human teeth, away in a murky tide.

Myrinda screamed for Derek, but the weight pressing her to the sink stole the force behind it so that it came out as a rasp.

She tried again, but couldn't draw in enough air to give it volume.

The mess that was the head twitched, the dangling pieces splattering fluid against the shower tiles. The figure took hold of the curtain with exceedingly long fingers, and it stepped over the edge of the tub. With a sharp crack, the knees caved in until the legs bent backward.

It spoke to her without words. It showed her images of her carving her own intestines out with a spoon from a gash in her abdomen. It showed her flowers in a field. It showed her peeling the skin off the muscle of Derek's thighs while he lay strapped to a gurney, screaming. It showed her a child's doll. A digital clock blinking 3:78 over and over and over. Aggie Roesler being pulled to chunks by disembodied fingers. Small children bursting open like blood-filled water balloons. Apple pie.

Finally it showed her the Old Ward, and she understood it wanted her to go there, to find a book and read it, to open more unhealing wounds in the ground. It made her see, so they could move freely from one place to the next, locking bloody hands and dancing and while their high-pitched screams of laughter pierced the night skies of many, many worlds. It promised her peace. It celebrated her uniqueness. It offered acceptance and comfort and showed her violence over which she could have total control.

Myrinda took it all in, mesmerized, neither terrified nor elated, but a terrible blending of both.

Then the thing gave its hands a good, hard shake and all its fingers fell to the floor. Its hands kept shaking, and more fingers kept falling until the bathroom floor looked like it was writhing with long, jointed maggots. Immediately the fingers turned themselves over so they could worm-crawl toward her. She screamed again, soundless, and kicked out at them with her bare feet, mashing some beneath her heel and launching others to crunch against the wall. There were just too many, though; they crawled over each other in their frenzy to reach her, snaking over her toes and ankles, clinging somehow to her pajama pants and working their way up her body. She batted at them, still unable to break free of the sink, her legs spasming in terror and her horror mounting as they crawled over her stomach, inched over her breasts, worked their way beneath her clothes. She felt them tugging on her hair, plugging her ears, and finally, working open her mouth so they could swarm down her throat. She gagged, choking on the rancid, rotting taste of them, the smell of them like skin left too long under a bandage. Her eyes watered and her vision swam in little kaleidoscopes of light. In the dream, she felt herself getting light-headed as they cut off her air. She clawed at her chest and throat. She could feel them inside her, burrowing down, down into her, and she couldn't scream, couldn't run.

She gave it one last effort to break into the hallway...and she woke up, tumbling out of her bed.

Now, as Derek breathed softly beside her, the feel of those fingers all over her made her gag. She wanted to run to the bathroom and throw up, but she was scared of what might be in there, waiting. Instead, she took several deep breaths, willing the gorge in her throat to sink again, willing the knot of revulsion in her stomach to untie itself.

As the night wore on, she found herself checking the clock periodically until the hour of three had passed. She thought if she looked and saw 3:78 on the clock, she might scream. At 4:11, she finally relaxed some of the tension in her shoulders.

That thing in the tub.... It had on a different face, but it was one of the things Aggie told her about. She was sure of it. She knew it like she knew her body—and Derek's, too. She didn't know about the rest, but there was no doubt in her mind that creatures born of and fed on madness had come through the wound. They were infecting her and maybe others in the building.

Maybe Derek—maybe he hid it better than she could. She was relieved when he rolled over, away from her, in his sleep.

If these things were affecting others, there would be no one she could trust. Anyone could have seen the images the thing in her dream showed her (having flashed before her eyes, those images themselves were gone, but had left their horrid afterimage).

She got out of bed and stood by the window, looking down at the Old Ward wrapped in night. Sometimes, she thought she saw jerking movements in the shadow, or snippets of chattered nonsense-words carried on the air. She stood a long time, filling up with thoughts that might not have been hers entirely. When Derek stirred in bed, it was light outside, the sky a soft pink dissipating to blue. She climbed quietly into bed next to him. She didn't want him to know. He couldn't know.

***

Derek woke suddenly, shaken from sleep by a feeling that vanished as soon as he opened his eyes. Beneath his arm, Myrinda's body lay rigid, so much so that he called to her softly to see if she was lying awake. She didn't answer. He peered over her shoulder and saw her eyes were closed.

He rolled out of bed and went to the window. Outside, beyond the apartment grounds, that last remaining part of the asylum stood silhouetted in the dawn. The Old Ward.

While Derek could appreciate the once stately and elegant architecture of the old building, there was something about it that Derek didn't like. It looked out of place, even out of time next to the modern facade of the apartment building. It was more than that, though. It was the nagging idea that whatever was going on with Myrinda was coming from that building—which struck him as stupid to even entertain consciously. Derek was reasonable, well-educated. He had experienced a number of different slices from the pie of life, and was no stranger to the odd and unexplainable, particularly in reference to the behavior of others. He wasn't the type to let feelings, especially seemingly sourceless ones, override logical thinking. There was something wrong, though, and not just with Myrinda. The old woman, Aggie, had worn the same distressed look just before she died. The cop—he had to be a cop, or ex-cop, the way he carried himself—and the guy from 2E both seemed jumpy lately. The latter could have been uncomfortable around big black guys, maybe, and the cop could have possibly been profiling him, but Derek didn't think either was the reason the one always looked so startled and the other always looked so hungry and haunted. Maybe that drove the old couple to steer clear of him (the way the sharp little woman looked at him as if she expected him to rob her at any minute), but not the others. No, it was Derek's job to be observant, and although he didn't know the cop, the couple, or the other guy, he did notice a distinct atmosphere of increasing unease, to greater or lesser degree, among the other residents that seemed to mirror that inside his apartment.

He wished Myrinda would talk to him about it. He was trying to give her space, to let her work through it in her own way and come to him in her own time. Often enough, he felt on the outside of things. He didn't like feeling that with his girl, nor did he like the insidious feeling that Myrinda and the others were all experiencing something in a language he couldn't hear, let alone understand.

Derek turned to the bed. Myrinda moaned in her sleep, shifting stiffly. He knew her; this was about more than just Aggie's death. It had started before that, with the tape on the vents, and it seemed to be getting worse, not better. If she wouldn't come to him, he'd ask her outright.

He went to take a shower. The hot water felt good; it washed the chill of the night and of his thoughts off his body. He dried off, wrapping the towel around his waist, then applied deodorant and cologne, brushed his teeth, and shaved before returning to the bedroom to dress.

When he got to the doorway, he saw Myrinda sitting up in bed, facing away from him, toward the window. He watched her unmoving form for a few seconds before entering.

"Morning, babygirl," he said, grabbing a pair of boxer briefs from a dresser drawer and slipping them on.

She didn't answer. Not a strand of hair on her head moved.

"Myrinda," he said, crossing around the foot of the bed to her.

For just a second, Derek thought he saw blood painting the side of her face. A second later, it was gone. A trick of the light from the window, maybe.

"Myrinda, we need to talk," he said. "You need to talk to me."

Her gaze was fixed on the window. On the Old Ward.

He took her shoulders, shaking them gently, and looked into her eyes. "Myrinda, I'm asking you. Please talk to me."

Myrinda's eyes changed then, and whatever haze she was in seemed to clear a little. "Derek," she said.

"I'm here, babygirl. Talk to me."

"I'm scared," she mumbled.

"Scared?" He looked around the room. "Scared of what, baby?"

"The fingers," she replied dully. "And the mouth-creatures in the Old Ward. And the wound."

Derek glanced out the window behind him, then back at Myrinda. He was getting really worried about her. Maybe she needed to see a doctor.

"Baby, I don't understand what you're talking about. Now, I want to help, I want to make it okay, but I can't do that if you don't tell me what's going on."

A little of the old Myrinda, the one he knew, flashed in her eyes. In a slow, rambling voice, she told him about the fingers that had crawled out of the vents. Then she stopped short. There was more that she was holding back. Derek knew it. And what she had told him made little sense. Dead fingers in the vents? Was *that* what the duct tape had been all about?

Derek settled back with a sigh. Something in his expression triggered an odd smile that made her face look cruel. Then it passed, and he was looking at the Myrinda he knew again.

"I don't know how to respond to that," Derek said.

"You asked me what was going on," Myrinda said. "I'm telling you the truth. I don't know why it happened, but it did."

"Baby, I think maybe the stress of the move—"

"No." She pulled away from him. "No, it has nothing to do with the move. I'm happy here, really. I like—I love it here. This is home now."

"Okay, baby. I'm not saying the move was a bad idea. I'm just trying to understand what's happening with you, that's all."

"I'm not crazy," she said, although the way she said it, it sounded to Derek like she was trying to convince herself more so than him.

"I know that. I know you're not crazy."

"Do you believe me?"

Derek considered how to answer that. "I believe you honestly believe you saw the fingers."

Myrinda frowned. "That's a nice way of saying you think I'm imagining things."

"I think even under the best of circumstances, all this change can cause a lot of strain. All this time cooped up in the apartment, away from family and friends, about to start a new job—"

"A new life. With you. It's what I want."

He reached out and touched her face. "Me too, baby. That's why I want to help you figure out what's really going on, what's weighing on you. I want you—us—to be happy. I need you to trust me."

Tears formed in her eyes. It took a long time for her to speak. "There's something wrong...here. On these grounds. Aggie was right. It's...making us, I don't know, sick or something. I feel it. It...makes me think things. Feel things."

Derek waited for her to continue. That there was something affecting the people in the building, well, he'd thought as much himself. When Myrinda started staring off into space again, Derek asked, "What do you mean, Aggie was right? What did she say?"

Myrinda told Derek all about what Aggie had told her in the basement about the wound to another dimension and the creatures that came through, the way they carried an insanity sickness that told her things, showed her horrible, horrible outcomes and promised life without consequence. She spoke in a slow, almost sleepy kind of monologue, and when the stream of words began to trickle, she looked lost and confused, like a woman who had awakened to find herself in strange and unfamiliar surroundings.

Derek took Myrinda's hand and stroked it for a while before speaking. He wanted to make sure he spoke carefully, so as not to upset her. He was nearly sure now that Myrinda needed a doctor, but he didn't want it to be confrontational. In her state, he was afraid he wouldn't be able to pry her through the doorway. "What do you think about what Aggie told you?"

She smiled thinly. "I believe she honestly believed what she said."

Derek frowned at her.

She looked at her hands in her lap. "I believe her," she said. "I—I'm starting to believe her. At least, there's something to what she was saying. I...I don't know all the details, but I can feel it, Derek. I can feel different thoughts in my head. Different ideas. Different moods. And they scare me. The ideas...they scare me."

He pulled her close, stroking her hair, and she seemed relieved to sink against him and let him hold her. "It's going to be okay, babygirl. We'll figure it out. Everything's going to be okay, I promise."

"I don't want to leave," she whispered.

***

In apartment 2C, slats of morning sunlight speared the gloom beyond the curtains, but reached nothing they could illuminate properly. Dust motes fluttered in the light.

Outside the front door, a little plastic bag lay, its contents congealing and curling with the onset of rot. A sickly-sweet smell of organic decay had begun to seep slowly from the seal. The bag had been there the better part of the night and into the morning, its donor dreaming of sex and violence across the hall.

The front door of 2C opened just a crack and a hand with long fingers reached for the bag. The fingertips groped the seal, pinched it, and pulled it over the threshold, leaving a small crimson smear on the hallway floor. The door closed. A lock clicked.

Inside, a woman's high-pitched giggling echoed through the rooms.

ELEVEN

It took Wayne three days to work up the courage to approach the Old Ward. When he thought about it, he supposed maybe he'd been hoping that the anxious, violent thoughts and the hallucinating, if that's what seeing the girl was, would just go away. Like shining light on the monster in the closet and making it disappear, a part of him had been hoping that his discoveries at the library would somehow have the same effect, that maybe he'd feel more in control knowing he wasn't crazy, wasn't growing a baseball-sized tumor somewhere in his brain.

The girl didn't go away. He'd seen her one other time after that day in the crowded parking lot, and that had decided it for him.

Wayne had woken up that morning early, while it was still dark. He'd been dreaming, although he couldn't remember all the details—something about a blue-lit alley and a man in gray sweats with a sharpened paintbrush jutting out of the bloody, jelly mess that had been his eye. The man had been surrounded by a crowd of shadowy waifs, each of them covered in some kind of thick black ooze. Whatever the ooze was, it bubbled and pulsed, fizzling and smoking as it ate into their skin. He remembered the tightened red skin patches just visible beneath the ooze splitting open. The old man reached out for him just before the crowd closed in on him. What happened before or after in the dream, though, had first blended into the blue-lit pre-dawn of his bedroom, then dissipated altogether.

He'd stumbled across the hall to the bathroom and urinated by nightlight, washed up, then shuffled groggily back to the bedroom. He hadn't even been near the window, hadn't been thinking about it consciously, until a gravelly voice had spoken his name.

He stopped, raising his head slowly to look around the bedroom. It was empty. He spun around, convinced from the sound of the voice that it was close, maybe behind him. No one was there.

"Wayne," the voice called again, this time from much farther away.

Without really knowing why, Wayne glanced at the window, all traces of sleep gone from his head. His stomach tightened. "Hello?" Fear strangled his voice to a whisper.

"Wayne," the voice called again. This time, it definitely sounded like it was coming from someplace outside. Strange, though—the volume didn't strike Wayne as being loud enough to carry from outside, even though the window was open. "Come out here."

With hesitant steps, Wayne made his way to the window and, in spite of the little voice screaming in his head to *look away, for godssakes, look away!*, he peered down onto the sparsely lit grounds below.

The girl was standing just off the walkway below his window, looking down. The jagged stumps of her legs disappeared in the long grass. Her arms were crossed over her chest in a dirty straightjacket, the areas where her hands would have been tucked under her armpits.

"Who—?" He breathed the question, but it lacked the force of breath to carry.

The bowed head lifted, its stringy black hair parting to reveal what might have once been a pretty face, before the latticework of scars on the left side. Wayne couldn't see the girl's eyes; even though the moon shone down on her gray and mutilated face, dark shadows pooled deep in the sockets.

"Do you want me, Wayne?" she asked in the same gravelly voice. "Do you want to see me fall apart?"

Before he could answer, the girl did just that. It was as if dozens of invisible fishing wires had diced her up. A chunk of scar-crossed face and a lump of hair slid away from the rest of her head, followed by another. One by one, pieces slid off the upright whole of her body, thumping to the grass, smacking wetly to the concrete walkway.

Wayne tried to look away, but he couldn't. His neck muscles strained, his eyes bulging at the grotesque horror going to pieces just below his window. His hands clutched the windowsill. What scared him maybe even more than what was happening outside was the fact that instead of feeling nauseous at the sight, he felt aroused.

"Stop," he whispered, as much to himself as to her.

The straightjacket cut away, still binding the pieces of her arms, and fell to the ground. The two standing legs collapsed in the grass.

Finally, the spell on him broke and he pulled himself away, breathing hard. He felt disgusted, confused, the sweat on him cooling and sticking.

"What the fuck is happening to me?" he whispered.

He'd run the shower in the darkness, sinking into a near-fetal curl in the tub and letting the hot water rain over him. Light began to come through the window before he finally shut the water off and got out. After drying and getting dressed (there was no way he could sleep, even now), he'd chanced a quick look out the window. As he'd expected, the pieces of the girl were gone.

It wasn't going to stop. Whatever was going on in this building, whether it was chemical waste or ghosts or something crossing through from another world, it was getting to him, getting inside him, and he had to get it out.

He wanted to see if there really was a *Book of Gates*. He had to know, actually. He couldn't get the thought out of his mind.

Now, with hours of morning sunlight putting distance between him and what he'd seen early that morning, Wayne stood in front of the heavy double doors of the Old Ward, taking in the warmth of the sun on his face (he certainly wasn't crazy enough to do this at night—why tempt fate?). Birds chirped overhead. A light breeze lifted his hair. There in the daylight, the Old Ward didn't seem so imposing. It looked smaller somehow, a sagging, decrepit monument to archaic ways, a soulless brown brick shell collecting dust, flaking paint, growing thick and muted with cobwebs.

The building was stoutly t-shaped. Wayne had downloaded and printed a floor plan of the asylum from the internet. Directly inside, he would find "parlor"-style waiting areas flanking the centrally-located lobby, each side with separate public bathrooms for men and women. Ostensibly, these areas were for family and close friends to wait while patients were checked in, brought out for visits, and the like. The front desk, usually set in the middle of the fairly large lobby pavilion, served as the face of the asylum in a way, the first thing patients and their loved ones saw. Behind it, beyond a door always locked by a card key, a long hallway stretched back the entire depth of the building. Along this hallway, closest to the lobby, were the administration offices, staff dining and bathrooms, a kitchen that took up the better part of the right-side length near the dining room, and some kind of greenhouse room for growing fresh herbs and vegetables across from the kitchen. The cross piece that made up the length of the building ran just beyond that locked door as well, perpendicular to the hallway. It contained all that was left of the asylum therapy areas, with a men's wing of patient bedrooms spanning the left side, and a women's wing to the right. At the far ends of each wing were staircases to the upper floors of the asylum, patient dining rooms and small bathrooms. There were places that weren't clearly labeled on his particular map, but he assumed from their placement in the structure that some of the larger ones might be common kitchen areas for supplying food to the different wards' expansive dining rooms. The other larger areas he figured for the common shower areas. In both cases, those large, unmarked rooms were located near what would have been turns down hallways to other wings, so it made sense that they might be commonly-shared areas. There were also areas labeled "drying room"; he wasn't quite sure what those were, but assumed they might have been locker-room-type places for patients to dry off after showers. The pattern on the map repeated with each zig and zag of the wings, with more unstable and more dangerous patients' sets of rooms, bathrooms, dining areas, and the like placed farther and farther from the administration, but these subsequent extensions no longer existed.

Wayne imagined pulling open one of those large wooden doors. He could see the lobby in his mind, its indistinct shapes of shadow scurrying as he entered. He imagined dragging open the door to the hallway, its dull, dusty creak echoing down the empty corridor. He pictured years-old untouched darkness punctured by sunlight, shadows forming slowly into mangled people, their hands and feet lopped off, their clothes stained with blood and body fluids, their hair thick with grime and their faces blank, the dead skin sloughing off in some places to reveal bone and—

He shook his head, snorting lightly at himself. He told himself it was just an empty building, like a thousand other old abandoned empty buildings all across the world. He didn't even think any part of the massacre had actually happened in the Old Ward itself, which meant there was nothing inside, nothing to be afraid of. Certainly no silent army of mutilated dead people.

With a deep breath, he took a step forward, then another, into the shadow cast by the Old Ward.

The sun passed behind a cloud then, and the sounds of birds immediately ceased.

Wayne stopped, listening carefully. The air was different, like he'd crossed into some barrier. He couldn't help thinking about what the old librarian had said about Symmes and La Claviére's gates. Maybe this wasn't such a good idea. Even if he found some moldy old book, what would it prove? Instead of standing out here in front of an abandoned building, he probably should have been trying to contact the EPA, maybe get an agent out here to find that chemical spill....

Except he knew there was no chemical spill to find. He knew that inside his head, inside his chest. Could breathe it inside of him from the soundless air. What was wrong with this place was inside that building sometimes, and when it wasn't, it was in and around the apartments.

He climbed the three wide concrete steps and grasped the metal door handle. With a grunt, he yanked with all his strength, and was surprised to find it swung soundlessly toward him.

The sunlight didn't penetrate too far into the darkness. He could make out a chipped tile floor of a nondescript neutral color, and nothing more. He pulled a pocket flashlight out of his jacket pocket and clicked it on.

The flashlight offered up pieces of the interior at a time—more tiles fading down a hallway beyond the scope of the flashlight, frames of cracked glass that reflected the flashlight glow, obscuring the prints behind, torn vinyl seating perched on rusting metal frames, a front lobby desk in the center with a large crack along the front of a wooden veneer and large, irregular stains dried beneath. To either side were doors to the parlor areas. Against the back wall stood a door. He thought he could make out a metal box affixed to the wall next to it—Wayne assumed it was a key card reader, probably the newest thing in the whole building.

He took a step inside, half-expecting the door to swing shut behind him, closing him off from the day. It didn't.

With a glance back at the outside, he exhaled, wiped his sweaty hands on his pants, and moved forward into the darkness.

Wayne approached the lobby desk first, skipping the flashlight over its dirt-gray surface. When he leaned over the top to look behind the desk, his fingers grazed the wood and he shivered involuntarily. Something about the silkiness of it, the way his elbows slid instead of sending up dry puffs of dust, made him cringe. It was like touching the muzzle of something alive, something unnatural and dangerous.

He quickly pulled away from the desk, again wiping his hands on his pants. The dust that clung to his fingers rolled into gray strings that he slapped away from his clothes. He didn't want any part of this place on him if he could help it. That he was breathing in the particulated remnants of the place occurred to him only peripherally, and he kept those thoughts out there where they were.

It was only a desk. Only an old piece of wood with some nails.

He shined the light on the doors to the parlors. They were as good a place to start as any. The one on the right was locked—even with a good, hard thump of the shoulder, he couldn't get it to budge. He crossed the room to the other door. It opened with a groan that sounded to Wayne like a giggle.

The little bit of light that slanted in through the front windows caught motes of dust and showed more ripped vinyl seats. He could imagine families sitting in those seats, anxious, crying, nervous, waiting on loved ones they would, in a sense, have to put on a shelf, out of sight and away from everyday life.

He shined the flashlight around, picking out torn, crumpled papers, old wrappers, and dead leaves in clumps on the dirty floor. No book.

At the far side of the room were the bathrooms. Wayne didn't think it likely that Symmes would have taken up in one of the public restrooms to open a gate to another dimension, but hey, what did he know about such things? A quick look around would confirm to his satisfaction that he wasn't doing a half-assed job of searching.

By force of habit, or maybe upbringing, he made his way to the men's room. Like the rest of the building, the bathroom looked pretty shabby. Few tiles stood intact around the bottom two thirds of the room. Grime had been worked into the grout between them to make it a dull gray. The sinks showed rings of rust like old bloodstains around the drains. The stalls on the doors were missing, and the urinals, when he passed them, gave off a faint, unwholesome smell mixed with bleach. The women's room he found in much the same state, and what he found in the parallel parlor area and its bathrooms very much mirrored what he had already seen, except for some spray-painted obscenities where the bland prints had likely hung, informing the reader of acts performed by Cassidy or requesting such acts be performed.

By the time he made it back to the lobby, he felt kind of silly. What was he doing there anyway? What did he really think he was going to find, and what good would it do if he did? In fact, he—

Wayne's thought broke off midway. The large door to the hallway was open slightly. Had it been open before? He couldn't remember, but he didn't think so. A breeze from outside, maybe? But that was stupid. A breeze from outside might blow the door closed, not pull it open.

If but if there was no electricity, it was possible that maybe all the doors on a card system had been sitting unlocked. The building was old. Maybe shifts in the foundation caused the doors to drift open.

He went to the door to wedge it open so he could fit through. It groaned on old hinges but opened with surprising ease. He paused under the door frame; he could have sworn, before the last of the echo died down the hallway, that he heard faint, high-pitched laughter from its far end.

He stepped through, clutching his pocket flashlight like a weapon.

According to his map, the two doors closest to him were administration offices. It made sense to Wayne that if Symmes was going to keep a book anywhere in this building, it would be in his office. Besides, he wasn't quite ready to tackle whatever was, real or imagined, giggling down the far end of the hall. He shined his flashlight on the little plaque affixed to the front of each door. SUSAN SNOW, MD, PSYD, read the one on the right. LEONARD ABRAMS, ED, PHD, the other read. Both these names he remembered from his research as victims of the massacre. Both these doors yielded rooms piled with splintered wood on the floor and spattered with dark stains over the once tasteful couches, the neutral walls, and the non-descript and deliberately uninspiring paintings on the wall. It amazed Wayne, in a way, that so much of this building had been left exactly as it had been—the furniture, the paintings, the rotting medical journals and books on the bookshelves against the far walls, even the paperwork which time, dirt, and water had congealed into solid, misshapen lumps. He would have thought much of it would have been confiscated by investigators, more by the evicted owners when the asylum shut down, and whatever was left, by looters and bored kids. But these rooms looked abandoned, as if everyone had suddenly been evacuated, or had simply disappeared.

He picked through each room's contents, paying closer attention to the books on the shelves, but found nothing of any real interest. He didn't think it likely, anyway, that Symmes would have trusted his colleagues with possession or even knowledge of a book like the *Livre des Portes*. He returned to the hall and was momentarily confused by the exceeding dark, then dismayed to find that the door to the lobby had closed. He didn't know whether to laugh or panic. *If this were a horror movie*, he thought, *that door would be locked, and I'd be screwed*. Immediately, he moved to the door to try the handle. It opened without a problem onto the lobby. He could see the rectangle of outside cut by the front door. Still sunny.

With relief, he let go of a breath he hadn't realized he was so tightly holding onto, then turned back to the hallway. *Screw this hunting and pecking*, he thought. *I don't have all day. I need to find Symmes's office*. He shined his flashlight on each door as he passed, reading off more names of people he recognized from his research had been killed or killed others. Finally, he came across a door whose plaque read GEOFFREY DAVID SYMMES, MD, PHD, PSYD. He pushed open the door, and fought an instant wave of nausea.

Unlike the rest of the Old Ward he had seen so far, which smelled musty, like old paper, dust, and faint antiseptic, this office assailed him with a smell like rotting meat. Maybe some small animal had wandered into the Old Ward, gotten lost there, and died in this room. Shining the light around it, though, Wayne saw that the place had been stripped nearly bare; no pictures hung on the walls, no desk or couch to afford the bland room an aspect of comfort. What was left of the wood paneling (it had been a Director's office, after all) hung in a bowed strip against a corner of the back wall. Most important to Wayne, there were no bookshelves and no books. Wayne remembered the librarian telling him that Symmes had been questioned about the massacre by the police. Maybe they had confiscated everything.

Maybe the *Livre des Portes* was in some evidence locker at the Bridgehaven Township Police Department, and he was wasting his time picking over old ghosts.

But something told him that wasn't true. For one thing, if the police had found such a book, it probably would have made enough news that the librarian would have known about it. And even if the police kept it quiet, as they did numerous aspects of the massacre, the townspeople would have found out anyway, which meant the librarian would have known. Besides, any man who had been lucky enough to find such an incredibly rare and, in his mind, powerful book, would probably have hidden it so even teams of police couldn't find it. To Symmes it was, after all, a kind of murder weapon.

So that was it, then. If there wasn't anything else there to see—

But there was. There, in the empty corner of the room, just behind the paneling, was a long, perfectly vertical crack and what looked like maybe a small latch. It was hard to tell in the gloom.

Bracing himself with a gulp of less noxious air from the hallway, he dove back into the office to inspect the crack. With his finger, he traced the rough line all the way up to a spot just above his head before it banked to the left.

It was a door.

He tried to open it, but the paneling blocked the way. Grimacing, he tried with one hand to yank the paneling away. It wouldn't budge. He clamped the small flashlight between his lips, pointing the light on the door, and with both hands, yanked the paneling with all his strength. It took two tries, but the paneling came away in a small puff of sheetrock dust. He tossed it aside and, taking the flashlight from his mouth, followed the crack with light all the way around.

The door, if it could be called that, looked like a crudely-drawn child's chalk outline. There was even a messily markered-in circle of black where a knob should have been. Graffiti, then. That was a disappointment. He flicked at the latch—that was real, at least—in disgust and gave the sheetrock a little shove, as if picking a fight with it.

The scored piece of sheetrock swung away from him into inkiness. Wayne stood there for nearly a full minute, dumbfounded. It really was a door.

When he got himself back together, he shined the flashlight into the opening, and discovered it was a small stairwell, with metal stairs leading down. Maybe it was a secret passage down to the tunnels. Wayne could see the forethought in building an escape route from the Director's office, in case...well, in case the patients rioted and massacred everyone in the building. He could have slipped down into the tunnels and out to safety.

By accounts, he hadn't. Maybe he hadn't known about the door. Maybe when Symmes took over the position and the office, the paneling had already boarded it over.

Or maybe, Symmes had known. Maybe he'd used it to find a nice, quiet, secret place to open a gate to another dimension, and when that went terribly, terribly wrong, to hide the book away from anyone else who might ever want to try the same.

From somewhere down below, he heard what sounded like a metal door swinging closed.

Maybe whatever Symmes had let through into this world had taken up residence down there in the dark.

What drove him to jog down those steps and pull open the door, even he couldn't identify. The impulse to do it was strong, though—overpowering and inexorable. He found he wasn't even too worried about it. After all, he was a journalist. Journalists observed. They watched like omnipotent spectators. They wouldn't be hurt, couldn't be killed. They were the ones who carried on knowledge of the Narrative, so others could find it and open doors. He would do that, would find the Narrative, would mingle with the chaotic ones and dance in the blood they spilled and howl at the alien moon with them and—

He shook his head, feeling momentarily dizzy. Those were not his thoughts...were they? He didn't even know what they meant. He didn't want to know.

At the bottom of the stairs, he shined light on the gray metal door. Faded strokes of red paint evidently marked it as something, but he could no longer tell what. He opened it, echoing that same sound he'd heard right back up the staircase, and slipped silently through.

The cavernous corridor he was standing in was no doubt an entrance to the underground tunnels. He swallowed dryly. The book was here. He could feel it. And by God, he wanted it.

But which way? The tunnel extended to the left and right, swallowed on either end by utter abysmal black. A thick pipe, bundled together with several thinner pipes, also marked by indecipherable red paint slashes, ran its length. A fat black spider, its bloated body shiny in the flashlight glow, scurried to get out of the light. In its temporarily abandoned web hung the carcasses of several tiny dead.

A ping against the pipes to the right set him walking in the other direction. A part of his mind was developing distinctly uneasy feelings about all this, urging him to turn around, to climb those stairs and run, don't walk all the way to the sunlight and fresh air and manicured lawns of the apartments. That part of his mind, though, evidently didn't control his feet, which carried him away from that metal door. Even with the flashlight, he felt swallowed by the tunnel, its lips blocking out his view of the door and its throat carrying him along to some awaiting acid gullet. That uneasy part of his mind, which so often seemed to take on the voice of his old partner, Jerry, tried to tempt him with cold beer and his DVR backlog. It tried to push its way to the front of his mind and make the other thoughts, the ones that didn't feel like his, shut up a minute so Wayne could listen to reason. It tried telling him it wasn't too late to get the hell out of there. But it would be, soon. Very soon.

A ghostly pulse of pale bluish light far down the hall did finally slow his steps. It had illuminated nothing, but it had thrown him, just the same. There shouldn't have been any source of light down there except his flashlight (the batteries of which, Jerry told him in that petulant way he'd always had, were gonna die and leave him stranded in the dark down there). He waited a moment to see if the light would pulse again, if maybe it was some kind of emergency system or something. Seconds ticked off in the murk. No pulse of light repeated itself.

Wayne had started to shiver. It was cool, but oppressive, the air stale and unstirred. He suddenly very much wanted to be out of there. He turned back toward the direction of the metal door, and his toe thumped against something. He shined the light down and in surprise, sucked in a lungful of tunnel air.

He crouched down slowly, his fingers first brushing, then lifting, the burled brown, cloth-bound cover of the old book. Gold-stamped in calligraphic text on the cover were the words *Livre des Portes*, and in the bottom left corner, the name La Claviére. For the most part, the damp and rats and whatever else was down there had left the book untouched. The papers crackled with age as he turned them. In the weakening glow of the flashlight, he perused the text. He didn't know much French, just the tidbits here and there that had stuck with him since high school French classes. Still, he could make out a few phrases. A chapter about securing the key (*Sécurisation de la Clé*), a chapter about doors and windows (*Les Portes et Les Fenetres*), and a lengthy passage about using *le sang des betes et des enfants*.

A shuffling sound in the direction of the metal door drew his unwilling gaze away from the book. He paused, listening again, and immediately he heard a low drag across the pebbled concrete floor and another loud bang against the pipe.

Something was down there in the tunnel with him.

His heart pounded so loud it thumped in his ears. He covered the tip of the flashlight with his palm so that it looked like he was seeping bloody light across the back of his hand. He didn't dare shine the light down the tunnel and draw attention to himself.

Whatever it was down there lurched forward, knocking chunks of concrete out of its way. A bang against the pipe following the dragging sound gave Wayne the terrible impression it wanted him to know it was coming. It was marking off the shrinking distance between them with each step.

"Oh shit," he whispered in a voice softer than a breath.

Suddenly, the other thoughts in his head were gone, and the Jerry-voice had full free reign to panic. *Run!* It screamed at him. *Run, for godssakes! Don't just sit there, waiting for whatever that is to reach you!*

While he agreed wholeheartedly with the sentiment, running away from the direction of the metal door would only plunge him deeper into an unknown length of tunnels. He didn't know where the far exit was; the map from the Internet didn't show the tunnel system. He would be down there for hours, maybe days, lost in a labyrinth with...Symmes only knew what. No one knew where he was. No one would come looking until his rent was due.

Whatever that thing was, it was blocking the sure and safe way out of there, and he sure as hell wasn't about to run *toward* it.

He felt sick and sweaty all over, in spite of the chill. He stood slowly, quietly, clicking off the flashlight. His breath came in puffs too thin to make him feel like he was getting enough air.

The dragging was much closer now, though with the acoustics down there, it was hard to tell how close. He took a few steps back, doing his best to mute the sound of his shoes against the gravelly floor. Terror pulsed in hot-cold flashes across his skin and deep in his gut, threatening to double him over in gut-clenching spasms to vomit.

He wished he had a gun, a knife, even a rock to throw. The pocket flashlight was little comfort.

The thing dragged itself forward. Banged the pipe.

He closed his eyes, fought off tears, fought off the scream building in his throat. He imagined something like the girl, dragging its jagged bone-shattered stumps across the rough floor of the tunnel, leaving viscous green stains mixed with dead blood trailing behind it. He saw in his mind the hand-less stump of its arm sliding along the pipe, the wrist bone slamming against it, the vibrations carrying its desire to play with him, its hunger to hurt him, down the pipe's length like some sick children's game of telephone.

It dragged forward another step. Banged the pipe. This time, a high-pitched giggle, drowned quickly in a wet gurgle, carried across the stagnant air between them.

He took another step back, and another. His legs felt like dead weights he had to drag, too, his own feet useless. The rest of him felt numb, the hot-cold panic drawing sweat from his skin. Every part of him thrummed with terror. He could imagine the black stringy hair of the girl-thing that had never been a girl, clumped with dirt and blood, falling away in clumps that curled like dead black snakes at its jagged ankles. The scarred gray flesh he imagined falling away too, clumps of a masker's clay muddied with whatever touched and stuck to it. These chunks of pseudo-flesh, he saw with stomach-turning clarity in his mind, would fall to the pavement like the decaying fat of rotting steaks, sizzling on the tunnel floor as if dropped into a pan, before melting away into little grease spots.

They were more alien thoughts—he recognized that now—but no less accurate for being so. It was showing him what it was, making him see in the dark.

It dragged forward. Banged the pipe. Both he and the Jerry-voice screamed silently in unison, willing the rest of his body to run.

The eyes of the thing, pits filled with the kind of lightlessness collected only at the very bottoms of underground chasms, spread like stain, engulfing the entire face, the neck, the body. It was becoming what it truly was; his mind saw it, and tried to reject such a shape.

"Wayne," it said with the last of the faked human elements in its throat, and sheer blinding-white panic finally launched him into a jackrabbit bolt—away from it, away from the door into the length of tunnel, away from that terrible voice on the verge of hysterical laughter, that voice that knew his name.

He stumbled as he ran, too scared to look back. He didn't need to. Over the clamor of his steps, he heard the drag-bang pattern of the thing's movements behind him become just drags, and those in turn pick up frequency until the thing behind him was sprinting. He could hear its jaws opening the expanse of its face, a gaping rip, a chasm, then snapping shut like a bear trap.

He fumbled to turn the flashlight back on, but he dropped it, his feet sending it spinning off into the dark. He swore and kept running. His heart thudded, dry and painful in his chest, forcing him to gasp for air. With each inhale, he felt like he was sucking up the madness around him, taking it into his body. He could almost feel it dilute his bloodstream.

A pulse of blue light shocked him into near blindness for a second. He cried out. His foot caught something solid and painful, pitching him forward onto the ground. He scrabbled over the concrete, his feet kicking out behind him, his mind searching frantically for the commands that would get his body up, get it moving again.

A loud bang against the pipes made him flinch. He rolled over onto his back, his breath lodged in his throat.

The blue light pulsed again, and for just a second, in its glow, he saw the blurred head of the thing towering over him, its vertical, needle-lined mouth working open and closed.

Wayne screamed. Then the blue light winked out, plunging them both back into blackness.

TWELVE

The sticky note Larson found on his fridge two days after his partial amputation startled him. He'd been taking it easy since that night, cognizant somewhere in the back of his head that the ball was in his court, so to speak. The woman in 2C had issued initiatives in her curtains, and now it was up to him to put those initiatives into action. In his opinion, he had started off on a high note, as draining as it had been. He hadn't expected communication so soon. Not yet.

The morning after had been rough. His stomach full of whiskey-rot, his head pounding and slightly dazed, he'd stumbled to the bathroom to change the bandage on his mangled hand. That had been painful, almost as painful as the cutting had been. Blood, which had leaked through to form a large, irregular stain on the couch, had made the bandage stiff, and it adhered to the wound like a second skin. Pulling it off ripped open what messy black clotting had sealed the wound, and his hand began to bleed fresh, dark red blood again. His middle finger was bruised around the base knuckle and up the side, and the raw edges of his palm, wrist, and the back of his hand were a waxy red bordering on purple.

He let the blood patter into the bathroom sink while with his good hand, he fumbled in the medicine cabinet for some Aleve.

He had some trouble getting the safety cap off with one hand and dropped the bottle so that the little blue ovals spilled across the sink and into the bloody basin. Slowly, he replaced each, one at a time, until three remained. He picked those up and swallowed them dry. They stuck in his throat, so he ran the water, cupped a palmful and brought it to his lips to wash them down.

After rinsing his damaged hand, he wrapped it in clean bandages, pulling it just tighter than was comfortable. Immediately, the layers of bandage took on a reddish tint that spread along the length of his hand but did not quite bleed all the way through. He grunted, satisfied, and went to make himself some greasy eggs to quell the roiling in his stomach.

He'd survived that morning, and the rest of that day. Two days later, the bleeding had mostly stopped. The pain had, for a while, receded but then returned with a vengeance. The way his middle finger had swollen and was intensely painful to the touch made him wonder if the wound had become infected.

Still, he believed he had survived the worst of it. He'd noticed that the little bag was gone from in front of the door to 2C, and felt confident that she had retrieved and approved of his gift. At first, he thought the little yellow sticky might be a thank you note. Maybe her need for proof of undying devotion was simple, and the other missives of the curtains were no longer necessary. All this crossed his hazy mind while he crossed the kitchen to the fridge. He reached for the note, realized his left hand was in no shape to do something as taxing as hold something, and switched hands.

There were only three lines written on the note, in that same script he'd come to think of as belonging to the woman of 2C. It read:

Keep going.
Take it all back.
I'm waiting for you.

So it was a note of encouragement, then. Just as good, almost. She was thinking of him and was pleased. He'd passed the first test. She had faith he'd pass the others. That's why she wrote that she was waiting for him. He had to keep going.

He crawled into his bed to sleep off his hangover first. He wanted a clear head to plan his next move. Besides, he was feeling dizzy either from the pain or the blood loss, and couldn't quite remember what else the curtains had told him to do.

When Larson woke again, late afternoon had cast its blue-gray shadows and orange highlights through the bedroom window. The thunder in his head had quieted to a dull roar and his vision was clear again. His hand still throbbed, but he could deal with that. It was time to start thinking about his next move.

With his bandaged hand thrust uncomfortably into the pocket of his overcoat, he made his way once again to a spot beneath the window of 2C and studied the curtains. The messages remained unchanged. Flipping open a notepad, he balanced it on his left wrist while he took notes with his right hand. Then he put notepad, pen, and bad hand all back in the same pocket, wincing from the pain. Even the lightest brush against the tender side of his hand sent screaming fireworks of pain up his arm lately. He'd have to douse it with Hydrogen Peroxide or slather it with Neosporin or something when he got back to the apartment.

Right now, though, he had work to do.

The curtains had suggested he do a very specific favor for a neighbor, one who didn't fully understand all the angles and layers and dimensions of the language which gave Larson purpose and direction these days.

Larson wasn't sure exactly what this particular request had to do with his woman in 2C, but he didn't question it. He'd done similar tasks before, and always to effect a necessary outcome. He didn't think of it as planting evidence so much as guiding an investigation to its obvious, inevitable, and absolutely true conclusion. Maybe this was a test of his empathy or his humanity, to see whether he'd help his fellow man. He got the impression from the messages in the curtains that what he was doing was necessary, at any rate.

It was quiet when he made his way out into the hallway. He paused, listening for movement in the other apartments. There was little more than the occasional muted thump or indistinct syllable. He felt pretty confident that he could move about undisturbed. He didn't even think Mrs. Sunderman would pose a problem. No one had seen or heard from her in a while, not that it was unusual. It was Larson's experience that she made herself scarce until rent time. And if there was a problem with a clogged drain, a loud or leaky pipe, or an appliance not up to snuff, well then, she was a phantom.

He glanced at the closed door of 2C, with its brownish smear at the threshold. He wanted more than anything to just open the door and take her up in his arms, to carry her to the bed and make love to her, to hold her through the night. He crossed the hallway and tried the knob. The door was locked. He'd expected that. It would remain locked to him until he'd proved he was worthy of opening it.

Other apartment doors, he knew, would not be locked. It was time to focus on them.

Outside apartment 2G, he paused again, listening. He was pretty sure no one lived there. He tried the knob and the door opened.

The apartment was vacant. It mirrored the same configuration as his own. The smooth, unmarred white walls, the new carpet and hardwood, the gleaming fixtures in the kitchen and bathroom all sat ready for a new tenant. Mrs. Sunderman's empties were, evidently, a pride and joy. He wandered the empty rooms, searching for some clue to what he was meant to take from the apartment. He found nothing in his room-by-room sweep—no boxes, no papers, not even an inspection notice. The kitchen cabinets and drawers were empty. So was the medicine cabinet in the bathroom. He even shined a penlight into the vents from the Swiss Army collection on his key chain. Nothing.

He'd just begun to think that maybe he was wrong about what this test was supposed to prove when he re-entered the den area and saw the box. He was sure it hadn't been there during his first pass through the room.

He frowned, and just below the surface of his conscious mind, something moved. It didn't happen often, dragged down in the depths of his mind as it so often was by alcohol, depression, anger, and the desperate desire inside him to win over his woman. When it did happen, it made him think of fingers struggling to claw out of a dirt grave. He wasn't sure if those fingers meant to convey something he needed to unearth, or something he needed to keep buried. Either way, it never lasted long enough for him to dwell on it.

He crossed the room and bent down in front of the box. It was mummified by packing tape. A large white label pressed to the top read DETECTIVE JACK LARSON. He got out his pen knife from the same Swiss Army set on his key chain and sliced through both sides of tape and then down the center. His bad hand throbbed beneath the bandage as if reminded of its own cuts.

The contents of the box surprised him. He supposed he was supposed to get creative. No simple plan of leaving strategically placed journals or file folders, no slipping extramarital love letters under a door or putting drugs into a car glove box. No guns or knives or even ice picks to wipe prints off of. He seemed to be tasked with planting evidence of something else.

There was a key; he recognized it as one of the set Mrs. Sunderman gave the new tenants. This one fit the 2A storage bin's lock. There was a bifolded paper he discovered to be a life insurance policy on a man named Wycoff for quite a hefty sum, naming as beneficiary his neighbor's wife. There was also a small gray paper envelope with the words "Roots, Water Hemlock" scrawled in the same script he had grown so familiar with from the sticky notes.

Larson put all these things into his pockets and rose unsteadily. His head felt continually stuffed with cotton now, his vision dimming if he got up too fast or turned his head suddenly. He figured that had more to do with the constant flow of booze in his system than because of any infection in his hand, but hell, he wasn't a doctor. He didn't think any of it was life-threatening, and that was all that mattered. He was still strong enough and whole enough to get the job done. His head, his hand, all of the little things could be taken care of later.

He closed the door of 2G softly behind him. He thought he heard a click like a lock falling into place, but he didn't bother to check. He walked briskly to 2A, doing his best to keep his footsteps light and quiet. He found the door to that apartment unlocked as well, and he let himself inside.

The apartment was tastefully furnished, a testament to upper middle-class security and comfort. It was empty; he knew it would be. The man worked from 8 to 6 or thereabouts. The wife no longer worked, but community event planning seemed to keep her from the apartment for the better part of most afternoons. He stood in the den, contemplating how best to incorporate the items from 2G. Too obvious, and either the wife would find them or the husband would discount them as harmless coincidence. Too subtle, and the husband might not put the clues together. He surveyed the den. The overstuffed recliner with the crumbs on the cushion and the remotes lined up in a caddy beside it on an end table seemed most likely to be the husband's chair. He dropped the key between the remotes in the caddy. The desk in the far corner of the room seemed like a good place to drop off the copy of the insurance policy; he slipped it into a side drawer, atop some banking papers. The envelope with the poison in it (Larson realized there was no less sinister a use for a packet of water hemlock roots) presented a trickier problem. The couple had struck him as pretty traditional the one time he'd spoken to them out in the parking lot. It was more likely that the kitchen was the wife's domain, so planting the water hemlock behind the spices or with the tea bags might alert the wrong person to the suggestion of murder. The envelope needed to look like something in the wife's possession without really interfering with any of her regularly used things. A jewelry box, maybe, or a hatbox in the back of a closet? He didn't know either nearly well enough to even take a stab at where the husband might search to discover his wife's possible secrets.

An idea occurred to him, and he smiled to himself.

When Larson returned to his apartment, his whole body ached. His hand pounded blood in painful splinters down his arm. His head swam, and with it, his vision. At first he didn't see it—another sticky note waiting on the television. He shuffled to the television and bent down, forcing his eyes to focus.

Instead of words, he found a neat little heart in the center of the paper. Smiling, he snatched it up in his good hand, crushing it close to his chest as he flopped onto the couch. He was asleep within minutes, the note crumpled in his fist.

He dreamt of the woman in 2C. In the dream, the door to her apartment was open and a bright light spilled from within to the hallway. He entered the light and felt safe. He dreamt her apartment was decorated with fine furniture, sensuous fabrics, warm and sweet-smelling. She stood in the center of the den, clothed only in silks that draped and swayed with their own life. She was so beautiful. Her arms reached out to him, beckoning. Her lips and eyes were hungry for him. He pulled her close and she took his hands, both of them, and slid them over her body. She was so soft, so smooth. He dreamed of taking her to the bedroom, of kissing her, of being inside her.

It was the last good dream he had.

***

It never really occurred to Hal that the fight with Eda that day had anything to do with thoughts or feelings other than his own. He was, for the most part, a reasonable, practical man, not given over to wanderings of the imagination. In his mind, the upside-down commercial man's appearance in his life was more likely a result of his own internal workings (or misfirings), rather than the other way around.

During the periods of time at work where no problem needed to be solved, the idea that Eda had been unfaithful vaguely irritated him, but not so much as it would have decades ago. What bothered him far more was the idea that she had been unfaithful because she thought she was better than him—and thought her lover was, as well.

He had looked up the name "Gerald Wycoff" on the Internet and had found a few pages' worth of articles relating to his moderately successful political career. These he found of little interest beyond the fact that they proved him to be the kind of man Eda had always tried to ingratiate herself to. Next, he had searched images, looking for even the briefest glimpse of him with Eda. He found none, and supposed that made sense. A man in Wycoff's position would have cloaked himself in discretion, would have known precisely how to carry on any number of political or personal affairs below the radar of the media and out of the public eye. Even gossip columns where his name came up focused on his sketchy finagling of financial records and community funds rather than any romantic liaisons with women other than his wife. He did finally find a mention of Eda in an article detailing his campaign committee's efforts to get him reelected, but it was just that—a brief mention of her fundraising efforts. In the accompanying picture, she was standing next to him. Leaning into him more like, he thought. And she was smiling and waving, just as Wycoff was. But the picture didn't really confirm or dispel the notion of an affair between them. Also, there was a brief article about his support of a particular corporation's efforts to demolish the Bridgehaven Asylum and make room for modern apartment housing; evidently Eda had been on that committee, too. That surprised Hal. Eda had been the one to suggest a move from their somewhat rickety Arbor Street one-bedroom ranch house to the new apartment building on the hill, but Hal had chalked up her discovery of the place to her religious reading of the local news, her keen eye for opportunity, and her juggernaut desire to move up in the world. He hadn't realized she'd had any hand whatsoever in seeing the asylum torn down and the land cleared, against the fervent wishes of the historical society, so that the very apartment building in which they lived could be built. It was yet another thing he didn't know about her. It made her seem all the more conniving to him. Eda had a plan for life which she intended to execute, with or without him. Maybe her political and community work put her in a position to cash in on favors (Eda would never suffer owing anyone anything if she could help it). Maybe she had more power to pull strings and manipulate circumstances than he had ever imagined. Hal was starting to believe that if he got in her way, she just might have the power to steamroll right over him. Maybe Wycoff had made that possible. For that, Hal felt a sudden and intense surge of hate for him.

He saved the articles and pictures about the fire for last. He wanted to enjoy those.

The fire had started, according to the articles, in the master bedroom on the second floor of the Wycoff family mansion in Idyll Hills, a wealthy gated community just outside of Bridgewood's center of town.

According to reports, Mr. and Mrs. Gerald Wycoff had returned from the funeral and memorial dinner of a well-known retired psychiatrist whose career and life had both ended under unpleasant circumstances—a man named Symmes. Wycoff and Symmes had been in opposition on the issue of rebuilding on the asylum's land, so as a show of good politics, Wycoff not only attended the services but also gave a fairly moving (if somewhat professional) eulogy.

Those whose job it was to notice and report such things to the public via newspapers speculated that the personal space between Wycoff and his wife was thick with tension. Neighbors confirmed hearing the sounds of arguing between the couple that evening in the driveway. Less than an hour after, the heat, light, and the crackling of flames drew the neighbors' attention again, and the fire department and police were called. It was too late, though, to save anyone. Mrs. Wycoff had died of smoke inhalation, the burns on her body nearly obliterating any way of identifying her. Gerald Wycoff had third-degree burns over 80% of his body. They found him down in his study. He'd died on the way to the hospital. No one else had been in the house, and no evidence found of foul play or escalated violence between the couple. Neither the local fire department or the arson investigators could pin down the exact cause of the fire. One of them (who'd asked to remain anonymous) had told the papers that it really seemed as if the entire bedroom had spontaneously combusted.

Given the reported date of events in the article, Hal brooded. It put Wycoff's death a couple of years before the final grand opening of Bridgewood Estates apartments, which was definitely a few years after Hal had affixed it in his mind. He'd assumed the affair and Eda's decision to leave him had all happened and ended seven years ago. He thought that was what the upside-down commercial man said, although thinking back on it, nothing Hal was told gave him any kind of time-line. For all he knew, the upside-down commercial man could have been sugar-coating his information, soft-shoeing the details of the affair. For all Hal knew, Eda could have been banging that politician right up until he'd been burned to a cinder.

Until she was done with him. The thought sprang suddenly to his mind, a staggering leap of logic even in his present mood. *Until she was done with waiting for him to leave his wife. Figured she'd kill two birds with one incendiary device.*

Hal scoffed. Eda might have been many things, but she was not capable of killing anyone. She would have considered it...vulgar. Unladylike. Then again, he thought with a sudden flash of bitter anger, what did he really know about her anymore?

He found Eda wasn't there when he returned home that evening. The door was locked, the lights all turned off. There was no note. No dinner waiting, either. He sighed, dropping his car keys on the kitchen counter. He got himself a beer from the fridge and microwaved some of the pizza from the day before. Nothing on the kitchen calendar indicated an event or meeting she was supposed to be at that night. She simply...wasn't there.

It occurred to him that this was a taste of what it would be like without her. Maybe it wasn't such a bad thing.

He settled into his easy chair and reached for the remote, then paused. What if the upside-down commercial man was waiting? What if that bright inverted smile filled the screen the minute he clicked on the television?

Hal set down the remote. He didn't have it in him to be badgered about Eda. He had enough to think about as far as she went, thank you very much.

He finished his beer and went to the kitchen for another. He considered it a moment, grabbed two to save him a trip, then made his way back to the chair. He sat staring at the gray screen of the television while working on his second beer. If he couldn't watch TV, maybe he could do a crossword puzzle...or fix the drip in the shower that damned Sunderman lady kept avoiding his calls about. Maybe that would make Eda happy, if he fixed something.

Hal settled back into his chair. Fuck it. Why did he need to make her happy? When was the last time she had made an honest, focused effort to do anything but criticize him?

He drained the second beer and went to put the bottle on the table when he knocked over the caddy. Remotes for the television, DVR, and even old ones he'd forgotten the uses for tumbled to the floor like pick-up sticks. So did a key. He leaned over and picked it up, the remotes temporarily forgotten. It was the key to their storage bin. He hadn't been able to find it for weeks—had told Eda, in fact, that it was the reason he hadn't done much around the place, as his tools were locked up in there. Had she found it, and dropped it in with his remotes as a reminder? That would be so like her, that passive-aggressive bullshit. He grunted. Well, two could play that kind of game.

He went to her desk across the room and opened a drawer. It seemed somehow fitting to bury it deep beneath her papers and checkbooks. He was about to drop it in when he noticed an official-looking paper that caught his eye. It was a copy of a life insurance policy. He took it out and read it. A life insurance policy for a Gerald Wycoff. He felt the heat rising from his chest to his face. Eda had been named a beneficiary.

His first thought, wildly, was to wonder how the hell he would have ever explained another woman's name on the policy to his wife. Assuming, of course, she survived him, which she didn't. His second thought was even wilder, obviously colored by his mood.

Maybe her not surviving him was the point. Had that fire been planned? Had Eda somehow convinced Wycoff to let her arrange for a fire that would kill his wife? Maybe Eda had double-crossed him, and set things up so both of them were killed. Then she wouldn't have to wait for the money.

Still...if she had been the beneficiary, where was the money? It was certainly enough for her to be able to leave Hal and live comfortably without him. Unless...yes. Unless she was deliberately distancing herself from the fire investigation, and had been waiting a safe number of years to cash in on the policy. He had never known Eda to be a patient person, but he was lately discovering she could be cunning. If waiting was a means to an end, he supposed she could do it.

He'd been through her desk before, looking for stamps or a stapler or a roll of Scotch tape. He'd never seen the policy. That it was now at the top of her things might mean she had grown tired of waiting. Maybe she wanted her money and an end to her simple life with Hal.

He put the policy back in the drawer where he'd found it and pocketed the storage bin key. He wasn't quite ready yet for her to know he knew. He wanted more information first before he confronted her. Maybe he ought to hire a private detective to see what she was doing with her free time nowadays, someone like—like that Larson guy across the hall. Or, he could just snoop around himself. She didn't have a cell phone—at least, not so far as he knew—so he couldn't call her. He had no idea when she would be home. For all he knew, there was some new

225

guy outclassing him, someone she might be out with right now. And she wasn't even bothering to hide it. No note pretending she was running late at a committee meeting or out shopping.

At the moment, though, she *wasn't* home. He figured he might as well not waste the time sitting there going over what he didn't know, and start adding to what he did.

He went into the bedroom, which had so often lately served as a sanctuary for her, away from him. It wasn't that he didn't sleep there anymore, but lately she went to bed long before him, and he fell asleep in his chair. By the time he awoke and stumbled into the bedroom, he had two, maybe two and a half hours before he had to get up for work. He felt almost like he was renting the bed space from her, that it was her room and he just used half of a mattress and a night table top to finish out the rest of the night.

He searched her night table, but nothing in it—aspirin, tissues, an earring missing its mate, a pen—raised an eyebrow. He picked through her cosmetics and perfume on the dresser then opened drawers and rummaged through her clothes and underwear. Nothing buried at the bottom of the drawer. He felt beneath the mattress on her side, then on his side, stood and flipped the pillows, sank to his knees and looked under the bed, and only found more nothing. He stood in the center of the room, looking around, when his gaze fell on the closet.

He opened the door. Eda wasn't one for clutter or sentimentality, so there was little to find in there except a shoebox of receipts and old holiday cards and a plastic storage container of winter hats, gloves, and scarves. As he was pulling down her old sewing kit, a small gray envelope fluttered off the shelf and fell to the floor. Hal put the sewing kit back on the shelf and bent to pick up the envelope. He didn't recognize the handwriting on the front, but he understood the contents: water hemlock roots.

His grandmother and his mother after her were avid gardeners. Between the two of them, they had every kind of flowering plant imaginable. The more exotic, the more it delighted them to cultivate and display it in their jointly-shared greenhouse. Growing up, his mother had taken care to make sure Hal knew, whether it interested him or not, which plants grew when and in what conditions, which ones were edible, which ones could be used for medicinal or health-related purposes, and of course, which ones were poisonous.

Hal had always been strictly forbidden to touch the water hemlock (its roots, specifically), among other poisonous plants.

"She's not trying to kill me," he had told the upside-down commercial man.

"Isn't she, though?"

Was she? Had Eda really decided that leaving him wasn't enough? That being the recipient of one insurance policy wasn't enough?

Dazed, Hal wandered out to the den and sank in his chair. Poison? How would she do it? Would he be able to taste it? Smell it? He reached for his beer, realized he'd finished it, and put down the empty bottle. He'd lost his taste for eating and drinking anything tonight, anyway.

He turned the TV on, determined to find something to watch to keep him awake. He didn't feel safe falling asleep before he saw Eda return home and go to bed. He didn't feel safe, and that made him angry at Eda. He stared at the television, trying to concentrate on some slasher movie in which beautiful, half-dressed twenty-somethings were being carved up in the woods by some silent, lumbering man with an axe.

Hal had an axe out in the storage bin.

Before the last of the twenty-somethings, a blond in a white tank top, could escape the woods and the man with the axe, Hal had fallen asleep. He never heard Eda return, change for bed, and go to sleep. He never heard the last of the movies give over to infomercials. He never heard the front door open, or the soft spasmodic footsteps that crossed from the door to the den and then stopped in front of him. He slept through the pressure of long, pointed fingers digging into his shoulders.

What managed to filter through the wall of sleep was a whisper whose cadence rose and fell hypnotically. It was in a language he had never heard but understood both literally and on subtle, symbolic levels. It made pictures in his dreams.

When the footsteps receded and the front door closed, Hal dreamed of murder. In his sleep, he smiled.

THIRTEEN

Two nights later, Myrinda slipped a little further away from herself, just far enough to be out of reach.

She felt jagged and bruisy, the clouds beneath her eyes threatening to squeeze up and cause rain. Derek had gone out for a late afternoon meeting with his new boss to square away some things before he started work next week, and he wasn't expected back until late that night. She was in the apartment alone. He hadn't wanted to leave her, not after the other night, but she'd insisted. His hovering was only making her more anxious, stirring up the thoughts in her mind that she'd wanted to settle to the bottom.

She looked out the window. Beyond the darkening hills, she could make out the brooding, stolid shape of the Old Ward. Its long shadow fell before it, and Myrinda thought it looked as if a giant hole (Aggie's woo-nnnd) had opened up, a gaping chasm to the other place that the Old Ward stood in danger of toppling right into. She imagined someone unwittingly looking to explore the lightless pain-soaked corridors of the building, wandering alone into that shadow, and just slipping away to some other place, another time. Just vanishing forever.

It might have been the angle from the window, or the way the moonlight fell just so on the rough bricks, but the building seemed to expand and recede, to breathe and—this was nuts—to actually titter over that death-lined throat into the center of the earth.

Still, a part of her—a very insistent part—wanted to go out there into the night alone. To be that explorer, searching through the dark, slipping in and out of the folds of the rippling, overlapping worlds outside and—

She shook her head, snapping off the train of thought. What in God's name was she thinking? It didn't even make sense. Rippling, overlapping worlds? What did that even mean?

What was happening to her?

A sudden bang from somewhere out in the hallway made her jump. She turned slowly from the window, annoyed. "Derek?" She hadn't expected him home so early. The way Derek had described it, his new boss was probably going to keep him the better part of two or three hours, showing him around the facility and discussing security needs and options. "Derek, is that you?"

She went down the hall to the den. Another loud bang made her flinch. It was the sound more than the suddenness; lately, she seemed more sensitive to loud noises and bright colors. The bang, like a metal pipe hitting a wall, left a wake of only a few moments' silence before a door slammed. She jumped, cursed softly, then crossed to the door and opened it a crack. Another door slammed, followed by a steady tolling of the pipe.

Myrinda peered into the shadowed hallway, searching for any indication that other neighbors were as disturbed by this as she was. The other apartment doors remained closed. She chewed her bottom lip, wishing Derek was home. She was the more likely of the two to engage in a confrontation, but it didn't mean she liked it. And she sure as hell didn't relish the idea of getting into a dust-up with a neighbor who obviously had some rage issues going on.

The dull clank of the pipe seemed to be coming from apartment 2C. She frowned. She could have sworn Derek told her that apartment was empty. Leaving the door to her own apartment open, she padded down the hall in her socks and with some hesitation, knocked on the door.

Immediately, the banging of the pipe stopped. From somewhere inside the apartment, a door slammed.

"Hello?" she called through the door. "Uh, hello?" She knocked again, louder this time, then put her ear to the door. She thought she heard voices speaking low, but it was followed by applause and canned laughter. The television, probably.

She knocked again. "Hello? Uh, excuse me, but whatever you're doing in there, you're making a lot of noise. It's kind of disturbing the rest of us." She put her ear against the door again.

The low voices snapped off and there was a thud, and then something like fingers scratching against the other side of the front door. She pulled away from it as if it were on fire. The scratching continued, so close to her, so close—just a door's width away. And its span was spreading—fingers scratching above her head, at eye level, around the door knob, and even down by her feet. She thought she could see the tiny moving shadows cast on the threshold.

She cried out. Long gray fingers were reaching beneath the door, scratching at the hallway floor. When one of the cold fingertips touched the edge of her sock, she screamed, jumping and kicking at the finger, which twitched beneath her blows and withdrew beneath the door again. She bolted back to her apartment and slammed the door, then locked it. For several minutes, she leaned with her back to the door, breathing hard, listening to the sound of those awful fingers. She could hear them on the carpeting now, those pointed, nailless tips digging into the pile and dragging their knuckled segments closer to her door.

"No," she said, "no no no no NONONONO!" She sank to the floor, then leaped to her feet again at the thought of those fingers reaching under her door and touching her.

Abruptly the scratching stopped. She waited, forcing each inhale and exhale to stretch over four seconds. She listened for what felt like a long time, convinced that the fingers were just outside the door, biding their time until she opened it.

She felt a knot in her throat. Tears made her vision swim. This place was very, very wrong. It was tearing her down. It wasn't fair. This was supposed to be her beautiful new life, her clean break. This was her chance to build a future with Derek free of the ghosts of the past. But somehow, new ghosts had found her, and they were, quite literally, driving her crazy. The laugh that escaped her was harsh and ugly. If the Puritan wagging tongues of the great New England gentry weren't satisfied with making judgments about a white woman dating a black man, well, they'd have a field day with her losing her mind. Zombie fingers and black, oozing pools of interdimensional gateway and blurry monsters in the dark. Oh yeah. A freaking field day.

She had to get out—soon, tonight, before she lost herself completely.

Myrinda turned and opened the door a tiny crack. The hallway was empty. No fingers. No monsters. She closed the door again, relieved. She was just about to return to the bedroom again when she heard the man screaming.

***

Larson's last gift of proof for the woman in 2C, the woman he'd come to think of as his new Julia, had proved to be the toughest to carry out. Like with his hand, he knew preparations would be essential. He'd picked out a penknife, some towels, bandages, and a plastic container from Chinese take-out that he found in the back of a cabinet on the counter in the bathroom. This time, he would need a mirror to see what he was doing.

To see. He'd laughed to himself. He'd still be able to see her with his good eye.

A friend of his from the force had given him painkillers from the evidence locker when he'd had his breakdown. He'd tried a few once to sleep, but they had made him feel paranoid and have given him night sweats and terrible nightmares. Tonight though, he thought they might be more efficient than a bottle of whiskey. He'd taken three—one dose and one extra. He could already feel a warmth numbing his face, his limbs. Even his bad hand felt okay. He used the remaining fingers to pull his eyelid open. The knife he held with his good hand. When he angled the point between the bottom lid and the eyeball, he felt pressure first, and then a far-away pain. Blood trickled from the socket like a tear, trailing red diluted with tears. His eyelid fought to blink, and his fingers strained to keep it open. He dug the knife deeper, under the orb, and his eye watered. A stab of pain broke through the haze of painkillers. He started moving the knife around lightly, afraid of cutting into something other than the muscles and tendons that held his eye in place. The knife caught against something stringy; Larson figured it to be a nerve. Sawing caused waves of blinding pain to blare through his head, so he flicked his wrist hard, to sever the nerve. His vision went white and then black in that eye.

With the fingers of his band hand, he dug in and tried to pull the eye out. Blood washed over his bottom lid and down his cheek. The eye caught, still attached. Growing impatient, Larson swiped the knife as best he could behind the eye and finally felt it cut through something thick. The eye popped out in his hand. He placed it gently on the counter so it wouldn't roll, then wrapped the bandage around his head, binding the socket tightly. He rinsed off the eye, then put it in the plastic Chinese food container.

He had done it all, finally—everything she asked for through the curtains. He had proved the lengths he'd go to show his love for her.

Larson carried the container into the bedroom and set it down on the bed. He kept his gun in a box in the closet. He took it out and put it in the waistband of his pants. Then he picked up the container. He made a quick detour to the liquor cabinet and took several healthy swigs from a bottle of Jameson. It splashed lightly into the cracks where the painkiller buzz couldn't reach.

Now, he was ready. With every step down the hall and through the den to the front door, Larson felt light. Free. He knew he'd accomplished something. One way or another, this night's events were his end game.

He opened the door and crossed the hall to 2C. He knocked on the door and waited. When he had confirmed to his satisfaction that no one was coming to answer the door, he turned the knob. It opened easily.

Inside, the apartment was dark. He flipped the light switch, but nothing happened. It took a few minutes for his one good eye to adjust to the gloom inside, but when it did, several realizations struck him at once.

There was no furniture in the apartment, no pictures on the walls, no rugs. Instead, a thick, fluffy carpet of dust lay across the floor and on the windowsill. Like he'd done with apartment 2G, he made a sweep of each room, looking for some sign of life.

In the bedroom, he saw the curtains. Those curtains had promised so much from the outside. They had been infused, embroidered with a strange language of terrible tasks and wonderful outcomes. He went to the curtains and picked them up. Between his fingers, the material felt threadworn. There were holes. No pink or gray threads. Just a cheap, gauzy material made for showing the apartment—something old and moth-eaten from the back of the landlady's closet. It wasn't the same set of curtains. It couldn't be.

He went out to the den and placed the container with his eye in it in the center of the floor. Then he went to a far corner of the room and sank to the floor himself. He took out the gun. He'd figured he might need it to...what, convince her to keep her promises?

No. He'd known deep down he would need it because the woman of his dreams wouldn't be there. That she had never been there. The apartment was empty.

He cradled his bad hand, which had begun to ache, along with his gouged socket, in spite of the painkillers and booze. Frustration wrenched tears from his eyes. Anger and disappointment blurred the gloom in front of him. But none of these compared to the pure depth and breadth of the despair that welled up in him. From his soul through his chest and lungs and up his throat, all the wretchedness of his life, all the mistakes he'd made, all the destruction that had left him scarred, drunk, high, and alone, broke free of him. With all his breath and strength, he screamed.

***

Myrinda ran into the hall and saw the door to 2C was open. Instantly, the bottom of her stomach dropped out, and she clutched at it. She glanced around nervously at the floor, searching for fingers. There were none, but still, her steps across the hallway were careful, almost tiptoed.

She poked her head through the doorway and called, "Hello?" Her voice sounded small and echoed through the empty apartment. "Hello?"

From somewhere inside—it sounded like the den—she heard moaning. Someone was hurt.

She hesitated in the doorway. What if it was a trick? What if she went in there to help whoever was moaning, and the fingers crawled out of the darkness? What if they jumped at her, clawing for her throat and trying to strangle her?

Another moan escaped into the hallway.

"Hello? Are you okay in there?"

She heard the sound of bodily movement, the shifting of weight against the wall.

"Do you...need help?"

"It's all gone," a voice from inside said. It sounded familiar, but from where? Was it the voice of a neighbor, or a voice from one of her dreams?

Taking a deep breath, she stepped inside. The door was open; she could run for it if there was even the slightest sign of something suspicious. She flipped the light switch, but no light came on, so she trudged through the darkness, waiting for her eyes to adjust. Her toe connected with something that slid a little across the floor of the den, and she stopped. Then she saw him in the corner.

"Oh my God, are you okay? You're hurt! Want me to call an ambulance, Mr.—?"

"Larson. Jack Larson." The mutilated figure on the floor sat clutching a heavily bandaged hand. More bandages dipped over one eye as they wrapped around his head. It was difficult to make out details in the dark, but so far as Myrinda could see from the moonlight filtering in through the den window, the man looked pale, with nearly gray lips and a heavy, uneven stubble on his jaw. His clothes were rumpled and he smelled like whiskey and staleness. His eyes, wild and empty, sat in deep reddish-brown bags.

She glanced back at the thing she'd accidentally kicked. It was some kind of container, and she bet it belonged to Larson. Given his condition, she didn't really want to know what was inside.

"Mr. Larson? I'm Myrinda. Just hang on, okay? I'm going to get you help."

"No! Stay."

"What?" Myrinda paused.

"I don't need help. It won't do any good, and I'll be gone before you make the call anyway."

Myrinda sat on the floor to look him in the eye. "What can I do? Are you sure I can't call an ambulance for you?"

"Just let me talk. I want to tell you something," Larson said.

Myrinda looked around, uncomfortable. "Uh, okay."

"When I was still a patrol officer in Boston, I responded to a domestic violence call one night. A neighbor called it in. She didn't have much good to say about this couple that lived next door. Twenty-somethings. Black hair, blue eyes. By all accounts, striking set, they were, both good-looking in that way that sort of hurts your heart. Like you, really. You and your man."

She smiled at him, not quite sure if that required an acknowledgment of the compliment, but he didn't seem to be looking for one. He went on before she could say anything at all.

"They were creepy, though. No family, no friends—they only had each other. For years, it was just the two of them. I knew this, because I had gotten to know the both of them a little. The woman, Julia, was worried about her boyfriend. Apparently, he was convinced that something...I don't know, some kind of entity, was stalking him, filling his head with diseased thoughts. Making him confused. Julia was afraid maybe he would hurt himself. Or her. It got so she was scared to be home alone with him at night. She wouldn't leave, though. She loved him. God, she loved him. She refused to go.

"So anyway, when the domestic violence call came in, I recognized the address. I was scared for her. I...I had fallen in love with her. She... her safety was everything to me. I don't think—no, I know—she never loved me back like that. I wasn't good enough. I could never prove myself. But it was enough to just be near her, to protect her. To see her once in a while.

"So anyway, my partner and I showed up at the house and found the door open, so we announced ourselves and went inside to check out the situation." His eyes filled with tears. His whole body shook now.

"When I found him, he was standing over her, holding onto the handle of an axe with both hands. I remember the blood more than anything else because there was just so much of it. His t-shirt and jeans were splattered and soaked through with blood, there was blood in his hair, blood dripping from his coated palms and down his arms. Blood dripping off his nose. The blade of the axe looked dull, a kind of dark gray that reminded me absurdly of tornadoes—funny, sometimes, what rolls through your head when you're trying not to think too hard about what you're seeing. Anyway, the blade was all slick with red streaks. Her hair—little strands of it—stuck to the blade. Her lovely long black hair. She lay there like a broken doll cracked all to pieces, and the cracks in her body swelled with blood that ran all over the floor. Her eyes just...stared up at him. All glassy, glazed over. Still loving, though—still loving. And her hair, the rest of her hair...." He shook his head. "It clumped in the pooled blood around her head, heavy, stringy, as lifeless as those cooling lips, those eyes...."

"God, how awful," Myrinda whispered. She was afraid to speak louder, afraid to wake him, in a sense; he spoke to her as if he wasn't really speaking to her at all, but rather, reliving it.

"I don't think he ever saw me," he added softly. "I watched him for a bit, trying to assess the situation. His head was bowed a little, smears of blood across his forehead, his cheeks, his mouth. And his eyes—he had cold eyes, and right about then, they looked as dead as the ones that stared up at him from the floor. They never left her face. I approached him slowly. I had my gun on him. Guys like that, you never know what to expect. They could fold up and sink to the floor, blubbering like a baby, or turn on you all growling and snarling and swinging the axe. He didn't do either. I think...yeah, I think what he did was worse."

"What did he do?" Myrinda wasn't sure she really wanted him to answer.

"He started laughing, laughing and then screaming, and the laughter came harder and harder, like waves—like convulsions, really—and the screaming was hysterical, high and thin. It was like he was strung up inside like a guitar, see, and all his strings were winding tighter and tighter and...snapping." He sighed. "Have you ever heard someone do that? Laugh and scream at the same time? I think it's the most awful sound in the world." He sank to the floor, looking very tired and very small just then.

"Did...did he ever, you know, say why he did it? Why he killed her?"

Larson looked up at her, but some part of his gaze was somewhere else, seeing past her, maybe to some cramped, cold, harshly lit interrogation room. "He said he loved her. He said—" He exhaled a shuddery breath, inhaled, tried again. "He said he loved her, had loved her many times in many lives on many worlds, whatever that meant. He told me she was...his sister, and that since their parents' deaths, they had become each other's worlds. They rarely left the apartment. They had no other friends, no individual hobbies. They had each other, they had the sex between them—the bond, he said. The love that no one else understood. But he was jealous, paranoid. He didn't want her to leave him, ever. He never said what it was that set him off, just kept telling me over and over that he loved her, missed her, wanted her back, and why the hell wouldn't we just let him see her, just for a moment?"

"He...didn't realize?"

Larson shook his head. "Not all crazy is dangerous. Not all crazy is real, honest-to-God crazy. Some people play at it. Some are even good at it. But that boy was the real deal, and he was deadly." Officer Larson seemed to come back a little then, and when he looked up at her, his eyes were stormy and troubled. "I didn't tell you about that for the shock value. I told you because I need someone to know I tried to love, and to be worthy of being loved. I tried. When I first moved here, I thought I could feel something...I don't know, inside me, maybe. Taking over in my head, like a cold. Something's been wrong with me for a long time, but here, it's gotten worse. For the first time, I understand—I mean, *really* understand what that boy felt. Why he did what he did. I've carved out the best parts of me and given them over to someone who was never there. Myrinda, I died in that room with Julia. Her death destroyed me. It ruined my career, my life. And something here—" he looked around the apartment "—made me believe I could get it all back. But it's gone. Everything...everything I was is slipping away. Now, I'm tired. Now, I realize I never had a chance. And...I don't know how to reconcile that with what I thought I knew. Maybe...maybe I really am crazy."

Myrinda crawled a little closer to him. She didn't question what he was saying; she didn't need to. She knew on a gut level that he was right because she could feel it, too. "I don't think it's just you. I think there's something in this building affecting everyone, making them sick. Confused. I feel it, too."

Larson stared at her.

"Do you think...well, I mean, could it be possible that the craziness is like an infection or some kind of poisoning? What if it's their exposure to something from...someplace else, something we don't have mental antibodies for?"

"What are you getting at?"

"There's no question in my mind there's a kind of insanity unbalancing people around there. But what if at least some of what these folks are seeing is real? That some kind of...external force is driving people crazy?"

Larson stretched out his legs. "I don't know. But I can't take it any-more. I don't have the strength to find out. I just want it all to stop."

"Mr. Larson—"

"Myrinda, have you ever seen someone die? Ever seen the color drain from their faces, their necks, their hands? Seen their lips turn a little bluish and dry around the outlines? I've seen that depth, that color and flicker, the intelligent *thereness* of life fade from the eyes. And that's the kicker, the eyes—that's when you really know, if you ever knew the person at all. Life doesn't wink out. It fades. And for several seconds after, you just kind of look in those eyes, expecting to see something of what used to be there. You want it so badly to be there still that maybe you drag it down for a time, that you keep it from flying up and away from the person you love. Bodies take time to cool from the heat that meant life. Eyes, too, take time to develop that glassy vacancy. And I don't think you feel true loss until you look into those eyes and know the person you loved isn't there to look back out at you."

"Mr. Larson, I'm so sorry."

He offered her a weak smile. "You know what's worse? Not getting to be there for someone while they make the great change from life to death. Knowing that she had to face death with no one to capture those last moments of her life in his memory, to cherish what she was before she became a shell, a nothing."

"I—I don't.... Please, let me call an am—"

"And what's even worse than that? Loving someone who never really was. There is no closure, there is no comfort in thinking circumstances beyond anyone's control took away someone who loved you. When death and death alone takes someone, she can still be yours in your heart because her life, her moments transitioning into death, were spent loving you. But when that person you thought you loved never was, it's more than death. It's living death. Pain that echoes on and on. It's death and rejection. There is no room for healing to get a foothold, because the hurt is too immense."

"Mr. Larson, I don't think I follow you."

Larson pulled a gun from his pocket.

Myrinda's eyes grew wide. "Oh! Oh no, Mr. Larson, please! Don't—"

"I tried to take it all back, and I failed," he said wearily.

"Please don't do—"

Larson pulled the trigger and a halo spray of red and gray spattered the wall behind him. Myrinda screamed as his body jerked and then slumped. The gun fell from his limp hand. Her hands shook as she clamped them over her mouth. Her breathing, even around the hands, was deep and ragged and she was afraid if she didn't hold it in, she'd scream again and again and never stop screaming.

She turned away from Larson's body and ran out into the hallway, where sobs exploded from her chest. She ran to her phone and called 911, and explained what Larson had done. The dispatcher asked her a series of questions, and she hung up. Then she went to the bedroom and stared out the window for what seemed like several very long hours.

Myrinda wanted to sleep. Every part of her body strained to hold her up. Her head felt light with exhaustion, and she couldn't focus. A mind deprived of sleep, after all, was like clay that could be molded any way that amused. She wanted sleep, but she knew the chaotic ones wouldn't let her. Too much was going on. She could hear things through the walls, for one. The damn idiots in 2G. She heard banging, doors slamming all over that apartment, and something that sounded a lot like dozens of fingers scratching on the wall, the same as she'd heard in 2C. Whoever was staying there had obviously moved apartments just before what Larson did, because aside from him, there had been no sign of anyone living in that apartment.

She thought she could hear voices periodically, and from the timbre of them, she supposed they came from the television. She didn't have the strength to stand up, let alone go tell them to be quiet, and frankly, she was a little afraid of who she'd be confronting if she tried to make it stop. So the banging of pipes went on and on. Pipes and doors and scratching fingers that sounded set up to go all night long. It was the kind of stuff that could drive a person crazy. She knew Derek worried she was stressed, but how could she not be? If she flinched a little at noises now and then in her waking life, or seemed a little oversensitive and jumpy, who could blame her, really?

Derek wasn't home to hear it. He thought that apartment was empty, but obviously, he didn't know what he was talking about. Of course there were people staying in 2G. Who else could be making noises like that? Rats, for God's sake?

She wished she could shut them all up so she could hear what the chaotic ones were saying. From the Old Ward, she heard the strains of their voices chattering and laughing. After a moment, through the tears, she started laughing, too.

FOURTEEN

Derek returned home to the blue-red-blue flashing lights of two police cars, an ambulance, and a stretcher carrying a black-bagged figure out of the front lobby.

"Uh, excuse me," he said to one of the police officers overseeing the scene, "what happened?"

"Suicide," the policeman replied, then moved to enter the lobby. Derek stopped him again, his unease ratcheting up to alarm. Myrinda had been off, but she wouldn't—

"Is it a woman?" he asked.

"Do you live in this building?"

"Yeah. Yeah, I live in apartment 2E with my girlfriend, Myrinda. She isn't—?"

"Myrinda Giavelli?"

"Yes. Why?" Derek looked from the cop to the EMT standing between him and the stretcher. He was truly afraid for Myrinda. How could he have left her?

The EMT exchanged glances with the policeman, who nodded. Then he said, "Your girlfriend was the one who called 911. One of your neighbors, a Mr. Larson—she found him in 2C. He shot himself."

"Oh, God," Derek muttered, and jogged into the lobby toward the elevator. The policeman called after him to wait, but

Derek ignored him. The elevator cars opened. He stepped inside and pressed the button for the second floor. The doors closed and the elevator started to rise.

Then it stopped mid-floor.

"What the—? Oh come *on*, man. Not now." Derek tapped the "2" button a couple of times, but nothing happened. "Shit." He was about to push the red alarm button when a voice close to his ear, just behind his shoulder, said, "Leave her, Derek." He jumped, wheeling around. Obviously, there was no one behind him. No one had been in the elevator when he got on, and no one had gotten on with him. So what the hell?

From somewhere in the car came the same low, humorless chuckling he'd heard in the bathroom. His gaze darted around the car, and for a second, even less than a second, he thought he saw a wide, vertical mouth set in an eyeless, mottled, misshapen head in the reflection of the elevator's shiny interior. He blinked, though, and it was gone.

"Fuck this shit," he muttered to himself, and turned to the call button. Just then, the elevator car lurched and began its ascent. When the doors opened, he ran to the apartment, as much to get away from the oppressive little box as to get to Myrinda.

The door was unlocked and opened a crack.

It wasn't a good sign. Derek shook his head, swearing to himself. He never should have left her alone. She wasn't well—

he could see that. He thought maybe she was hearing or even seeing things. She certainly believed things that couldn't be true...could they?

He thought of the chuckling and the blood in the bathroom. He'd thought it was Myrinda, but it couldn't have been. He knew what he'd seen, what he'd heard. But the next morning, he'd looked into the waste basket for the bloody wad of toilet paper. He'd been surprised to find it wasn't. Something else was there, though, curved over an empty toilet paper roll and sitting snugly against a crumpled tissue, was a finger. It was gray, slightly pointed at the tip, the nail bed wet and devoid of a nail.

"Geezus!" He'd flinched from its obvious grotesquerie, its misplacement among the normal things of his everyday life with Myrinda. But what made him sick around the edges was that it was just like Myrinda described, just like what she saw coming out of the vents.

And if they both were seeing these phantom fingers, then it couldn't be just some stress-induced hallucination on her part.

And what about what he had just seen in the elevator? What the fuck had that been all about?

Maybe she had reason to believe what Aggie told her. Maybe they both did.

"Myrinda?" He went into the apartment. He felt apprehensive, wanting to find her, to see she was okay and yet afraid that if he did, he'd find....

What? What did he think would be there? A Myrinda he didn't know? Or one of her wound-monsters?

"Talk to me, babygirl. Where are you?"

"In here." Her voice was an echo, a shade of itself, coming from the bedroom.

He found her sitting on the bed, rocking a little. She was staring out the window.

"Babygirl, what happened? The EMTs downstairs said you found Larson, that he committed suicide? What's going on?" It wasn't lost on him that this was the second death in their apartment building that she had been witness to. At best, it was a terrible case of being in the wrong place at the wrong time—twice.

She turned to face him, and he felt the bottom of his stomach drop out. The shadows beneath her eyes, the gauntness of her cheeks...she looked broken to him. His beautiful girl, his partner in crime. Oh God, what happened to her? He rushed to the bed to sit next to her and took her face in his hands. He couldn't lose her. He wouldn't. Not many things scared Derek Moore, but losing the love of his life topped that short list.

"Myrinda," he said softly. "What happened?"

"They got him," she said.

"Who? Who got him. The EMTs said—"

"The chaotic ones. They made him...hurt himself. Badly. He thought they tricked him. He killed himself." She cupped the hand that touched her face with her own. "They told me. I can hear them sometimes, out there in the Old Ward. They hurt Aggie, and then they took Mrs. Sunderman and threw her into the abyss, and then they made Mr. Larson kill himself. There are others. 1D. 1C. 2A. 1F. 2F." She gave him a sad smile. "They couldn't let go and just be free."

Derek slumped a little, feeling defeated. "What are they?" he finally asked. He wasn't sure he ought to be entertaining her ideas, but...well, there was the finger in the bathroom. The blood. The laughing. The deaths. The elevator. "What the hell are they?"

She glanced at the window. "They are chaos. Wild abandon. Insanity. Psychosis. Sociopathy. Their world is a black chasm steeped in madness. It's all they know. It's all they are. They call themselves hinshing. I don't know what it means. I don't even know if that's how you say it out loud. But that's what it sounds like in their language in my head."

"Are they...talking to you now?"

She shook her head. "They're off playing. Pretending to be other things."

"Look, baby, we have to get out of here.

"No!" she jerked out of his grasp as if he were on fire. "No, we can't! They need us! They're going to make us free. It'll be different with us, Derek. They promised. They'll take all the worry away. We'll never have to worry about dying or getting sick or—"

"Stop. Just stop it. Myrinda, listen to yourself. Do you hear what you're saying?"

Myrinda stared at him, perplexed.

"Baby, whatever these things are, they're hurting you. They're changing you. You've got to be able to see that, can't you?"

Myrinda looked down at herself, her face a fixed but sincere expression of confusion.

"They're making you sick, just like they made Aggie sick, and Mr. Larson."

"Just like Wayne?" she asked. She sounded small.

"Uh, yeah, just like Wayne." He had no idea who Wayne was, but if he was in this building, it was very possible he was as bad off as Myrinda.

She sighed. Tears filled her eyes. "I'm tired of worrying. Tired of being judged and—and caring that I'm being judged. I want a home to be proud of and a family to love. I want peace of mind."

Derek hurt for her. He wanted those things too—even more so for her. He loved her and her happiness meant the world to him. He wanted to take her into his arms and stroke her hair, to tell her everything would be okay, that he'd make it okay. But he was going to lose her if he couldn't get through to her.

People were dying all around them in that building. Myrinda believed these hinshing were responsible. She also believed they were tied to the Bridgewood Estates apartments. That meant the best plan for her mental and physical well-being was to get her far the hell away from there.

"Myrinda, do you love me?"

Her eyes reflected pain. "You know I do."

"Do you trust me?"

"Of course."

Derek nodded. "Then you need to hear what I'm saying. You and I are not safe here. We have to leave, maybe for a little while, maybe for longer. We need to be better, first. Stronger. Then we can have all those things you wanted."

She frowned, the tears finally spilling down her cheeks. In her eyes, he saw a change. She was back a little, at least enough to trust him, to resign herself to his plan.

"I'm scared," she said. "What if they won't let me leave?"

"They'll have to go through me," he said.

"Tomorrow," she said.

Bewildered, he shook his head. "What? Why tomorrow? Why not now?"

"I need one more night in my bed. Please, Derek. Just give me that." Her voice pleaded. Her eyes searched his. "Please."

He knew it was a bad idea, but he gave in. He had always had a tough time saying no to her. One more night couldn't hurt, could it? He sure as hell hoped not. He helped her out of her clothes and handed her a nightgown, which she slipped into like an obedient child. He changed to sweat pants and climbed into bed with her.

With his arm protectively around her, his chest pressed to her back, he whispered that he loved her and that he would keep her safe. She was asleep in seconds. He drifted off not long after, and his sleep was long, deep, and dreamless, unbroken until when he turned over and felt the empty space beside him. He immediately sat up in the pre-dawn darkness. "Myrinda?"

Derek checked the bathroom, swung out into the hall, checked the kitchen and den. He opened the front door and looked up and down the hallway. There was no sign of her.

Myrinda was gone.

***

The irony of the police and EMTs swarming the building on the night he'd planned to kill Eda was not lost on Hal. They were there a good 45 minutes. The upside-down commercial man had told him earlier in the evening that the old cop was going to shoot himself, and so it was a perfect night for him to get rid of Eda.

At first, he'd balked at the idea if for no other reason than because his committing a murder with cops around seemed absurd. What if they stuck around, knocking door to door to investigate the guy's death? What if they came back to peruse the crime scene?

The commercial man dismissed all of that. He explained that it was perfect, like getting away with speeding on a highway because a cop had already pulled someone over. Hal would be working, essentially, under a cloak of invisibility. He'd be invincible. If he waited until just after they left, just as everything was settling down for the night, then he'd be operating in the one window where police would be least likely, for any reason, to be there. They would already have their hands full with processing a late-night suicide. Even they wouldn't think of returning to the same building that night.

The upside-down commercial man had a way of making everything sound reasonable.

Eda was already asleep; she had, in fact, been asleep long before the police arrived. He'd seen to that. He'd ground up some sleeping pills to a powder and slipped it in her iced tea, which she drank black, cool, and bitter anyway. Why she chose to drink something unpleasant-tasting with dinner and caffeinated so close to her usual bedtime was another thing he didn't understand about her.

When Hal asked her where she'd gone that night he'd discovered her intent to get rid of him, Eda had told him (with a marked degree of disdain, he'd thought) that as usual, he didn't listen to anything she said. She said she'd already told him all about the cooking class she was taking at the community center. She told him it had run late, and that she'd found him asleep in his chair when she got home and thought it better not to wake him.

She was lying. He felt it with every fiber of his being. He didn't know where she was, but he was sure she'd never told him about any class.

It was no matter. Hal was done with her and her lying. After tonight, there would be no more Eda. No more worries. There would only be Hal and the rest of his blessedly quiet, judgment-free future.

In the night that rushed to fill the vacuum left by the police's and ambulance's departure, Hal almost skipped across the parking lot. The key to the storage bins was in his pocket. He had a partial erection from the excitement of thinking about what he was going to do.

The storage bins were actually little more than chicken-wire cages wrapped around 2x4s. These bins stood along the back wall of the garage units which lined the parking lot. For a couple hundred extra a month, tenants could rent a garage space for their car as well. Hal knew that someone in the building owned a '68 Chevy Chevelle, and another (possibly the same tenant) owned a '57 Ford Fairlane. Both were kept under canvas covers. Hal thought that his renting an apartment at Bridgewood was evidence enough that he couldn't afford to breathe on either of those kinds of cars, but hey, however people spent their funny money was no big thing to him. He had his storage unit to keep all the holiday decoration boxes, a tacky patterned couch that Eda's parents had given them so generously right off the goddamn garage sale driveway, and the extra vacuum that he swore didn't work and she swore they couldn't throw out. Her gardening paraphernalia was stuffed in there, too—the terracotta pots, the potting soil, the little shovels. And his axe.

He turned the key in the storage bin lock and it clicked. Pocketing the key, he pulled the creaking slab of a door open and stepped into the gloom inside. The axe was laying on top of an old Farmer's Fresh produce crate in which Eda had packed the barbeque supplies. In the dim light of the storage unit, the blade looked a dull gray, its wooden handle worn. He'd kept the edge of the blade still sharp, though. The axe was old, like him—old, but sturdy and useful. Old but reliable. Like him. An extension of his arm, in a way. There could be no other tool to use. He imagined for a moment the feel of the smooth wood in his hand, the sharp end of the blade buried in Eda's head above her right eye. He allowed himself a small smile.

He didn't pick up the axe; the handle somehow slid into his hand. Suddenly, he was holding it, heaving it above his head, flooded with confidence and conviction that its heftiness provided.

Hal turned and walked out of the storage bin without bothering to relock or even close its door. As he passed the Ford Fairlane, he dragged the sharp edge lightly across the length of the quarter panel, just enough to leave a long scratch flanked to either side by tiny curlicues of paint. The faint whine of steel against metal made him smile even bigger.

He slammed the garage door down behind him and crossed the parking lot in the darkness. No one else was around. Nearly all the windows of the surrounding apartments were dark. His anonymity, the delightful secrecy of his whereabouts and intentions as he strode toward the lobby cloaked in the night, made him feel powerful. He giggled. The axe handle felt warm in his hand.

The lobby was empty and dark. As he got into the elevator and the doors slid closed, he stood with axe in hand and a content expression on his face. From the corner of his eye, he noticed a scrawl written on one of the steel panels in dark blue marker which read *I tried to take it all back.*

Yes, he thought. *Yes. I'm trying to take it all back—my life, my confidence, my peace and quiet. I'm taking it all back.*

With a ding, the doors opened and Hal stepped out onto the second floor. The hallway at that hour fell mostly in shadow, except for the soft lights at either end where the exits stood. The door to 2A was closed, the thin band of space beneath it dark, just as he'd left it. Eda was likely still in bed, asleep. He crossed the hall and let himself in.

The furniture of the apartment swam up from the darkness, taking shape. It was so quiet. So peaceful. His heart was at ease. After tonight, he'd have all the peace and quiet he'd ever want, inside and out.

The television came on, and although the volume was turned down low, the sudden bright box of static made him jump. Hal frowned. He knelt in front of it and leaned his head in until his ear was nearly touching the screen. There! There it was, just beneath the low buzz of static—voices talking. He couldn't make out what they were saying, but at times they sounded desperate or feverishly gleeful. Once he thought he heard his name, but he couldn't be sure. Then the television went dark and silent. A note of subtle encouragement, maybe, from the upside-down commercial man.

His attention returned to the bedroom. Its door was ajar. From the darkness within, he heard the bed creak lightly as she turned over. Hal rose slowly, clutching the axe handle in both hands, and moved toward the dark enshrouding his sleeping wife.

He hovered in the doorway for several minutes. It wasn't hesitation on his part; even in the deep folds and tucked-away places of his mind, there was nothing of the old Hal's thoughts or feelings toward Eda left. It wasn't quite that he was savoring the moment, though, either. Rather, it was as if his life had been a long highway with a series of exits. For so long, he had reluctantly passed those exits, hoping to get somewhere, anywhere, faster without running the risk of a detour's delay or derailment. Tonight, he was taking an important exit that would change the course of his journey forever. It would reroute him to a new destination. And as he stood in the doorway, his breathing soft and even like hers, he reflected that in making that turnoff, he was admitting to himself that there had, at least for the last few decades, been no end destination to reach—at least, not one he could clearly qualify to himself or justify anymore in whole or in part. That realization, that all of it was Eda's fault, spurred him forward into the room.

Eda snored softly into the pillow. She had managed to tangle part of the sheet around her waist and legs; it was a small thing, really, but caught Hal off guard, given the unnaturally stiff and unshifting way in which she slept.

Like a vampire in a coffin, he thought, and a grim smile spread across his face.

Eda turned over, her eyelids fluttering a moment before closing again. "Butter," she mumbled. Another thing that threw him; she never talked in her sleep.

"What?" he whispered.

"You got the wrong butter," she mumbled. He supposed she was dreaming, but it irked him. Even in her dreams, he was doing something wrong.

"You need to take it back. I can't do anything with it," she mumbled, snorted loudly, then resumed her light snore.

Take it back.

He looked down at her, at the sharp cheeks and chin on the pillow, the brow creased in disappointment and disapproval even in sleep. The lips were pursed in a smug sort of smile, as if his dreamed-of mistake reaffirmed her opinion of him in the waking world. That was not the face of the woman who had smiled to see him come home from work in their early years. The gray hair fanned soft and thin on the pillow behind her was not what he had stroked and smelled as he held her close. He studied the pointed fingertips that had poked his arm so many times at social affairs in her "subtle" attempts at correcting his boorish behavior. Those fingertips curled inward toward her palms now like shriveled flowers, little angry, razorboned fists on the pillow beside her face. Those were not the hands he'd held during courtship. Her bony shoulders, the one exposed bony knee—the body laying beneath the sheet was not the one he'd touched, caressed, made love to when sex was still more important than Wheel of Fortune. And none of that, he realized, was the problem. That her body had changed—that had never phased him. That her mind and heart had changed...that had made all the difference in the world.

Take it back.

She couldn't—she wouldn't—do anything with what they had become. But he could.

Damn right. I'm taking it all back.

He raised the axe. He could destroy the part of her that had changed.

As she moved to turn over again, her eyes opened. It was as if she sensed him, smelled the metallic tang of the axe blade, felt his anxious heat, heard his breathing. She just had time to open her mouth and say "Ha—" before he caught her above the right eye. He was surprised by how little force it took to bury the axe so deep into her head. The momentum carried his motion through for him. Her skull made a sound like an egg cracking and her hair caved in a little along the fault line where the blade had hit it. She made a strange little sighing sound and dropped onto the pillow. There was a lot of blood, but not nearly as much as on television. It seeped into the crisp white of her pillowcase, staining a halo around her disarranged hair. Her legs, hooked around the edge of the bed sheet, twitched feebly and the unpainted, neatly pedicured toes spasmed toward his thigh. Her shriveled flower-fists trembled. Although Eda had always been fastidious about using the bathroom first and last thing of the day to, as she put it, "remove as many toxins and impurities as possible," the smell of urine emanated from a different dark stain which spread across the tangle of sheet around her waist.

Then she stopped moving, ceased to be a person at all, and an empty thing blue-gray in the moonlight, a mere bundle of sticks over which a thin canvas had been stretched, lay in lieu.

Hal was alone. Even the commercial man was silent, gone off to wherever commercial men go when they've gotten old husbands to finally get rid of old wives.

He wondered if he should close her eyes—the blood from her head wound was collecting and dripping off the lashes of the right eyelid—and decided against it. He liked the wide white orbs caught like that in a perpetual state of surprise. He grinned as he studied the slack bottom jaw, where indignation had been overcome by fear. God, how he'd loved knocking loose that tightly smug smile, that expression of grim self-satisfaction, as if always having to nag him was a burden, but one that would nevertheless be sure to propel her straight to the top of the list for sainthood.

Hal dropped the bloody axe by the side of the bed, then made his way to the kitchen. He got two beers, one for now and one to save him the trip later, and then settled himself in his chair in front of the TV. With confidence, he picked up the remote and clicked on the television, half-expecting the upside-down commercial man to be there waiting to congratulate him. An infomercial man with a beard yelled about his excitement over a cleaning sponge. He changed the channel. An old black and white Western. He waited. Closed his eyes and opened them. No sign of the upside-down commercial man. He clicked to a static channel, feeling vaguely perturbed. Still no sign of his mentor in murder.

Hal felt slighted and a little scared. Had the commercial man abandoned him, after all that? Or had he been dismissed now that he'd killed his wife?

He gulped his beer, and with each listless click to a new channel, his eyelids grew heavier. Halfway through his second beer, he fell asleep with the bottle in his hand. About four in the morning, the glow of the TV and voices breaking through the edge of his sleep woke him, but there was only static on the screen. He reached over to the remote, which had fallen from his grasp, and clicked off the television.

Leaving the half-drunk beer on the end table, he trudged to the bedroom. Eda lay stiff as always, cooling and congealing on her side of the bed. He climbed in next to her and within minutes, he had fallen into a deep sleep.

FIFTEEN

When Wayne awoke, he felt disoriented and groggy. Remembering the tunnel, he jumped and promptly fell off the bed in a tangle of sheets. It didn't stop him from scrabbling across the floor, away from the bed. Part of his mind was still in under the Old Ward, feeling the cold breath of the gaping mouth bearing down on him. After a moment, the details of the room shaped themselves in his periphery, and his gaze darted around, confused. He was...in his own bedroom. His own apartment. But how?

Something...something had happened down there in the tunnels, some kind of violation. It wasn't a physical assault, but rather, an invasion of his mind. He couldn't be sure, but he felt sort of bruised inside his head, like someone had hurt him deeply. But he couldn't remember anything beyond some hazy images which ignited such intense anxiety that he was okay with letting them sink below the surface of consciousness.

He untangled the sheets from his legs and stood. He was still wearing the jeans and t-shirt he'd worn in the tunnel. He was missing a shoe, and the bottom of his sock was black. He had scratches all over his hands and his cheek throbbed.

Wayne looked out the window, noted the daylight, and then glanced at his digital clock. 3:00. What day was it? How long had he been gone? Where was Warner? He had to be starving.

He found the cat batting an empty food bowl, sloshing water onto the tiled kitchen floor. He immediately filled the bowl with kibble and fresh water, but when he went to pet Warner, the cat hissed at him. He drew back his hand, puzzled.

He got himself a bottled water from the fridge and went back to the bedroom, to his desk. What he saw on it made him drop the bottle, its contents spilling in a tiny waterfall onto the floor.

The book from the tunnel was there. La Claviére's *Book of Gates*.

Recovering himself, he swooped to pick up the water bottle and brought it sloshing to the desk. His fingers ran over the aged leather cover, then traced the letters of the title. Here it was, but why? Why had the chaotic ones brought him back, and why had they left the book there with him? He was fairly sure they didn't tuck him into bed and then offer the very book he'd been looking for as a kind of apology. Did they want him to use it to close the gate? That was doubtful. That they were hoping he'd blunder blindly into opening another gate seemed more likely.

He opened it, turning the old pages slowly so as not to tear them. Warner rubbed at his legs but he paid no attention. The words were occasional glimpses of lingual clarity in an otherwise storm of unfamiliar words and phrases, but the pictures told a lot. He counted about 13 plates in all. Whether La Claviére had drawn them or not, Wayne couldn't tell; they weren't initialed. Wayne suspected they were copied from the original manuscript parchments brought out of Egypt. One depicted a long table on which a woman was laying. Her mouth was slack, her eyes rolled upward, and from the back of her head, a long tube looped over a wooden frame and dripped into a large bottle. In another found in the chapter on keys, an assortment of men, women, and even children were shown strung upside-down over a large black pit over which a swirling black cloud was forming.

There were brief mentions of *les fantômes* (ghosts) and *les monstres* (as side effects, he guessed from the text, of opening various gates). There were also supposed locations of the gates (*Où Trouver des Emplacements de la Porte*). What he found interesting about that chapter was, considering the supposed origin of the information dated back to ancient civilization, it was something akin to prescience that the author gave locations all over the globe.

At least four of the plates had an odd quality uncharacteristic of the style they were usually drawn in. It was almost as if they had been done by artists who had never before encountered human people. One of them showed a black whirlpool surrounded by stars and overlaid with complex 3-

dimensional symbols, while another showed three faceless figures pointing at wavy lines meant to indicate some type of ripple in the air. The third showed what looked to Wayne like an immense alien city hovering in the sky just below a smaller, far simpler village. The fourth one really chilled him, though—so much so that his shoulders shook the hairs on his arms and neck stood on end. He went to get a throw blanket off the couch and then returned to study it.

In that plate, a large black chasm seemingly deep enough to reach hell had split the ground in a wooded clearing nearly in half. Rocks protruded from the insides like broken teeth. Scrabbling along those rocks were figures he had spent the last few days encountering both in subterranean tunnels and in nightmares. Their long fingers clawed at rocks and grass. Their mouths reflected in miniature the origin of their ascent. The ink of the drawing trailed their backs out behind them. The more he studied the picture, the more the image of those things made him shake.

Those were the chaotic ones, crossing over from their world of madness. The caption, neither in French nor in English, simply read: HINSHING.

It occurred to Wayne then that maybe the chaotic ones had left the book there for him to see what they were and what they could do. He tried to decipher the French on the pages surrounding that last book plate, and found what little he could pick up seemed to be about insanity and death. There was even mention of Le Diable, and he supposed to a 16th century mind, the chaotic ones would have appeared very much like demons. *Hell*, he thought. *They're very much like demons to this 21st century mind, too.*

He turned back to the Table of Contents to see if there was a chapter on closing gates that had been opened, but evidently, La Claviére wasn't as interested in that. He found some mention toward the end of the book about opening other gates, but Wayne couldn't tell whether that meant gates opening in the opposite direction to existing ones, or new gates inviting potentially worse monsters to this one. A portion of that chapter was composed of incredibly complex mathematical formulas and those same intricate symbols he'd seen written over the black hole plate. He thought the symbols might be some kind of hieroglyphics of the ancient language of the manuscripts, and if that were so, they might be the words used in the incantation to open a gate. All in all, just opening a gate looked to be a very complex and multi-stepped process. No wonder there was nothing about closing the gates. It appeared that symmetry and balance were important parts of the ritual; that much was suggested by another illustration that showed a scale weighing some of the symbols stacked atop body parts evenly against a vortex from which long tentacular appendages were climbing through. Any upset to the balance seemed to cause the ritual to fail.

Wayne closed the book and shivered. He knew he couldn't have gotten all those nuances from his limited French and his beginner's perusing of occult illustrations. The chaotic ones had been feeding him interpretations and he had been too engrossed in the book to realize it. It made his head ache, thinking about them whispering with manic glee about gateways and alternate dimensions, about how most occult rituals in this world were no more insane than what they lived and breathed every day.

He didn't like their violation of his thoughts. It made him hypersensitive. Of course, overthinking it was making him tired and achy. In fact, his last thought before laying down on the couch with the blanket wrapped around him was that he thought he might be coming down with their sickness. Then he stared at the wall and ceased to think at all for a time. He just gave up and listened to the things the chaotic ones told him.

***

The first place Derek thought to look for Myrinda was the Old Ward. Her fascination with it over the last several days had made it an obvious choice. If she'd wandered off in some kind of trance, she would have gone there, and if she were right about those things and they had taken her, they probably would have taken her there.

Derek had always prided himself on being a man who thought things through before acting. In his experience, jumping blindly into a dangerous situation got people killed, and rarely put a man in a position to get a job done. He was not completely innocent of wild risk-taking when the situation warranted it, but in his mind, the risks were calculated. Derek was solidly aware of his strengths and weaknesses, and knew when to drive fast, to jump away, to tackle someone. It was his job to know, and he didn't mind saying so himself that he did his job well.

Therefore, it didn't really surprise him to find seven distorted figures standing in front of the Old Ward, silhouetted by its bulk in the early rays of the rising sun. One opened its vertical mouth and a horrible, hysterical high whine descended into a growl. The hinshing, the chaotic ones, had come to greet him.

Still, it was a shock to finally see physical proof of creatures he'd had a great deal of difficulty even entertaining as possible. They were, to him, the stuff of fever dreams—vaguely human-shaped, but clearly not human, their mottled skin slick and shining as they stepped into the daylight. They were humanoid, but completely hairless and sexless. The faceless heads worked their zipper mouths open and closed, chattering in a language he had never heard. Their backs, as well as the backs of their heads blurred out behind them, neither a solid part of them nor a vapor, but something oddly in between. Those heads twitched as they studied him with a kind of sociopathic curiosity. Their grotesquely long limbs spasmed and bent in ways limbs shouldn't ever bend. When they stepped closer, their jittering bodies seemed to steal seconds so that the natural flow of movement was broken.

He couldn't go into that building and get Myrinda without knowing what he was up against. He was no good to Myrinda dead.

That was when he'd decided to find Wayne.

Down in the lobby, there was only one mail box assigned to someone with W as the first initial; a W. Tillingford of 2B.

He considered taking the elevator, thought better of it, and jogged up the stairs to the second floor. Checking his smart phone for the time, he saw it was still early. 7:24 a.m. He'd have to get this Wayne guy out of bed. He didn't have time to wait, and he didn't think Myrinda did, either.

He knocked loudly on the door to 2B.

"Wayne Tillingford?" he called through the door. "I need your help." He knocked again. There was no answer. He was about to pound on it a third time when he heard the sound of shuffling feet from inside.

The door opened, and a short, pale guy with floppy hair and glasses answered. His bulk was soft but fairly tidy, like he was used to eating for fun but tried, at least occasionally, to reign it in. He wore jeans and a faded gray t-shirt. In spite of the thin blanket wrapped around his shoulders, he was shivering uncontrollably.

"Excuse me. I'm sorry to bother you so early in the morning, but it's an emergency. Are you Wayne Tillingford?"

"Yeah. Who are you?"

"I'm Derek Moore. My girlfriend and I live across the hall in 2E. She's actually the reason I'm here. Do you have some time to talk?" Derek hoped, as he stood in the doorway, that his larger presence and the tone in his voice left Wayne with no other option than to make time. Wayne seemed to pick up that vibe, because after a moment, he stepped aside to let Derek in.

"So what's this all about?" Wayne led him to a tastefully masculine den and flopped on a leather couch. Derek sat in a chair across from him. A black and white cat sidled along with them and hopped up onto the couch beside Wayne, curling into a ball.

"This might sound crazy. Well, it is crazy. But maybe...maybe not to you." He paused. Wayne said nothing, so he continued.

"My girlfriend, Myrinda, has been seeing things. Hearing things. At first I thought she might have just been stressing out over our move here, but now I think it might be more than that."

Wayne leaned back, pulling the blanket tighter around him. "What kind of things?"

Derek tented his fingers and leaned his elbows on his knees. "Okay, here it goes. I'm just gonna lay it out for you like she told me. She says there is some kind of...of hole, or something. Some kind of opening, and she says these creatures have come through from some other world. She told me they're hurting people, driving them crazy. Now look, before you say anything, I know how this all sounds, but—"

"She's right." Wayne was wracked with a powerful shiver then, and he shook his head. The cat beside him twitched, then went back to sleep. "I've seen them."

"Well, uh, okay, then you know there is evidence all around this building that being here isn't safe. These things are driving her over the edge. I need to get her out of here."

Wayne snorted. "Not safe. Ladies and gentlemen, the award for Most Obvious Understatement goes to Derek Moore." He leaned forward, an odd smile stuck crookedly to his face. "But you can't go. They aren't done here yet, and they won't take the bad thoughts and feelings away until they're done. If they've already touched her, they have her mind until they're finished playing with it. Leaving won't fix that."

"Well, then, they're going to have to give up their toys a little early," Derek said. Wayne's words annoyed him, but beneath that annoyance, Derek was afraid. What if it was already too late to help Myrinda? Still, there was a chance for her to get better outside of this place. Continued exposure certainly wasn't going to help. "I'm taking her out of here, and if I have to cut down every single one of those ugly motherfuckers, I'll do it. But I need to know what you know. Myrinda mentioned you. She said they were stalking you, too."

"I don't know your girlfriend."

"Well, she knows you," Derek said impatiently. "Or at least knows of you. And she's in trouble, and right now, you're the only person left alive in this building that I know of who's seen these things and knows what I'm up against. I am not going to let these things take her away from me, you hear? So whatever you know, you need to tell me."

Wayne paled at Derek's mention that he was the only one left alive. He stroked the cat's head absently and looked away, considering something for several long seconds before looking Derek level in the eye.

"Where is she?"

"I don't know," Derek admitted truthfully. "I think she's somewhere in the Old Ward. She told me that's where they go when they aren't working over someone in the apartment building."

Wayne shivered, but it looked disjointed to Derek. His head and limbs twitched independent of the others instead of as a whole. He said, "If she's there, check the tunnels first. Save yourself some time. Find Symmes's office. There's a passage leading down from there."

Derek nodded. "Okay, thanks. Now, what can you tell me about these things?"

Wayne sighed. "Look, you seem like a nice guy, and I can tell your girlfriend is very important to you. But really, I don't have the answers you seem to be looking for. It sounds like she told you more about these things than I know."

"What are they? Can they be hurt? Killed?"

Wayne shook his head helplessly at each question. "I told you, I don't know. I really don't. All I know is, they came because of the book. It's what caused the massacre. Then they go and build this apartment right on top of the old ground. It was like dumping new fish in a barrel for these things."

"What book? What are you talking about?"

Wayne pointed to the bedroom, and Derek stood up. He glanced at Wayne, who gestured for him to go and get it.

The bedroom contrasted sharply with the rest of the apartment. A tumble of sheets lay in a heap in the center of the room. The bottle of water on the night table sat in a whitening ring on the wood, its contents splashed over disarrayed magazines. On the desk by the window lay an old book of moldy leather, dust worked well into its cracks. The cover was in French. He picked it up gently, and it emitted a puff of paper dust that smelled crumbly and old to Derek.

He carried it back out to the den. Wayne shivered again beneath his blanket seemingly at the sight of it.

"What is this?" Derek asked, handing it to Wayne before returning to his seat.

"The *Book of Gates*. It was written, supposedly, from ancient languages of faceless demons or something. All these old books have stories like that—murder, blasphemy, secret rites and societies dedicated to protecting the knowledge contained between the covers."

"What does it have to do with what's going on at Bridgewood?"

"It's a detailed account of descriptions, prime locations, and means of opening gates to other dimensions. Gates to alien worlds, where alien things can come through."

"Aggie's wounds," Derek muttered.

"I'm sorry?"

He shook his head. "Go on."

"The director of the asylum, this guy Symmes, he used the book to open the gate. He lost control, though. He brought them here, and they incited one of the worst events in this town's history. When he found out a new building—residential apartments, of all things—was going to be built on the spot, he killed himself."

"Jesus," Derek muttered.

Wayne leaned back. "You and your girlfriend know the history of this place before you moved in?"

Derek nodded. "Yeah, Myrinda told me all about the asylum that was here before. She told me about the massacre."

"Right," Wayne said. "But what about what came before? Before the asylum was even built? Native Americans sent their insane up the hill to be fed on by the spirits. Colonists claimed devils passed between earth and hell there so frequently that they caused it to be a 'weak spot.' There was a reason Symmes chose this place to try and open a gate."

"Okay, so if he opened a gate and these things came, then maybe we should just close the gate. Is there something in the book for that?"

"There is no way to close the gate so far as I can tell," Wayne said. "Symmes couldn't do it. My French isn't great, but I think it says the only option is to replace it by opening one somewhere else."

"That doesn't make sense," Derek said. "You said that book's been around for hundreds of years. How come there aren't gates open all over the place, then?"

"It isn't that easy to open one. The chapter on keys says that even if you can find a spot for a gate, you can't open it if it's locked. You need to have the right keys." Wayne shrugged. "You need the right conditions—certain spots, certain times, specific elements that form the keys. Special, and I'm guessing pretty rare, circumstances."

"So we can't close this gate...but what about sending these things back through it?"

"I haven't come across anything that even suggests a way to do that," Wayne said.

"Well, I don't like the idea of messing with another gate," Derek said, shaking his head. "Forgetting for a second the fact that you're forcing these things on some other unsuspecting world, you just said conditions have to be right. We don't know what those conditions are. We don't know what could happen if we screw up. There are too many ways this could go sideways in a minute."

Wayne sighed. "Told you I couldn't help much, big guy."

Derek thought a moment. "If we can't send those things back, we kill them. All of them. And if we can't close the gate, well, what about blocking it?"

"Blocking it? With what?"

After a moment, Derek threw up his hands. "I don't know. Anything in that book we could use?"

"No, noth—wait. Wait a sec." Wayne flipped through the book. He pointed at a paragraph in French. "This here says the gate can't stay open if conditions change. It doesn't close, I don't think. Not exactly. I don't know what that word means, but here I think it's saying it—" he gestured, looking for the right word, "—folds. Sounds like, in essence, if the angles aren't right to hold it open, it folds in on itself."

Derek clapped him on the shoulder. "That'll work. How do we get it to fold?"

Wayne smiled, but there was no pleasure or humor in it. "Doesn't say."

"Damn it!" Derek bolted up out of his chair. "Are you going to help me or not?"

Wayne flinched and the cat, startled, jumped off the couch and trotted out of the room. "I don't know how." He pulled the blanket tight around him again. "Look at me. I lost, geez, I don't even know how many days. I went into the Old Ward, into the tunnel. That's where the book was. And I saw one. It...did something to me. I don't know what, but I can feel it, like a tide, trying to draw thoughts away from me, trying to wash over me. Like how it feels when you can't keep your eyes open anymore, you know?"

Wayne searched Derek's steady, disapproving expression but didn't seem to find what he needed. He sighed.

"Myrinda was right," he said softly. "They *are* hurting me."

Frustrated, Derek turned to go. He'd made it half-way to the front door when Wayne spoke.

"Wait."

Derek turned. Wayne, looking sicker than when he had first answered the door, said, "I'm sorry. I'd help if I could. Hell, if I could, I'd burn that fucking Old Ward to the ground, with those things inside it."

Derek felt some of the frustration dissolve. He offered Wayne a nod of thanks. "That, actually, might not be such a bad idea." Then he walked out the front door, leaving Wayne Tillingford to whatever was eating him up inside.

***

Not long after he was left alone his apartment, the chaotic ones started talking to him again.

He hadn't told Derek how they stroked the violence in him, nor did he mention how he'd spent the better part of his first morning back pouring through the book they'd left with him, trying—and failing—to find something he could use against them. Leaving the book with Wayne had been a tease, a rug they'd yanked out from under him. They knew Wayne wouldn't be able to do much with that book. Even if he could speak fluent French, which he couldn't, he was no experienced occultist, nor was he in any kind of shape to fight back. What they'd done to him in the tunnel made sure of that.

Having resigned himself to the fact that he'd get nothing useful out of it, he'd set fire to the book in the bathtub. As he stood watching, waiting for it to catch and spread the flames, it occurred to him that fighting all the thoughts the chaotic ones were feeding him was really what the problem was. If he just gave in, just let those urges flow, they'd set him free. He smiled to himself, amazed at his own stubborn blindness. They had only been trying to unlock the other facets of his soul, to complete him. He needed to embrace all of what he was, and what he could be, and all he could accomplish if he let go of the fear of consequence. That fear, he realized, was the single most damaging and restrictive human quality to the progress of the species as a whole.

After a good hour and a half of standing there (time flew when you were self-discovering), he came to the conclusion the book wasn't going to burn, so he buried it way in the back of his closet, done with wasting time over it. It was no matter. He had other things to do this morning anyway.

SIXTEEN

Hal Corman woke to see the dead body of his wife in bed next to him. Her skin had taken on the color of ashes mixed in milk. The wide, surprised eyes had developed a white film that reminded Hal of an undeveloped Polaroid. He kept waiting for it to clear, for the picture of her irises to emerge, but it didn't. She was still laying on her side, her body stiff and cold, and what blood was left in her had pooled dark purple in the areas that touched the pillow and mattress—the side of her face, her arm, one of her legs.

Eda was dead, and Hal had killed her.

He was acutely aware of the silence, of being the only living, breathing thing in the whole apartment. Beyond that, he reached inside himself to feel something about Eda's death—guilt or grief, shame, anger, joy, relief, anything. He felt nothing, and that, at least, scared him.

He rolled out of bed, not yet awake enough to consider what to do with her body, and sat down in his chair—maybe the only thing in the apartment that was really, truly his. He turned on the television, flipping idly through the channels. He had thought, maybe even hoped, that the upside-down commercial man would appear again. He supposed it was a matter of closure. However, as he went from channel to channel, there was no sign of the man. There was one channel which gave him temporary pause; he noticed manicured green lawns and a few dazed-looking people milling around, but it was just a documentary on the history of mental hospitals and asylums in the New England area. He shut off the television and sighed.

He glanced at the kitchen, where no coffee was brewing, no snap of newspaper pages being smartly turned and folded. It was his kitchen now. The food in there was his to cook any way he wanted. The coffee could be brewed as strong as he liked, and he didn't have to wait for newspaper sections like a dog begging for scraps.

Still, he didn't feel much like cooking, anyway. Instead, he took a shower. While he got dressed, he made small talk with Eda, explaining how he was going to play hookie from work today and maybe tomorrow. Work just didn't seem all that important anymore. She said nothing.

She was starting to look funny, all half-purple like that, and he told her so. With some effort, he rolled her over to her other side so he could talk to her as he crossed the room to the dresser. He put on sweat pants and a faded green t-shirt with a pickle company logo on it. It was, to say the least, not her favorite item of his wardrobe. He was actually surprised to find it buried at the bottom of his t-shirt drawer; he'd assumed she'd thrown it out months ago. He explained that since it was his day off, he wanted to lounge in comfort. He giggled thinly when she didn't answer, and then responded in the best impression of her voice.

"Stay there," he told her, giggling uncontrollably to himself. "I'll be right back."

He picked up his wallet off the dresser and grabbed the keys he'd left by the front door. He felt lighter once he was out in the hallway, and surprisingly, he felt warmer, too. He hadn't realized how cold Eda kept the apartment all the time. Well, that would change now.

He whistled as he walked down the hall to the elevator. It felt good not to think or feel, not to have to worry about anything. It felt very freeing.

He pushed the down button and waited, still whistling. The doors opened, and he stepped inside. He thought maybe he'd get one of those egg white omelets from...where was it, McDonald's or Dunkin Donuts? He couldn't remember. No matter. He'd try both and see. He'd get one of those omelets for breakfast and a large cup of coffee and sit a while, and just enjoy the day. Maybe he'd even—

The doors opened and he stepped out into the lobby. That was when he heard the growl.

He turned and saw the mottled thing with the long, pointed fingers and pivoting legs scaling the wall next to the elevator. It paused, hanging upside down with its strangely blurred back to him, and as Hal stood rooted to the spot, wide-eyed and gaping, its head turned around with a horrific bony crack. Its head looked like a leathery ball unzipped, its lipless mouth and little needle teeth filling his vision. From that mouth, beyond those teeth, it laughed.

Hal knew for certain it was the upside-down commercial man.

The thing leaped at his throat, cutting off his scream.

***

Wayne had thought—hoped, even—that the compulsion would leave him once he was out from under the heavy miasma of Bridgewood's influence. It didn't. He carried it with him like cold germs. Like the black garbage bag whose drawstrings were balled up in his fist.

Inside the bag, Warner dozed. Wayne had drugged the cat, not from any vapid sense of affection for or memories of their history together, but rather, for a more practical reason. Cats had claws, and the plastic of cheap garbage bags could rip under an onslaught from an angry enough feline. He knew if Warner clawed a hole through the bag and his mission was foiled, reduced to a sloppy half-attempt, it would somehow be more awful, more horrific than the simple, blunt, quietly efficient act itself. There was no freedom to be found, no sense of completion and restoration, if he didn't go all the way through with it.

Warner shifted in the bag, thumping against Wayne's thigh. The cat was starting to wake up. Wayne reached the highway's sloping grass embankment, and made his way down toward the nearest lane. It was fairly quiet at that time of day, that pocket of time after morning rush hour and before the lunch hour. A car passed every five or ten minutes. That was good.

Without any further sentiment or thought, Wayne tossed the bag onto the highway. It landed with a soft thud near a pothole. From within the bag, Warner uttered a hung-over warble, followed by a kind of gurgling sound. He'd never heard the cat make a sound like that before. But his hearing seemed sharp today—all his senses did—and he found that beneath that steady, dull roar of traffic past and traffic to come, he could hear the soft crinkling of the bag as the cat stretched and tested its surroundings, and the bag stretched and shifted to accommodate it.

A sky-blue Buick Skylark, one of those big old boats, came steadily up the lane. With the sun glare, Wayne couldn't see the face of the driver, but he hoped it was someone focused on the road and not the bag, someone who, like countless daily commuters, paid no more than passing attention to trash in the road. He held his a breath a moment for fear of the driver's reflexes, but within seconds, saw he had nothing to worry about.

The car passed him—a chubby silver-haired old lady, he saw, sat behind the wheel—and rolled straight over the bag. And beneath the engine, Wayne could hear the crunch of bone, the strangled cry crushed in the throat, even the frenetic twitching of the limbs shocked into separation from crucial nerve centers.

Then the car did swerve, skidding to a stop in the shoulder several hundred feet away. Wayne didn't wait for the driver's reaction. It wasn't, and had never been, about the driver at all. He turned and walked up the embankment. For the first time in weeks, he felt like he could sleep.

He made his way along the forest-flanked road that wound up the hill to the apartments, huffing slightly by the time he reached the parking lot. He had lost a lot of his energy with each breath. Slowly, a liquid weight seemed to be spreading unevenly through his body, dragging at his limbs and numbing his head. It made his trouble breathing even worse. He looked at the Bridgewood Estates apartment building, and then at the Old Ward, and a sudden flash of memory shook his body as well as his thoughts; the thing that attacked him in the tunnel had injected the stuff of the gate in his head. The liquid abyss flowed with his blood, taking over each piece of him, changing it.

Maybe it was a side effect, but he really couldn't muster up enough energy to worry. Everything was what it was, and that was okay. There was no dwelling on the past and no worrying about the future. There was only the right now, and the odd sensations the stuff inside him caused in his extremities.

And the cuts.

He stood for a moment at the edge of the parking lot near the Old Ward, staring down at his wrists. Uneven abrasions formed a band of red around each one. He winced at the sting of the bands separating the skin and drawing beads of blood to the surface. He felt the same stinging sensation just above each ankle. From somewhere deep beneath the endless night in his veins, something fought to warn him, to shake him out of it and make him do something...something. It was washed over again by the tide of black.

"Oh," Wayne said, "shit. Oh shit." The feeling of drowsiness pulling at him deepened with the cuts to a feeling of being drugged. It didn't do much to dull the pain, but he found the situation sort of funny in spite of that. His left hand was pulling away from his wrist, dangling from seams of skin veined with blue. With a wet ripping sound, it flopped to the ground. Blood flowed from the split in his right wrist and down the back of his hand.

He took a step forward and stumbled onto the grass. When he rolled over, he noticed that his bloody shoe stood a few inches away from him, the jagged separation above the ankle clearly visible over the shoe. His left foot, hanging by a strip of skin, had twisted nearly backward. That panic from below tried to resurface and this time he felt it more clearly. It was wrong that his foot and hand were over there on the ground. His right had tumbled onto his chest and the new stumps each began to ache through the haze in his head.

Then the panic broke through to his forethoughts and he realized he wouldn't be able to walk. The helpless horror of it, the sense of loss for the completeness of his person, struck him as unbearable. He felt pegged to the spot. He couldn't walk, would never walk again unless he dragged himself like...it was just like.... *Oh God ohGODOHGODMYFEET IT'SLIKETHEDEADGIRL* he thought, and then he closed his eyes and started to scream.

He heard the arrhythmic steps of something crunching the grass, and his eyes opened.

Above him, one of the chaotic ones stared down at him. It tilted its head as if puzzled by the curiosity of Wayne. He started to whimper, remembering the tunnel.

"Please," he croaked. "Please—"

The hinshing reached down and snapped his neck.

SEVENTEEN

Derek had grown up with religion, and had always credited that with his distinctly nonreligious lifestyle as an adult, but to him, religion was a separate aspect than spiritualism. He had always thought that even if the fervor for church services and prayers and the intangible interpretations of the Bible didn't stick with you and inform your character, it was almost impossible to escape certain spiritual concepts tied to your soul like little ribbons. His need, for example, to believe there was some force in the universe (he was okay with calling it God for lack of a better name) that would guide his judgment and give him strength when he needed it. It wasn't the basis of religion, which to him, was the crux of spiritualism, that he had taken issue with. He did believe in doing the right thing, in thinking of others and in helping those who needed it. What he could not abide was the stubborn interpretation and execution of those interpretations. He put "Judge not, lest ye be judged" before just about all the other commandments, so to him, the refusal to accept certain lifestyles, certain practices, and frankly, certain people as one big spiritual family seemed hypocritical.

He thought a lot about what he believed as he gathered what he'd need from the apartment. He had been taught as a boy that there was God and the Devil, demons and angels. As a teen, there were other gods that seemed more pressing—the gangs in the streets and then, to prevent him from ending up affiliated with one, the football team his mom made him try out for at the rec center. Neither the streets nor the church ever allowed for the possibility of alien beings. Monsters, yes, but they had faces and bodies like men, dealing drugs, paying too much attention to one kid or another, hitting someone's mom and walking out on her. Monsters existed in the church and in the streets, but those kinds of monsters never challenged the way the world was.

The thing that terrified Derek about these chaotic ones was that they challenged everything—not just on a spiritual level, but on an everyday thinking and functioning level. It was one thing to come across evidence that challenged what, exactly, hell might be belching up and what kind of God might exist to protect folks from it. It was another thing entirely, somehow more real and immediate, to find oneself questioning the ideas and truths that delivered folks through everyday living. He could only imagine what Myrinda was going through. To second-guess every idea, to feel control slipping away—to really feel like she was going crazy...it made Derek's heart ache for her.

He got his Glock 19 from the safe in the bedroom. As part of his job, he'd been licensed to carry a concealed weapon, and had developed a fondness for that particular handgun. He didn't know if it would work against those creatures in the Old Ward, but it made him feel safer to carry it. He loaded it with ammo he kept in a second safe, made sure the safety was on, then put it in a shoulder holster he'd strapped on.

From the key hook hanging by the front door, he grabbed his set of keys, checking to make sure the storage bin key was there. He had a gas can in there, and a lighter for the grill he'd hoped to have when they bought a house together. She had always seemed to need to go slow in their relationship, and he was okay with that, especially in the beginning. He didn't push; his job could be demanding and sometimes even dangerous, and the thought of being responsible to a family at home that needed him whole and safe and alive had always seemed like an added pressure he didn't need to take on. He'd bought the lighter, though, on a whim, on Valentine's Day after picking up roses for Myrinda. He didn't think she'd ever really understand the significance of it to him, but that was okay. He remembered how much he'd felt for her then. It made him feel warm and good, the thought of marrying her and buying a house together and having kids and having barbeques in the back yard where he could grill up burgers for his family. He didn't have all that with her then, but he bought the lighter to remind himself that he would some day, to keep it in perspective that he had a great thing going with Myrinda.

He got both the lighter and the gas can from the storage bin and grabbed the heavy duty flashlight as well, locked up, and brought them to the car. There was a gas station down the road where he could get gasoline. The plan then would be to figure out how to find Myrinda and get her out of the Old Ward first, and then splash enough gasoline over everything to burn it and its monstrous inhabitants to the ground. He hadn't gotten much farther than planning beyond that. Wayne couldn't tell him what the book said about the conditions for opening the gate had been, so he had no idea what he had to undo to cause the gate to collapse on itself.

Maybe Myrinda would know. Her...exposure to those things and interaction with them might have given her some insight.

One thing Derek was sure of was he was going to get Myrinda away from that hill, no matter what. He was prepared to leave everything they owned and put as much distance between them and the Bridgewood Estates apartments as possible.

He felt a kind of weight lifting as he drove down the hill and away from the apartments. It was tempered by his discomfort at leaving her up there. Every second they had her, anything could be happening. He hated to think of her alone with them in that musty old relic. It made him want to kill every one of those things.

Derek filled up the gas can and paid for the gas, then sped back up the hill and parked the car. He carried the gas can to the front door of the Old Ward and set it down.

He switched the safety off his gun and clicked on the flashlight. He could feel an almost tangible force pushing him away from the Old Ward. The thinnest beginnings of a headache were starting behind his right eye, and he thought he heard rushed, frantic whispering.

They knew he was coming to get her.

His resolve gave him the strength to break the hold against him and move forward to the doors. They opened with a groan, and he stepped inside to the waiting area.

"If she's there, check the tunnels first," Wayne had told him. *"Find Symmes's office. There's a passage leading down from there."* Wayne hadn't been much help otherwise; Derek suspected he knew more than he was telling Derek, more about the Old Ward and the monsters inside it. Derek wasn't sure if Wayne had willfully lied, or if the chaotic ones had exerted just enough influence to keep Wayne from spilling everything, but either way, Derek had gotten the message that his neighbor wasn't going to be able to offer much more than a place for him to start looking. And for now, that was okay, even if the only reason he'd gotten that much information was because the chaotic ones wanted to lead him right into a trap.

Derek had done some security briefly in a mental health facility just after college. He shined the light around the lobby, taking in the marred and stained front desk and skeletal seating. He figured it was a pretty good bet he'd find the offices through the large door against the far wall. It was open a crack, just enough to let a man through. An invitation.

He squeezed through and found himself in a hallway that extended ahead of him into an impenetrable darkness. He shined the flashlight ahead of him, but the gloom seemed to swallow the light the way it swallowed the floor tiles. What he could see were doors to either side of him with name plates and credentialed suffixes. Wayne had told him to look for Symmes, the director.

He made his way down the hall on high alert, sweeping the flashlight ahead of him to check the space for possible danger. Then he shined the light up on the doors to read the name plates. A little way down the hall, he found it: GEOFFREY DAVID SYMMES, MD, PHD, PSYD. He pushed open the door and was immediately hit with a stench like decaying meat. He pulled back, trying to clear the smell from his nose and throat with the musty but cleaner air of the hallway. He turned back to the office, his nose pressed into the crook of his elbow, and shined the flashlight around the room. It was empty; nothing in there accounted for the smell. On the back wall, though, Derek saw the shadowed outline of the passage Wayne had told him about.

Next to it was a crude rectangle of sheetrock and some splintered paneling.

With a last gulp of hallway air, he dove into the room and to the passage as quickly as he could, climbing onto the descending staircase. Immediately, the smell dissipated. Derek shined the flashlight down the staircase. Metal stairs led down into an inky nothingness. He headed down the stairs.

At the bottom, the flashlight picked out the outline of a metal door. He opened it and found himself in the tunnels.

"Okay, now," he said to himself. "Which way?" Both directions led off into pipelined darkness. From what Myrinda had told him, the administration at Bridgehaven Asylum had used these tunnels to travel from one building to another, to transport patients in bad weather, to move the extremely sick or dangerous without incidents, or to remove the dead without upsetting the other patients. It had also been considered that if an uncontainable riot were to break out, the staff had access to the tunnels to escape. Still, for all its uses, as Derek panned the walls with the flashlight, he could make out no indications of directions. How people managed to come down here without developing a file folder full of new phobias was beyond Derek. It was little more than an oblong cave.

Derek swore to himself. He didn't have time to choose the wrong direction. She didn't wear jewelry she could have dropped, nor did he think she was in the right mind to think of leaving him breadcrumbs anyway. He'd just have to guess, unless....

There, just a few feet ahead to the right—there was a small smear of blood. It was dried on the wall, but it coated the spot without any appearance of fading. That could mean it was fairly recently spilled. Mixed feelings of hope and fear assailed Derek. He tried not to think too hard about the circumstances surrounding the little blood smear. Instead, he took off in that direction.

He'd walked about an eighth of a mile when he heard the whispering again. With the acoustics of the tunnel, it was difficult to tell where, exactly, it was coming from, but it sounded like it was originating up ahead of him. He shined the flashlight down the length, but could see nothing. With cautious steps, he moved forward, ready to grab the gun at a moment's notice.

Then he heard laughter. At least, he thought it was laughter. Maybe it was the tunnel, but the phantom sound was difficult to qualify; it could have been crying, too. Either way, it sounded like Myrinda, and that moved him forward faster—so fast, in fact, that he didn't see the large prone objects on the floor until he stumbled over them and nearly fell. Recovering before he went down, he turned and shined the flashlight on them.

They were bodies. The first Derek only recognized by sight, an older man who lived in the building. It looked like his skull had been caved in by something very powerful. His chest looked abnormally narrow, and Derek realized with horror that something had crushed his ribcage so that the ribs overlapped each other. Derek turned away, shining his flashlight on the other body.

"Ahh. Ahh, man, Wayne. What the hell happened to you?" he asked softly of the broken body. He swallowed the lump in his throat. Wayne's neck had been broken so badly his chin rested on the back of his shoulder blade. Where his hands and feet should have been were ragged bloodless stumps from which shards of the broken bone protruded.

Derek turned away from them, sickened. He had seen dead bodies before—not often, though sometimes he came across them in his line of work—but the brutality against these bodies only served to heighten his worry for Myrinda. He took several deep breaths to steady himself and then continued down the tunnel, fighting the urge to run blindly.

He hadn't gotten far when there was a whistle and suddenly, a form was flying at him out of the darkness. He leaped out of the way as something landed heavily on the ground. It moaned. He shined the flashlight on it.

Myrinda lay in a heap, her nose bloody and her nightgown torn to shreds around the hem. Another rip ran between her breasts down and around to her side, revealing bruised ribs. Her hair clumped with grime. A cut on her forehead bled down the side of her face. She curled into a fetal position as Derek ran to her, scooping her up in his arms.

"Babygirl, talk to me. Are you okay?"

She struggled a little in his grasp and then opened her eyes. When she saw his face in the flashlight glow, she went slack. "They took me. They went inside...." She began to cry. "Inside my head."

He pulled her into a hug. "It's okay, baby. Everything's going to be all right. I'm going to get us out of here, okay?"

"I want to go to sleep," she murmured.

"No," he told her. "Stay with me, babygirl. I need you to stay with me." He pulled her to her feet and looped her arm around his shoulders so he could hold her up with his left arm and help her walk. "We're going to make sure they can't ever hurt you again."

"It's too late," she whispered, and her thin giggle echoed around them in the tunnel. "They're here."

Derek shined his flashlight behind them and in front of them, searching. As far as the light could show, nothing was there. Then a flash of blue, followed by a low pulse of sound that Derek felt more than heard, lit the tunnel behind them. In the brief glow, Derek saw two of the hinshing, moving closer in its erratic, jerky way. Then the tunnel went dark. Another blue flash and pulse ahead of them in the direction of the door illuminated another one. A chattering sound above his head drew the frantic flashlight arcing upward. One of them crawled on the tunnel ceiling directly above them, skittering toward a wall.

"Myrinda," he said in a low, firm voice. "Run." He bolted forward, half-dragging and half-carrying her with him, in the direction of the metal door. He switched the flashlight to his left hand near Myrinda, and drew the gun with his right. A second later the open mouth of a hinshing swam up in front of him. He fired, and the creature jerked back, oozing a black ichor from the hole in its chest. It bellowed in pain and anger, and he shot it again, right down its tooth-lined gullet. It roared in surprise and pain, and the gloom of the tunnel swallowed it.

Derek yanked Myrinda forward again, acutely aware of the angry sound of a thousand nonsense words spoken as curses that the hinshing behind him were closing the gap in the darkness.

"Come on, babygirl," he coaxed. "Move with me, sweetheart."

She seemed to find her feet then, doing some of the work for him, but he had to guide her. Another reached with long, sharp fingers for his shoulder and Derek shot at the approximate height of its mouth. It screamed and the fingers fell away.

Derek maneuvered Myrinda around the bodies of their neighbors. He worried how she'd react when she saw them, but she paid them no mind. He wasn't even sure her eyes were open.

That's okay, babygirl, he thought to himself. *Keep on thinking this is just a bad dream.*

Pointed fingers dug into his shoulder and shoved hard, and he felt Myrinda jerked from his grasp. She sank to the floor by his feet. He whirled around and put a bullet down the throat of the hinshing right behind him. It bellowed, already beginning to come apart like flaking paint, the chips of its skin flying away. It spasmed once and stumbled back to the depths of the tunnel behind it.

He swooped down and grabbed Myrinda around the waste again, pulling her to her feet, and plowed forward again. After what seemed like an eternity, the flashlight glow by Myrinda's side picked up the metal door, and he dove for it, yanking it open. He had some trouble getting Myrinda up the stairs. About halfway up, she began to sink on her feet, claiming she was too tired to keep going, and for one terrible moment, Derek thought he was going to die with her in that stuffy passage on a metal staircase. Already, he could hear the remaining hinshing scrabbling at the metal door.

"Baby, please get up. We've got to go."

"Go home?" she asked blankly.

"Yes, yes," he answered, glancing back at the metal door. It was opening, and those pointed fingers were wrapping around the door frame. "We've got to go home," he said. "Please."

She blinked a few times, then rose and began climbing the stairs. The two of them finally tumbled out into the foul-smelling office, and Derek lead her back down the hall to the lobby door, shoving her through and then following behind. He threw his shoulder against the door, pushing with all his strength to close it. It skittered heavily across the floor, stuck, then slid into place. Derek turned back to Myrinda and led her through the lobby and out the front doors.

"Stay here," he said, parking her on the lawn several feet away.

By sheer force of luck (or maybe it was that force in the universe most called God), the gas can was still where he left it. He holstered the gun and dropped the flashlight, then uncapped the gas can just as the remaining four hinshing emerged from the front doors.

EIGHTEEN

Before they could move toward him, he splashed the gasoline at them, aiming for those terrible mouths. Some landed in their throats, and they gurgled. Some landed on the concrete steps. Others tried to shake it off by twitching their heads. Triumphantly, Derek pulled out the lucky lighter and clicked it on.

Nothing happened. He checked the handle, making sure to execute the sliding of the safety wheel and the pressing of the ignition button. Still no flames.

"Fuck," he said, pocketing the lighter. As one, the four moved forward. He pulled his gun out and aimed at the top concrete step on a slight angle.

"Derek," one of them said, trying out his name with some contempt.

Another laughed, and the sound was steeped in resignation.

He fired and the ricochet off the step created a spark. There was a single second of confused twitching among the four and then flames roared across their bodies and down their throats. They screamed, babbling different words from a myriad of languages until the words blurred into nonsense. Beneath the sheath of flames, they began to flake apart, the pieces rising and melting and winking out like the embers and ash. They jumped off the stairs and Derek backed up, pointing his gun at them, but they were beyond caring about Derek now. It looked like they were trying to make it to the apartments.

Derek watched as the burning bodies jerked and jumped and finally fell forward, one by one, onto an ugly black puddle whose septic veins had worked their way up one corner of the apartment building. They broke apart then, crumbling into powder and ash, and the fire surrounding them burned over the puddle for a minute, then winked out.

The puddle seemed to deepen then, bubbling and spreading outward. Derek took Myrinda's hand and they moved a little closer to it.

From his new angle, he saw the puddle wasn't really that at all; it was a growing, yawning chasm. Derek looked down into it; bluish light swirled and pulsed, and beneath that, a black hole. He felt dizzy, and he took several steps back to avoid pitching headlong into it.

"That's the gate, isn't it?" he asked Myrinda.

"Their bodies are not the right sacrifice for the gate," she said. "They died inside, and skewed the proportions. It's collapsing."

"You sure?" To Derek, it looked like it was widening, pulling rock and dirt down into it and expanding to fill the space.

Myrinda didn't answer. She wiped the blood from her nose and sniffed, then turned to Derek. She looked weak, and swayed where she stood. "I can feel the abyss." She stepped forward and swayed on the edge. Panicked, Derek grabbed her around the waist and yanked her back.

"What the hell are you doing?"

She offered him a weary smile. "I can feel the abyss," she repeated. "It's calling. I don't want to hurt you or me, like they told me. But they're gone and they can't undo what they did in my head. The abyss is the only way. The gate is collapsing and then it'll be too late."

"No," he told her, and she stopped her feeble struggling.

"Everything is going away," she whispered, and closed her eyes.

The gate stopped widening, but Derek could still see the swirling of its substance welling up. It didn't seem to be collapsing at all, but rather, gathering strength. Anxious, Derek tugged Myrinda back, putting several feet of space between them and the gate.

"I don't think it worked," Derek said, exhaling defeat. Then a deafening crack and boom made them both duck.

From the depths of the hole, wailing mingled with ecstatic laughter, creating a sound that jarred Derek to the bones. Myrinda, standing next to him, began to shiver violently. Rumbling preceded a sudden geysering of the substance of the abyss, which splashed onto the ground and across the side of the building. Just as suddenly, a liquid bluishness like plasma leapt from the hole, devouring the black in bright light and cold. With a roar, the hole belched out a plume of it that licked at the side of the apartment building. It was unlike anything Derek had ever seen; it ate through the brick facade like acid and scorched the grass around the base. It glided across the face of the building, the inkiness from the hole racing just beneath it. Fingers of the blue plasma stretched and flexed toward windows, punching through the glass. Shattered fragments rained down on the walkway just seconds after Derek yanked Myrinda out of the way.

Again the gate vomited its substance from its throat, and Derek just managed to jump out of splashing range. He couldn't begin to imagine what that stuff would do to his body.

He saw what it did to the Old Ward, though, where the majority of it landed. It ate into the brick and cracked the concrete steps. It ate through the doors. There was a groaning sound as it acidically lacerated the building, and then it began to crumble. Large chunks of brick fell to the ground with deafening crashes, windows shattered, and all along the empty, echoing hallways, the stains of insanity and tragedy, horror and death were buried under in waves of destruction. The last remnant of the Bridgehaven Asylum, historical landmark and monument to the treatment of madness, tumbled in a spray of brick and mortar to the ground. The Old Ward was obliterated.

The charred ground began to heave upward in a spray of rocks and dirt then fall back heavily, crumbling and sinking into the growing abyss at the building's foundation. As Derek watched, a swirling black space coated with tongues of flickering blue spread like an enormous blood stain beneath the apartments. The building hovered over the widening chasm, shaking and tilting downward. Cracks splintered across the bricks, sending fragments tumbling into the nothingness beneath.

"Derek," Myrinda said, tugging his sleeve. Her voice sounded small and terrified.

He followed her wide-eyed gaze to the parking lot. The ground had caved in along a fault line straight to the parking lot. The asphalt rippled, and the metallic groan of cars being shoved aside mingled with the wailing from the pit.

"Go," Derek said. "Come on, we gotta go, *now*." He grabbed Myrinda's hand and pulled her toward the lot. "Run, babygirl!"

They flew over the mangled landscape, keeping just ahead of a new fault line behind them. Ten feet from the car, there was a loud boom from below ground and the car launched into the air. Derek skidded to a stop, throwing out an arm to stop Myrinda and protect her. The car came down hard on a blue sedan, both of them crushing on points of contact. Glass shattered outward.

Derek pulled Myrinda away from the lot and toward the road. There was no choice but to flee the hill on foot. All around them, the woods magnified and echoed the terrible wailing of those things that had been just at the edge of the abyss, the crackling of the substance of the gate folding in on itself, the whine and shatter of the apartment building twisting and sinking into depths beyond anything ever seen. He ran, sweating and bleeding, tugging Myrinda behind him. He didn't stop or even look back until they had reached the main road to town, and only then, he looked long enough to see flashes of light from the top of the hill and hear the final thundering crash of the Bridgewood Estates apartments sinking into a fracture in the earth.

AFTER THE END (AN EPILOGUE)

Derek arrived at Bridgewood General Hospital at the usual time and signed in with Lois at the front desk. He took his visitor's pass and was buzzed into the psychiatric ward of the hospital to see Myrinda.

When he got to her room, Dr. Alice Edwards was just leaving. A short, thin woman in her late sixties with a thatch of blond hair going gray and glasses just a shade too big for her face, Dr. Edwards had immediately made an impression on Derek as being both warm and caring, and very good at her job. That was important to him. It hadn't been easy to turn Myrinda over to strangers to care for.

She winked at him encouragingly, clapping his biceps with her strong but tiny hand, and told him they could catch up after his visit.

He went in and sat down on the bed next to Myrinda. "Hi, babygirl. How're you feeling?"

Myrinda looked at him. It took her a moment to recognize him, but then she smiled. That was progress. "Hi, Derek." She leaned over and kissed his mouth lightly. "I've missed you."

"I've missed you, too, babygirl."

"Dr. Edwards was here. She says I'm doing better. And no nightmares last night."

He smiled, took her hand and squeezed it. "That's great. I'm glad to hear it. That's a good sign, baby, a very good sign."

She smiled. She was talking, and that in itself was a good sign, too. Sometimes, trying to talk to her was like trying to jimmy open a lockbox for which one had lost the key. He'd check with Dr. Edwards, but if the nightmares were going away, that was good, too. For weeks after what happened, she'd wake up shouting or crying.

***

On his way out, he stopped by Dr. Edwards' office, knocking in her doorway. She looked up and smiled at him. "Let's take a walk."

As they strolled down the glass breezeway connecting the psychiatric ward to the rest of Bridgewood General, she told him about how therapy was going. Myrinda was making progress, in her professional opinion. She was, as Derek had seen, regaining her ability to recognize faces. She was recalling memories from before their residence at Bridgewood. She seemed less paranoid, too, about people judging and plotting against her, and had given up the idea that the whispering demons would give her no peace unless she hurt people. She had, in fact, told Dr. Edwards earlier that week that Derek had killed the whispering demons, the ones she called hinshing, and so they couldn't make her hurt anyone anymore. It had been almost three months since Dr. Edwards had been able to get her to speak about anything that had happened in the apartments or in the Old Ward, and she couldn't always remember who Derek was. Her statement, then, had showed Myrinda had taken the first small step in overcoming both of those hurdles at the same time.

Dr. Edwards told him Myrinda was responding well to the medication and that with a little more therapy, she would be able to go home. Whatever Myrinda believed to have experienced at Bridgewood, Dr. Edwards told him, had knocked down certain walls in her mind, in essence burying her conscious self alive. But over the last few months, she had slowly managed to dig herself free, to climb over the rubble, and work her way toward sunlight again. It was possible she'd have some scars, some residual traumas they could deal with in outpatient therapy such as her nyctophobia and nightmares, but Dr. Edwards was firmly convinced Myrinda was getting better.

Derek smiled at her. "I can't thank you enough for everything you've done for her. You've worked miracles."

Dr. Edwards chuckled, gesturing modestly. "I am only as effective as the strongest link in her support network, and that's you. Even before she remembered it, I could tell how much she loves you by the look in her eyes when you'd visit—and how much you love her by the way you are with her when you're here. People need something to come back to, something to get better for. You're as good for her recovery as I'll ever be."

They walked in silence for a while, Derek chewing over what the doctor had said.

"Derek, what's on your mind?"

He shrugged, looking out the glass windows of the breezeway at the parking lot. He was still strong and healthy, as his employment physical and psych evaluation post-Bridgewood had confirmed. There had been a new reliable car and a beautiful new rented house that was beginning to feel like home—all it needed was for Myrinda to come home and add her style and her presence to make it so. There was the lighter waiting on the mantel, and next to it, a small jeweler's box with a diamond ring inside for when Myrinda came home and was well enough to move on with life. There had been time off from the new job to care for her and ultimately, to get her a spot in the hospital facilities where she could receive the help he just couldn't give her. His boss had been understanding, and had even given him Dr. Edwards' name because she'd worked wonders with his sister-in-law. Derek's life was mostly good now. He knew life had a tendency to move on with or without a person so he did his best to keep up, and to carry Myrinda when she couldn't. But it was his job, for chrissakes, to protect people from danger. Why hadn't he been able to protect her? And had what kept him from going crazy also prevented him from seeing the illness in her until it was too late to fix it? "Just wondering why it didn't affect me the way it affected her."

"Well, these kinds of things are dependent on a lot of factors. Everybody processes external forces and experiences differently—it's why psychological therapy is really a form of art as much as a science. It could be that, given time, whatever made her unwell would have worked itself on you, too, but you just had a better initial tolerance." Dr. Edwards paused as if to give herself time to choose her words carefully. "If Myrinda's symptoms are the result of greater exposure to some chemical or natural force or some experience that diverged from your own, then her reaction to that stimulus or stimuli would naturally be different." They reached the end of the breezeway, turned, and headed back toward the office.

Derek nodded. He had told the doctor he thought Myrinda's state had been the result of exposure to something up at the apartments. The doctor ran with that, citing possible exposure to high levels of some chemical either naturally occurring in the area or dumped there. Derek didn't see any need to refine that diagnosis, as it was pretty damned close to the truth as it was.

Dr. Edwards was an astute woman, however. She knew something had happened up on that hill that for reasons she respected, he couldn't or wouldn't explain. She had told him as much, and had never pushed for details. When he had told her, during one of the early-treatment darker moments, that the demons Myrinda feared were more real than anyone would believe, Dr. Edwards had simply nodded. The next week when Derek came to visit, she'd had article print-outs by a Wayne Tillingford regarding the Bridgehaven Asylum, as well as some paperclipped notes about the place's history.

She squeezed his arm again with her little mothering hand. "You can't feel guilty for not being sick, too."

He smiled at her. She had a way of knowing how he was feeling. Experience, he supposed, but it endeared her to him all the same. "I just want her to be able to let go of the dark memories someday, ya know?"

"Well, all memories are dark, aren't they? Shadowed, as they are, by time and distance and the merciful ability to forget the sharper details."

"I guess you're right about that."

"No worries," she said as they reached her office door. "Someday, you'll both be able to put all this behind you and live the life you wanted. And I'll do everything I can to help you get there."

"Dr. Edwards," he began, the overwhelming gratitude leaving him at a loss for sufficient words."

She smiled at him. "That's why I'm here. Now go on; you'll be late for work."

He offered her an appreciative smile and then headed out to his car. Although Derek had his doubts, the doctor seemed convinced the damage was not irreversible. He hoped for that. He really did.

The fire and the unexplainable collapse of the apartments on the hill the day of that freak electrical storm had been enough to convince the corporation that rebuilding there would bad idea. They claimed that a third attempt at construction would only be a money sink, but more likely, it was the discovery of the tenants from apartments 2A and 2B, found buried under the rubble of the apartments, necks snapped and bodies and skulls crushed by debris, and the subsequent bad publicity for the corporation that decided them. The land would be turned over to the town to establish a park or some other shared community space. It was rezoned as nonresidential. Everyone thought that was best.

As Derek drove to work, he passed the old hill. He deliberately gave it no more than a passing glance. That land could rot right down to rock for all he cared, and take its ghosts and demons with it.

On the hill, the ruins of the Old Ward's foundation poked out of the season's first snowfall. A blanket of white covered the remnants of the parking lot, the sweeping lawns, the walkway. To look at it, one would find it difficult to imagine the chaos that had consumed the area only three months prior.

Of course, the deep split in the earth where the Bridgewood Estates apartments had once stood served as proof, though.

What was left of the debris of the building still filled it in like a rushed and slipshod grave. Snow had filled in the indented tracks of the heavy digging machinery that had sifted through a good portion of the debris already, before the weather turned the ground too hard to dig the building's remnants out.

There was no sign of movement or life, no sound of laughter or chatter. There was only silence beneath a slate gray New England sky, a crisp chill in the air, and a sensation, too faint to even crystallize like a puff of winter breath, that nothing mattered and anything can happen. It was the remnant of wild abandon, the last of the abyss's germs of insanity strangled from their source and dying in the cold air.

At the bottom of the hill's chasm, the tenant of the slipshod grave buried deep beneath glass and brick, was a single small pool of black sludge reflecting a pulsing blue light from somewhere in its depths. It was folding in on itself, though, its physical and metaphysical asymmetry unable to support its structure. Surely nothing could crawl through the collapsed gate now; it was unstable.

The long hand with the pointed fingers feeling its way around the edge of the gate would soon discover that, surely. There were other gates besides, and other worlds.

7219945R00190

Printed in Great Britain
by Amazon.co.uk, Ltd.,
Marston Gate.